Peter Murray

A Passion to Build

clip-kit.com

Author's note

This book is a work of fiction. Although some well-known people are referenced by name, none of the other characters are real.

Published by Clip-Kit Ltd 2011

©Peter Murray 2011

Clip-Kit Ltd
31 Priory Avenue
London W4 1TZ England

e-mail:_info@clip-kit.com

www.clip-kit.com

Twitter: @pgsmurray

This book is printed on demand
and is also available as
an e-book on the internet.

Paperback edition:
ISBN 978-0-9570702-0-2

Cover photograph by Alan Williams,
art direction in homage to
Len Deighton and Raymond Hawley

Si monumentum requiris - circumspice

If you seek his monument, look around you

Epitaph of Sir Christopher Wren in St Paul's Cathedral
and of all architects who build

For David Pearce

Part 1 – Selection

Chapter 1

Harry Jamb, soon to become the most famous architect in Britain, was sitting in the meeting room of his Clerkenwell office, right in the heart of London's designer district. The building was a converted clock factory and the shiny steel and black leather chairs and long glass-topped table formed a foil to the shabby-chic background of bare brickwork and cast iron columns. Around the walls hung large photographs of buildings designed by Harry Jamb Associates, their clean, modernist lines creating almost abstract images against bright blue skies and rich green landscapes. At one end of the room was mounted a giant plasma screen.

Harry stroked the infrared mouse across the table top and the screen sprang into life. He clicked on the BBC News bookmark; right at the top of the page came the headline he'd been hoping for: "E U Sports Minister to announce host city for EuroGames".

"Cup of tea Harry?" Harry's long serving PA, Jenny, asked rhetorically as she placed a large mug in front of him.

"This is the moment of truth," Harry waved towards the screen, "will Frampton-on-Tees pip Warsaw or Seville on the shortlist? And, if Frampton wins, who's going to design the showcase buildings the city will need? I bloody well hope that we can win one of them, at least."

"We could certainly do with some new jobs now that the work on the Kensall Museum and the Sawditch Library is coming to an end" Jenny added.

On the screen the short, bespectacled figure of the European Minister of Sport walked up to a forest of microphones. The camera panned to the expectant crowds gathered in each of the candidate cities.

"Look at all those people," Harry waved towards the screen, "they've been working for years to get their bids together, and it's all such a lottery. A lot of them are going to be disappointed. Remember what it was like when London won the Olympics? The French couldn't believe it! They were in tears. But over here even people who were pretty cynical about the whole thing were suddenly delirious – cheering, hugging and kissing. They were right to be excited – these things change lives and they change cities. And it means work for us."

***

John Veduty was fed up. As the Chairman of the Frampton Civic Society it often fell to him to give tours of the city's historic buildings to visiting dignitaries. Today he had a group of half a dozen Japanese businessmen to show round; it was raining hard and Victoria Square in Frampton was packed, quite spoiling his well honed route. He was feeling cold and wet.

A tall and imposing figure, Veduty was usually immaculately turned out. He wore a traditional belted riding mac over his three piece Harris Tweed suit, a wide striped shirt, stiff white collar and old school tie. But today the fawn-coloured mac was darkened by the rain, the collar soggy, and his trouser creases non-existent. His leather brogues had also sprung a leak.

The people of Frampton had gathered in the square in their thousands to hear the live announcement about the Games. A massive screen had been erected in one corner and spectators were excitedly clambering on walls, up lamp posts and hanging out of the windows of the buildings to get a good view and soak up the festive atmosphere. Veduty managed to squeeze his charges into the corner of the city's most important public space.

"God, I hope we don't win the Games – what an absolutely ghastly nightmare that would be" Veduty said under his breath as he surveyed the crowds and then launched into his well-rehearsed tour.

"This square," he shouted slowly above the hubbub, "was named after Queen Victoria, Empress of India, in the days when the steelworks of Frampton were sending sheets and girders to all the corners of the globe, including of course Japan! During the road building boom of the 1960s, its magnificent 19th century buildings were lucky to remain intact while the rest of the centre was destroyed by traffic engineers and the insatiable demands of the motor vehicle!"

"You will note that the square is dominated by the bright red brick and terracotta of the Civic Centre, designed by Giles Gilbert Scott in 1865, which has been recently cleaned at great expense," Veduty continued stoically as rain started to drip down his neck. "The building's exotic gothic style and pointed arches are reminiscent of the same architect's masterpiece at St Pancras Station in London. In the carved niches you can see the statues of civic dignitaries who have contributed to the life and wealth of Frampton over the ages. The building houses the offices of the City Council and contrasts in style with the Classical portico of the Frampton Art Gallery opposite, designed by Charles Cockerell in 1850. It was described by Pevsner as 'one of the finest neo-Grecian buildings in Britain'. The triangular pediment that sits of on top of the fine Corinthian columns contains sculpted scenes of Frampton's 19th century industries."

He turned abruptly. The Japanese dutifully followed as their guide made his way towards George Street and the older part of the town, leaving the noisy citizens behind them.

***

Sir Richard Jarvis, Mayor of Frampton, looked up at the Civic Centre as he waited impatiently for the Minister's announcement. Standing next to him was Ed Clutton his charismatic head of city planning, or Director of Infrastructure and Wellbeing, to give him his official title.

9

"Bloody wonderful building that, Ed," enthused the Mayor. "It sums up what Frampton's all about. Out of all the muck and the brass comes something really beautiful. Pity we don't do architecture like that today!"

"If we win the bid we're going to have to find architects who can create the twenty first century face of the city. And it's not going to be anything like this if I have anything to do with it!" responded Clutton. "We want to get the best modern architects in the world to build here. That will be your legacy to the city. The Games will give new hope to Frampton; we can regenerate all the run down industrial lands. We have to believe in the future and not build some sort of Disneyland pastiche!"

Jarvis wasn't quite sure what Ed was getting so excited about. He looked at the row of statues of former Mayors and dignitaries that decorated the Civic Centre facades. If he pulled off the EuroGames, Jarvis would deserve to be up there too. There was still one unoccupied niche which he had mentally reserved for himself.

***

The sodden crowd had been kept amused by the choir of Frampton-on-Tees Comprehensive with a medley of pop and show tunes, a set by the cast of Riverdance who were doing a two week stint at the Frampton Theatre Royal, and a stirring speech about the significance of sport in today's world by the Olympic Gold medallist Martin Hester who was born and bred in the city. Hester was prominent as a key member of the Government's "Healthier Britain" campaign to tackle the nation's growing obesity problem.

The tall, bronzed, ex-athlete shouted into the microphone.

"And now, as we get closer to the moment which could make such a massive impact on our proud city and on all our lives, please welcome the man who has led the bid for Frampton-on-Tees to host the EuroGames, and who is the inspiration for the regeneration of our run down areas. . . please welcome Mayor Sir Richard Jarvis!"

The Mayor led the official party onto the stage. Behind the group was the giant screen erected for the announcement ceremony and a huge banner proclaiming "Go Frampton!" The local Councillors lined up on either side of the Mayor in his ceremonial garb. The bright red robe stood out among the grey suits.

All eyes were on the big screen. The crowd cheered loudly as the European Minister moved up to the microphone; he held a large gold envelope in his hand. They cheered because hosting the Games would bring jobs and a new spirit to Frampton.

The EU Sports Minister coughed. The crowd instantly went silent. Despite the lashing rain, people put down their umbrellas so others could see the screen. As Jarvis looked out over the expectant faces he sensed the unity that his daring bid for the Games had generated among Framptonians.

There were plenty of doubters and critics when he announced that the city would apply to host the Games. He had had to make a lot of promises to Councillors to ensure he got their vote. But now, as the city held its breath, Frampton-on-Tees was united. It was Frampton against the rest of the world. The Mayor adopted a fixed smile, conscious of the television camera a few feet away which was focused on his face ready to record his reactions to the announcement. He wondered if he would be able to maintain the smile should the Minister give the wrong result. If Frampton won he wouldn't care what the cameras caught.

"As Minister of Sport for the European Union, first of all I would like to thank all the cities who had made excellent bids for the Games. I would also like to thank. . ."

"Get on with it!" shouted a voice.

". . . the Games Committee who have studied the various proposals. Each of the cities could have put on an excellent Games, but only one can win." He lifted up the envelope and started to open it. "It is my proud duty to announce that the EuroGames is awarded to the city of. . ." he paused for effect. The crowd watched his lips; would they be pursed for a "W". . . or stretched for a "S"? The expectant throng only needed to hear the first syllable.

He drew a card from the envelope.

"FFra. . ."" started the Minister. The rest was drowned out by a huge roar from the Victoria Square crowd, a forest of arms punched the air in triumph. Confetti canons exploded from the roof of the Civic Centre. Queen Victoria's statue had not seen anything like it since the relief of the siege of Mafeking or VE Day. Framptonians of all ages whooped, jumped for joy, waved their arms and made 'victory' signs at the TV cameras.

***

"Yeeess!" Harry exclaimed and gave a modest air punch. He was more than pleased. A major sports building was just the sort of job the office needed.

"Jenny, can you get our credentials information together. I want to start working on the material we need for the Frampton sports buildings tenders. And keep an eye on the website for the tender documents."

***

Mayor Jarvis and Clutton were the sort of dream team that all hard pressed cities need: Jarvis the politician, the facilitator; Clutton the visionary who believed that by improving the quality of places and the smooth functioning of the city the Council could give the inhabitants of Frampton better lives. The Mayor had made no bones about the scale of the task when he first interviewed the planner for the job.

"Frampton has been in desperate need of regeneration for years," he explained. "Its wealth in the nineteenth and twentieth centuries was built on steel. Competition from countries with cheaper labour took its toll in the post war period, but the killer blow was delivered when Margaret Thatcher told us to pack up making stuff because the future was in services, not steel. Call centres were to become the backbone of the Frampton economy – at least, they did until they were moved to bloody Bangalore."

"The traffic engineers ripped the heart out of Frampton in the 60s with an inner ring of motorways just as they did in Birmingham and Newcastle," the Mayor warmed to his theme. "The Market Retail Mall replaced old Georgian squares. Thousands of 'slum' dwellings were cleared and residents moved to tower block estates on the outskirts of the city.

Since the riots of 1981 a series of regeneration projects have tried to take the place of the factories and mills. A hell of a lot of money has been pumped into new housing, but nearly thirty years later many parts of the city are still suffering from long-term unemployment, while the city centre at night has all-too familiar binge-drinking problems. It's a mess, but I love this city and passionately believe in a better future."

The two made an odd pair: Jarvis had made a lot of money when he sold his Ford dealership business and he retained some of the slickness of the car salesman, his smooth charm masking an aggressive ambition. Clutton was equally steely in his desire to deliver his vision for the city and provided an academic foil to the Mayor's plain speaking, man-of-the-people persona. Jarvis was tall, rather vain and prone to wearing shiny suits; Clutton was considerably shorter with a rumpled air, an unruly mop of fair hair, and fine gold-rimmed glasses. Aside from their commitment to Frampton-on-Tees, the two had little in common.

"We should put in a bid for the EuroGames," Jarvis had said one day to Ed Clutton. "they would bring new investment to Frampton, create jobs and generate tourism. It's not just about hosting the two weeks of the Games but about the long term legacy they can deliver for the city."

The area around Frampton's redundant steelworks was in dire need of major investment and regeneration. There were large tracts of low quality housing, vacant industrial sites and areas of major deprivation. Frampton had the highest unemployment rates of any city in the region.

"It's a once in a lifetime opportunity," the Mayor enthused "for you, me and Frampton."

***

Jenny downloaded the entry forms for the Frampton EuroGames architectural competitions from the internet and handed them to Harry.

"I've got a good feeling about this one, Jenny. It's just our cup of tea!" Harry said.

"You always say that when we start on a project – the eternal optimist!" Jenny replied with a laugh.

"Architects have to be optimists, we have to believe in a better future otherwise we might as well give up!"

Jenny had heard that one before too. She had worked with Harry since he first started up in practice. She was committed to the firm, just as she was committed to Harry. Her life was focused on ensuring that Harry's was made as efficient and effective as she could make it. She accentuated her efficiency with her Miss Moneypenny appearance – heavy horn-rimmed glasses, pencil skirt and tight white blouse that accentuated her hour glass figure. Harry admired and appreciated her dedication to her job, but was blissfully unaware of the passion that drove her to such perfection.

Harry Jamb Associates was one of Britain's best regarded architectural practices. It had won masses of awards for its buildings, but had never done very well commercially. Harry liked entering competitions. He only got paid on a few of them, most were purely speculative and the odds of winning were long.

"Why do we keep going in for these competitions, Harry?" Jenny asked. "We seem to lose such a lot of money doing them."

"I love competitions," Harry replied. "They're a gamble, sure, but the rewards are great – you get chances for which you'd normally have to wait years. Look what happened to Richard Rogers when he won the Pompidou Centre or Zaha Hadid after she got the prize for The Peak in Hong Kong. Competitions give us a chance to do buildings we would never be asked to do otherwise. The problem is that in England we don't do enough of them. In places like Germany, they're more common and the risks involved, the wasted hours, are less."

"But even after we've won a competition, the jobs are hardly ever profitable," Jenny wouldn't let this one go. "The problem is that you're much more interested in taking on projects you like, rather than making money."

"I'm very lucky that I've got a wealthy wife then!" Harry laughed.

His father-in-law, Riccardo Scappi, started Marsoni – "Makers of Modern Masterpieces" – in Milan after the Second World War and was part of the renaissance of Italian design that took place in the 50s and 60s. Riccardo liked commissioning new designers to produce ranges of furniture for the company. He owned houses in Chelsea, Milan and Tuscany where he entertained those he commissioned and who, in return, bought lots of his furniture for the buildings they designed.

Ever since Harry had married his daughter, Eleanor, Riccardo had helped to support Harry's business – he wanted to make sure that neither Eleanor nor his granddaughter, Amelia, would suffer for Harry's art.

Eleanor was beautiful, impetuous and spoilt. She was an only child and Riccardo doted on her. Anything she wanted he was happy to give. He had allowed her to do just about anything she wanted as a teenager; he would send his chauffeur to pick her up from parties (staying out all night was not on the permitted list); she could bring as many friends to stay in their Tuscany villa as she liked. On her 18th birthday he bought her a Series 2 Alfa Romeo Spider sports car. Riccardo saw the car with its Pininfarina styling as the epitome of post war design excellence. The image of his beautiful daughter driving this thoroughbred masterpiece of engineering and design was, to him, the essence of *la Bella Figura* – the epitome of Italian style.

Her father gave way on most things, but put his foot down over Eleanor's plan to go to university. She was keen to study English; he was adamant she should do a design degree. He had hoped one day that she would join the board of Marsoni and continue the family connection. Eleanor enjoyed the world of design but, unlike her father, she didn't want it to take up her entire life. On the subject of what to read at university, however, she reluctantly agreed to go along with his wishes, knowing how much it meant to him.

Harry for his part was grateful for the financial support Riccardo gave him, but he did not like being in his debt. The young architect knew that if he won one of the Frampton jobs, it would finally make the practice financially independent. He was not alone among the successful architects of his generation in having family money behind him. It was tough carving out a reputation as an independent architect without a sizeable financial cushion. Less fortunate, cash-strapped firms often had to take jobs not because they wanted to, but in order to pay the rent and salaries; they were thus in a much weaker position negotiating with clients.

"You've got to be able to tell clients to 'fuck off' if you don't like what they are telling you to do," Frank Cummins, his tutor at architecture school, and his mentor, had told him "if you want to be a famous architect and haven't got any money, marry it."

Harry was not in the habit of telling clients to "fuck off", but he took note of what his tutor had said.

***

Riccardo fixed a place for Eleanor at the London Academy of Architecture, the leading school in the country. The Academy was housed in a powerful 1960s Brutalist block which sat incongruously among the polite Georgian terraces of Gibberd Square. It was run by the inspirational Norwegian Thor Christensen. Christensen was not a designer himself, and he didn't have a clue about basic architectural tasks like keeping the rain out or costs down – in fact he didn't care – he was interested in the academic investigation of new ways of designing and new patterns of living.

"The practice of architecture is the practice of innovation," he would tell his students. "Architecture is all about change and about progress."

"I'm having a great time at the school, thanks Papa," Eleanor responded to her father's interrogation on one of her regular weekend trips home. She didn't mention that nobody made you work if you didn't want to and the social life was heaving. Eleanor was always the life and soul of any party, outgoing, often loud, always laughing. She wasn't tall but her Manolos added a good three to four inches to her shapely legs, and her shock of black hair framing her fine tanned features making her a powerful presence. She showed off her comely figure to great effect, squeezing into her size eight Vivien Westwoods and Jasper Conrans when someone more cautious might have gone for a ten.

"But it's a really long time to study, I'm not sure I can stick it out. It'll be seven years before I'm fully qualified. I'm not sure I can stand being a student for that long."

"It's important to me, Eleanor that you work hard. At least do the first three years which is like a normal university degree – you'll learn a lot about design and make good contacts for the future."

"Si, Papa!" Eleanor laughed and kissed her father affectionately on the cheek.

***

Eleanor and Harry had met while they were queuing for drinks at the Student Union Bar.

"Hi! I'm Harry Jamb."

"Yes, I know who you are. I've seen you around the school. I went to your crit last month when you were presenting your designs for the new Bank of Britain."

17

"That was a hard one," Harry replied, referring to an established part of architectural education in which a students hangs his or her drawings and a jury of three or four architects and critics quiz the victim about the design, and deliver their (often crushing) criticism. "The jury showed little mercy. Thor sees crits as a way of toughening us up for the slings and arrows of professional practice. He thinks that if a student can't hack a crit, they'll never make it in the real world."

"But you were brilliant! All the younger students want to come to your crits to see how it's done," Eleanor thrilled.

Harry was certainly one of the school's top performers. He was engaging, fluent and on top of all the facts. Good looking, his open but thickset features gave him an air of strength and trustworthiness. He smiled easily and he used his penetrating brown eyes to great effect.

Harry knew how to respond quickly to the most aggressive juries. Like hyenas, practised jury members snapped in turn at the heels of their terrified victims. As the responses got slower and less coherent, the interrogators went in for the kill, ripping the project to shreds. After weeks of work, drawing through the night – often with the help of amphetamines to stay awake – students, male and female, frequently left the room in tears. Some never returned, seeking a more comfortable life away from architecture.

"I'm working on a project to design an academic institute in Ireland," Eleanor continued breezily. "I'm absolutely terrified at the prospect of a crit. I don't even understand the brief. Look at this."

She delved into her bag and drew out a crumpled sheet of paper. Harry read from the typescript.

"Avoiding the tangential invention of increasingly bizarre activities we return via ritual (the re-mythologised event) to orchestrate the object itself. Literacy is sublimated as background (content being different from virtuoso performance), 'invento' takes precedence over 'imitatio naturae'."

"What the hell does that mean?" Eleanor asked.

"It's something you'll just have to get used to. A lot of architects speak in a language that no one else can understand, but this place is the worst. It's a useful defence mechanism when you haven't a clue what you're talking about."

Harry was well aware of Eleanor's background; every student in the place was. Her father's Sunday lunches were legendary and every student prayed to be invited. Those that succeeded returned with tales of meeting the great architects of the day – Gropius, Kahn, Johnson, Kikutake, Foster, Stirling regularly ate at Riccardo's table.

"Look, if you're really worried about the presentation I'm happy to help you get it all together."

"Wow, that would be great. My father will be absolutely furious if I flunked my first year."

The next day Eleanor went round with her portfolio to Harry's flat. He was renting the top floor of a crumbling mansion block on Shaftesbury Avenue in the heart of Soho with three other Academy students. Harry answered the buzzer and she made her way into the hallway with its period checkerboard floor tiles. The lift looked distinctly dodgy and she decided to use the wide stairs taking care not to trip on the peeling linoleum.

The door to the flat was open. A sign asked visitors to take their shoes off before coming in, Japanese-style. She was amazed, it didn't seem like a student flat at all. It was spotlessly clean, everything was white, even the floor. Cardboard models of student projects were arranged around the walls, futon beds doubled as sofas and the second hand TV was given design-cred by removing the timber casing. The exposed wires, however, looked very dangerous.

Harry and Eleanor didn't leave the flat for a week. They spent most of the time in bed – although the futons were excruciating –

19

making love, talking and making love again. Eleanor failed to turn up to her presentation.

She moved her stuff into Harry's flat. They were inseparable in the bar and studios at the Academy, much to the disgust of most of the students who had lusted after her since the day their course had started. Eleanor's outgoing manner, Italian vivacity and general flirtatiousness often gave hope to eager suitors where there was none.

On the last week of term Thor Christenson called her in to his office.

"Eleanor, I'm very, very disappointed and I know your father will be too. You seem to have done nothing at all this year." He said as he looked at the tutor's report, which was indeed blank. "You didn't even turn up for your crit!"

Eleanor leant forward as though to check what her tutor had written. She had put on a particularly low cut top and short skirt that day. Thor enjoyed the company of his female students and Eleanor calculated that a suggestive pout and view of her revealing cleavage might at least soften the tone of the Head's letter to her parents. Had it been anyone else Thor would have fired her on the spot, but earlier in the year he had approached her father about setting up a bursary for disadvantaged students to attend the Academy under the Marsoni name. He was still waiting to hear Riccardo's answer.

"I don't want to be an architect anyway," she said in her little girl voice, leaning over the glass-topped table. Thor had a panoramic view of her long, slim legs through the glass.

Thor was not an unattractive man. He had the rugged look of someone whose forefathers fished the fjords, his lived in, lined face reflecting his love of sailing – the fiercer the weather the more he loved it – and of brandy and cigars. He was rarely without a glass in his hand and a Cohiba Robusto stuffed either into the corner of his mouth or between his thick fingers.

"And my father will be really cross." Eleanor fluttered her long Italian lashes. "He'll probably cut me off without a penny."

"He will be justifiably cross. But if it helps I'll write a letter to your father to say what a good student you are but that you are just not cut out for architecture."

"Thank you," Eleanor smiled as she stood up. Thor came round the table and took her arm as though to guide her to the door. He pulled her towards him. She caught a powerful whiff of cigar smoke. She knew what was coming. God! I can't let him kiss me, she thought.

"No Thor," she said gently as the large Norwegian leant down towards her "Not now. I'm engaged to Harry Jamb and he wouldn't be at all pleased to find me with your hand up my skirt!"

Chapter 2

It was a chilly November evening as Harry, in his last year as a student, and Eleanor made their way across Gibberd Square, drawn to the thumping music which was already shaking the sash windows of the surrounding buildings. The London Academy of Architecture building was bathed in a red glow. Suspended above the concrete structure were six-foot high helium-filled inflatable letters spelling out the word SEX and picked out by spotlights hidden amongst the foliage in the square gardens.

Even before she arrived at the school, Eleanor had heard lots of tales about the Academy's Winter Fiesta and its reputation as the most dissolute of London's student parties. New arrivals at the school were regaled by hardened veterans with tales of drink, drugs, group sex and compromised staff. The decoration of the building was a major feature. It was done by the Second Year students and was the first real project many of the students would deliver. The transformation of lecture theatres and studios into Roman Temples, Rococo grottoes or velveteen cocktail lounges was viewed by tutors as a real test of their charges' architectural skills.

The event itself was traditionally organised by the Student Union, a group of hard-partying public schools boys who formed the focus of the Academy's social life and whose aim was to make each Fiesta more extreme and radical than the last.

Harry had bought two tickets. They were expensive, since they covered the cost of unlimited alcohol as well as a selection of several good and upcoming bands; but there was no shortage of takers – once the Academy students had bought the tickets they needed, they were put on sale to students at the other architecture and art schools – the Slade, Bartlett, Central Poly and the RCA – who snapped them up.

Inside, the Second Year students had developed the theme for the night with interpretations of the bordello through history. From the seraglios of the Turks to specially-designed quarters to serve oil men in the Arabian desert, the architects-to-be created seductive interiors which provided the ideal environment in which guests could act out the planned debauchery.

Harry and Eleanor wandered through the various rooms, admiring the handiwork of their fellow students, cardboard painted columns, swags of fabric, painted views and lewd Pompeii-style murals had taken the place of the drawing boards and lecture room seating which occupied the rooms for the rest of the year.

The place was filling up fast and in some of the rooms there was an uncomfortable crush, made worse by the number of couches and beds that had been provided to create the appropriate atmosphere. These were already occupied by kissing couples or younger students who had already succumbed to the copious supply of alcohol.

Eleanor complained of claustrophobia and Harry steered her into the staff room where things were a lot quieter. A group of tutors, unconcerned at the intervention, propped up the bar. They had clearly been there for some time; Jim Bragg the history professor with his purple, whisky-ravaged nose was holding court on the subject of Colin Rowe, Collage City and Camillo Sitte to half a dozen or so other drinkers who nodded blankly as he spoke.

A baggy-suited figure slowly raised his hand in salute to Harry. Frank Cummins was thought by many to be one of the best architects in the land and the prestigious *Architectural Review* had recently published a whole issue devoted to his university buildings and high-density housing. Harry had worked for Cummins during his 'year out', when he had learnt more about architecture and how to do it than in the three previous years at the Academy.

Cummins taught one day a week, partly because he enjoyed the intellectual stimulus, but largely so that he could scout for talent. The best students were cultivated, given temporary jobs while at college and then invited to join Cummins and Partners, generally on a subsistence wage, when they graduated.

As one of the brightest in his year, Harry had been invited for an interview at Cummins's South Kensington offices, housed in a magnificent Regency terrace. Only a modest brass plate defined the house as the home of a major architectural practice, for this was before the days that architects were permitted to promote themselves. They were expected to get new clients only by recommendation or through entering competitions. Almost anything that today goes under the heading of 'marketing' would then have been described as 'touting' and the architect doing so could be struck off the register of architects and sacked from the Royal Institute of British Architects.

Harry pushed the shiny black door and walked into the spacious entrance hall. Exquisite boxwood models of Cummins's projects and buildings were displayed on minimal white plinths spread generously across the pale polished wood floor.

"Mr Cummins has been expecting you." The forty-something secretary led the way to a large office with three drawing boards on stands. Wagner wafted from the sound system as Cummins sketched on a roll of yellow tracing paper, seemingly unaware of Harry's presence.

Behind the great man sat two others, ignoring their drawing boards they worked at office desks. Harry was to discover these were the less well known partners, one of whose responsibilities was to run the office – to make sure costs (that is, staff) were kept low and the partners' fees high – and the other was to run the projects, while Cummins focused on design.

As he waited, Harry's gaze wandered around the room. The walls were covered with framed drawings in the practice's signature style of hard lines and soft crayons. There were also certificates of the many awards won and a framed letter of congratulations signed by The Queen following the opening of the Oxford Medical Research Laboratory.

Cummins looked up from his board "I've been watching your work – you produced some really mature designs in Third Year". He was a man of few words – except when he was presenting one of his own projects – and went straight to the point. "Why don't you come and do your year out here? You won't get paid much but you'll learn a lot. Dorothy will sort out the details and give you a quick tour of the office."

Harry realised the question was rhetorical. No one turned down a job with Cummins. Dorothy came up behind him.

"Let me show you where the others work," she said briskly, as Cummins went back to his sketching. Harry followed as the grand stairs narrowed and he was shown into a smaller room packed with drawing boards where a dozen men, and one woman, were busy drawing with pen or pencil. Large drawings of current projects were pinned around the walls and product catalogues of the latest bricks and drainage systems were scattered round the room. Harry recognised some of the people from the Academy, bright students who, like him, were being fast tracked through Cummins' own form of practical training.

"This is Harry Jamb everyone," announced Dorothy "and he'll be joining us for his 'year out' next month." Some of group looked up and nodded, others were so engrossed in their work they didn't seem to hear. "We'll find you a board when you get here," she added.

And that was it. As Harry left the office he realised he could learn a lot in a year with Cummins – but he had no intention of making a career there. He would try a different practice when he finished his training to get the broadest experience, and then set up on his own as soon as he could.

Harry watched how Cummins ran the office, observing the things they didn't teach you at architecture school. First of all there was Dorothy, Cummins's PA, who it turned out was a power behind the throne; she ran the great man's life for him, juggling professional and personal commitments, a go-between linking staff and partners, and a confidante.

Cummins had organised the office so that he could concentrate on what he liked to do most, which was designing. His two other partners took on the admin chores inside and outside the office. He would study the brief of all the new jobs that came in and do a series of sketches and notes on how the office should approach the problem. It would then be passed down to one of the job architects to start drawing it out more accurately.

Cummins would tour the office looking over the architects' shoulders, frequently leaning over to draw in suggestions with a soft 6B pencil. He was invariably right. That was his genius. He could look at a drawing and immediately see where the problems and possibilities would be in the finished building. He could see the building in three dimensions in his mind.

As the drawings developed he would sit down with the job architect and go through every detail, marking up the changes he wanted made. He never missed any mistakes, even when he had been drinking.

And that was often. Cummins was a bon viveur, he enjoyed a good meal and a good wine even better and luckily he had the constitution of an ox. As his drinking chums from the Academy staff room gradually succumbed to the depredations of Bacchus, Cummins would continue to down two bottles of claret over lunch.

Harry joined him one day at Chanterelle, a classic French restaurant in the Old Brompton Road, and as the great architect shovelled a dripping Camembert into his mouth, the young man marvelled how, , flushed and rotund though his boss appeared, he did not collapse into the cheese with a coronary. But entertaining was important to the business. Cummins entertained clients, critics, editors, and journalists as well as colleagues. Before the days when public relations consultants were permitted, he had few equals when it came to self-promotion.

"It's essential," he once lectured Harry "if people don't know you're out there they won't give you any work. If you don't have work you don't have a business. We're not like artists – they can go off and do a painting – we need a client to pay for the job first. So the three essentials of running a successful practice are 'get the job, get the job, get the job'. Without a job you've got nothing."

"Look at Vitruvius, Palladio, Corbusier – they all knew the power of the publication – Corb would never have had the massive influence he did without the books he published."

Harry listened and learnt. Indeed, the first job he was given when he arrived for his 'year out' was to redraw plans so that they would reproduce clearly in magazines and books.

"As an architect, you've got to be both a charmer and a shit." Cummins continued. "Once you've won the job then the battles start. You've got to fight the client to get the sort of building you want, fight the neighbours, fight the planners to get it through, fight the contractor to get him to build it properly, fight the suppliers to get the quality you want, fight the lawyers who try to sue you and then fight the client again over the final fees. People often think architects are arrogant. They need to be, to hold onto their vision through years, sometimes decades, of battles."

Harry watched Cummins in meetings. Yes, he was arrogant, and yes he could be totally stubborn, but he also had a charisma that helped him convince doubters that he was right, or at least there was no point in them continuing any resistance. And then a strange thing happened. Even as a student, at meetings, people started to speak to Harry as though he was an avatar of the master. And in turn he found it came easily to take on some of the characteristics that he had seen in Cummins. He became expert at sticking his heels in where he knew Cummins would have done so.

"Arrogant little fucker" he heard a contractor say to his colleague as they left one of Harry's meetings having lost an argument over the choice of a material.

And he knew he was learning important lessons that would set him in good stead for the future.

The noise of The Fiesta subsided as Harry let the Staff Room door shut. He walked over to the bar and shook Cummins's hand.

"Aren't you joining the party? It's heaving out there."

"Not my scene, old boy, this is as close as I want to get."

"Can I introduce Eleanor Marsoni, who's just joined the First Year."

"Yes, I'd heard Riccardo's daughter was at the school. Thor keeps going on about a big Marsoni endowment. Do tell Daddy to make his mind up, the school needs the money!"

Eleanor bridled at the reminder that she owed her place at the school to her father.

"Tell him yourself – he's more likely to take notice of you!"

"I think you're right!" Cummins laughed not at all bothered by her response. "I'm just about to buy 250 very expensive chairs from him for a new university hall of residence. I'll use that to twist his arm!"

***

"That man is so arrogant!" complained Eleanor as they slipped out of the room.

"It goes with the territory, you'd better get used to it" chuckled Harry.

A roar rose from the ground floor lecture room.

"Get 'em off! get 'em off!" came the repeated chant.

Harry and Eleanor squeezed in through the door and could just make out the half naked figure of a young girl writhing provocatively to the music of a modern jazz quartet squeezed into the corner of the room. Around her neck was draped an enormous boa constrictor. Following the drunken instructions of the almost totally male crowd she expertly removed her knickers and then

28

grasped the tail of the snake and waved it provocatively at the crowd.

"Put it in! Put it in!" the chant changed.

"My god, she can't be serious!" exclaimed Eleanor as the reptile slid down the girl's stomach.

"What the hell is going on?" Thor's powerful voice rang out. The quartet stopped mid-bar and the girl let the snake's tail drop. Open mouthed, the students turned to see what the clearly incandescent head of the school was about to do. Thor ignored the stripper but made his way to the group of Student Union reps who had been orchestrating the event.

"You bloody idiots! Not only is what was about to happen disgusting, it is also illegal. What do you think this sort of thing will do for the school? I don't mind you all getting pissed out of your minds but this sort of obscenity is another matter! That's it! I'm closing down the party, you can all go home!"

Thor had been pretty relaxed about the debauched nature of the event, but after a worried member of staff had let on what was planned and warned him that in England zoophilia was an imprisonable offence, he had no option but to take action.

As the stripper sulkily put her clothes on and the deflated students shuffled out into the night, Thor shuddered as he imagined the possible headlines in the next day's tabloids.

"For god's sake don't mention this to your father," Thor said rather nervously to Eleanor, "I can't see him funding us if this gets out."

The next day the tabloids lead on the latest IRA bombing and, luckily for Thor, there was less space for tittle-tattle. A few weeks later Cummins and Partners confirmed their order for 500 chairs with the Marsoni Furniture Company, and not long after the Academy of Architecture received a substantial endowment for the Marsoni Student Scholarship Fund.

Chapter 3

Harry sat staring at the TV screen as the celebrations in Frampton continued. He was determined to pull out all the stops to make sure Harry Jamb Associates was on the roster of firms to design the new buildings for the Games.

"A big project like that would be great for business," he said to Jenny as he switched off the TV, "but more importantly, it would be one in the eye for Freddie."

Frederick Shaw was Harry's ex-partner and major competitor. The two architects' early collaboration and friendship had turned into an increasingly bitter feud . Their firms vied for the same jobs, for the same awards and the same critical recognition. So far each had matched the other in terms of honours and rewards, but the Frampton Games would be different. Such a high profile project would put the winners right at the top table of world architects. A project like this could win him the prestigious Frazer Prize.

When they had finished their training both Harry and Frederick went to work at AAP Architects, one of the largest firms in the country. They sat at adjacent drawing boards and talked frequently about setting up an office of their own. AAP designed a lots of university buildings and, as the most junior members of the office, the two young architects found themselves doing the most boring jobs. This usually amounted to endlessly drawing by hand (this was before such mundane tasks were done on computer) student bedrooms, lavatories and shared kitchens.

One day the senior partner of AAP proudly announced that the practice had won the job of designing the student accommodation for the University of Rutchester.

"God! Not another thousand student loos to draw!" groaned Freddie. "We've got to get out of here. This wasn't what I trained for as an architect!"

"Come on let's take the plunge!" said Harry excitedly. "We'll have to do it one day. Why not now?"

"But it might be a good idea if we had some jobs under our belts," cautioned Freddie.

"I'm sure I can get my father-in-law to give us a bit of work. He's very well connected through the furniture business. You know we'd work so well together – I'm keen on detail, you're a broad brush man."

Freddie agreed. Detail bored him, he enjoyed the grand vision, he liked coming up with the ideas but not delivering them. He was only too happy to pass that bit on to others. Where Harry was open and frank, and people immediately trusted Harry, Freddie was more difficult to gauge. Those that knew him said he was shy; those less familiar thought he was arrogant. He certainly had a chip on his shoulder and resented his lowly background. Nevertheless, like Harry, Freddie had an unquenchable passion to build.

Frederick Shaw was an only child. His father had left home when he was three. His mother Winnie had a modest but secure job in the local council. She committed her life to the clever boy who did well at grammar school and, she knew, was destined for great things. He was brilliant at drawing and the school's art master had taken Freddie under his wing, hoping that he would be the first of his students ever to get a scholarship to the Slade School of Fine Art or Central St Martins. When Winnie heard of the plans she put her foot down. A career as an artist was far too risky. A compromise was reached. A career in architecture provided an outlet for Freddie's creative talents but was also a "proper and respectable job".

Freddie was taller than Harry, with aquiline features and long flowing blond hair. He wore the same black unstructured suits and white collarless shirts every day, and for every occasion, whether a client meeting or a black tie function. It was a habit which started for convenience – he never had to waste any time deciding what to wear and there was always something clean in the wardrobe – but as time went on it became something of an affectation. Freddie once punched a porter at the Reform Club when the hapless servant insisted he put on a tie before entering the hallowed portals.

Shaw, Jamb and Partners – SJP – opened up in a small office just off Charlotte Street close to Goodge Street Station in the heart of Fitzrovia. They did well from the start – AAP generously passed on jobs that were too small for its practice to take on. A wealthy uncle of Harry's commissioned a house on the cliffs at Harlyn Bay in Cornwall, while Riccardo asked them to design a range of office furniture. They took part in the 'Forty Under Forty' Exhibition, were featured on the cover of *Blueprint* magazine, and selected by *The Gazette* – the only national newspaper with decent coverage of architecture – for their New Year feature in the annual Cultural Supplement on 'Young Talent to Watch'.

The seeds of distrust between the partners were sown in a small but significant incident on the night that the Harlyn Bay House won a National Architecture Award. The whole of the five-year-old office, all eight of them, went to the presentation ceremony in the Royal Institute of British Architects building in Portland Place. Eleanor came too. In those days the awards ceremony wasn't a big sponsored dinner event – there were no drinks or food at all. Award winners gathered in the Wren Lecture Hall and were called up one by one to receive an inscribed certificate from the President.

Feeling elated and very hungry, the whole team from SJP went for a celebratory supper at Efes Turkish Restaurant on Great Titchfield Street where they gorged on kebabs and much too much retsina.

The architects were all either just out of college or taking a year out from their course to pick up practical experience, except for a quiet young Asian sitting at the end of the table. Tariq Shah had joined SJP from a large commercial practice where he had learnt how the business of architecture operated. But Tariq didn't like the buildings the practice were doing, they just weren't good enough in his opinion. Tariq was ambitious and wanted only to work with the best. He had pinpointed SJP as a practice that was going places. His family had been disappointed that he hadn't become a doctor and he wanted to prove to them that he had made the right choice.

When the group finished supper they tumbled out into the balmy Fitzrovia night. They were all too excited to break up the party.

"What shall we do now?" asked Jenny, surrogate mother to the young staff.

"There's plenty of drinks in the office fridge," said Harry. "Let's go back there."

Harry was keen to get back so he could check on some faxes he was expecting about a possible job in Hong Kong. Even in his current befuddled state the chance of a major new project set his adrenalin coursing.

Tariq gave his apologies.

"It's way past my bedtime".

Tariq always like to be in full control. He drank, but only in limited quantities, he never liked to be tired in case he under performed at work. He also wanted to get away because he knew that Freddie would get out the office stash of marijuana. Tariq hated drugs and felt very out of place when anyone was using them in his company.

The remaining group meandered back through Fitzrovia. Harry, Eleanor and Freddie walked in the front, arm in arm. Eleanor had drunk as much as any of them and was in flirtatious mood. She looked fantastic in a green tight cotton dress with a short flared skirt and vertiginously high heels. As they walked Freddie could feel the warmth of her body against him.

They tumbled into the office – a single open space that took up the whole of the ground floor of the converted Georgian terrace house. They had fitted it out very simply and cheaply. They used hardboard flush doors as worktables fixed in rows along each wall. Painted in clear matt varnish, the brown tones of the hardboard reflected in the cheap coconut matting carpet on the floor. The white walls doubled as pin up space and were covered with plans, sketches and photos.

Drawing boards lay in neat rows along the worktables. In the front of the space was Jenny's desk on which was proudly displayed the office's new Mac Classic computer and dot matrix printer. A spiral stair in the middle went up to spare office space that the practice hadn't yet grown into. Beanbags on the floor provided space to relax and discuss design issues. When working late staff, would sleep there rather than going home. Freddie tended to use it more than any of the others.

Harry went straight to the fax while everyone else staggered up the precarious spiral staircase. The machine had spewed out yards of thermal print paper, a concertina of drawings, charts, calculations and text covered the floor. He looked at his watch. It would be half past six in the morning in Hong Kong and they would be starting work in hour and a half. He had to see what they wanted straight away.

Harry sobered up in a flash as he read the opening paragraph. "It is the intention of the Hong Cho Property Company to built a major shopping centre in the New Territories. You are invited to submit your proposals. A brief and a site plans are attached. Please let me know by return whether you are willing to take on this important project." Harry sat down and started reading.

Upstairs (as Tariq had anticipated) Freddie removed a plastic bag from the back of the fridge, tipped half the contents onto the low table and started expertly rolling joints for his staff. They passed them round to the sounds of Phil Collins, Police and Blondie and the room vibrated to the bass sounds emerging from the new Bang and Olufsen speakers Freddie had splashed out on to celebrate the award.

As the time of the last tube train drew near, the staff members slipped out into the night leaving Harry downstairs in the office and Eleanor and Freddie lying next to each other on the bean bag in the upstairs room.

While Harry was totally devoted to Eleanor, Freddie was a serial adulterer who was addicted to sex He openly confessed that he found it impossible to go to sleep if he went to bed on his own. At the sight of an attractive face or a great figure, Freddie's shyness seemed to disappear; his winning smile and piercing blue eyes transfixed his prey and his usual laid back manner was transformed and animated by the prospect of coition. Freddie rarely seemed to have any problem finding attractive girls to join him in bed.

He moved closer to Eleanor, rearranging the beanbag so that he pressed against her body. Eleanor didn't move away. He sensed her respond to his touch. All evening she had been laughing and paying extra attention to Freddie. He needed no more encouragement. He pulled her close to him, quickly moving his free hand under her skirt.

"No! Freddie! Don't!" she said firmly and pulled sharply back and Freddie rolled away.

"I thought you were up for it! You seemed keen enough!' Freddie retorted, insulted by the rejection.

As Harry recognised their urgent tones from downstairs he rushed up the spiral stairs, two steps at a time, until he could dimly see Eleanor lying on the bean bag with her cotton skirt rumpled around her waist and Freddie lying on his back next to her. Harry was stunned. It looked worse than it was, but it was clear Freddie had been trespassing in forbidden places.

"What's going on?"

Harry tried to sound firm but suddenly found himself shaking as feelings of betrayal and jealousy swept over him. He wasn't often jealous. Eleanor's outgoing personality, familiar manner and Latin ease of getting very close to, and touching, people naturally meant she had a lot of admirers. Not infrequently men made a grab for her which she fended off with practised ease. But this was different.

"Nothing" answered Freddie glumly.

Eleanor could see Harry's shocked expression, his shoulders slumped as though a load has been dropped on him from a great height. His open face was contorted with . . . was it hate? Or jealousy? She rearranged her dress.

"What the hell do you think you were doing Freddie?" Harry said quietly.

"I'm sorry," Freddie mumbled and got up silently. He couldn't look at Harry, who did not know whether to punch his partner in the face or to drag Eleanor away. This was his friend! His business partner! They were going to be famous together, build towers and spaces that would change the world! The biggest job they had ever had was their's for the taking in Hong Kong! How could Eleanor do this?

Freddie realised he'd overstepped the mark that defined his relationship with his business partner. He hung his head looking shamefaced, vulnerable even, like a schoolboy about to receive six of the best.

Harry turned and walked down the spiral stairs.

Suddenly, and unusually for her, Eleanor started weeping.

"I'm so sorry Harry! I'm so sorry! Please don't go!"

Harry strode out of the office and into the still warm, empty night. The sky was clear, the dark shadow of the Post Office Tower loomed above the Georgian terraces of Fitzrovia. He was still shaking. He needed a stroll through the quiet London streets to calm him down. He loved to walk and soak in the atmosphere, the history, and the buildings of the city, tracing the outlines of the ancient farms and estates that determined where developments took place, and the drovers' routes that set the pattern of the city.

Less traffic and fewer people gave Harry a feeling of freedom and ownership of the streets. He liked to see the insides of buildings – by day solid and monolithic, but at night, peering into illuminated rooms, he could understand their internal spaces and their three dimensionality. Harry's own work was all about the geometry of space. At night he saw the city as a continuum of interconnected volumes, some enclosed, some open.

He walked up the Euston Road and along Albany Street towards their Chalk Farm flat, skirting the great blackness of Regents Park.

Eleanor was already at home when he got back waiting in the kitchen, her face streaked with tears, her green dress exchanged for her familiar woollen dressing gown.

"I didn't mean anything to happen, Harry. We'd had such a lot to drink. . . and then the grass. . . I like Freddie, but that's all. It happened so quickly and you *know* what he's like."

Harry accepted Eleanor's description of events, but everything had changed. For the first time, Freddie had become a threatening presence in their relationship and Harry felt a new sense of uneasiness .

***

"This Hong Kong job is potentially the biggest that SJP has ever attempted. We've really got to pull the stops out on this one." Harry was guarded with Freddie at the partners' meeting the next morning.

Each of them knew that it was too dangerous to argue about the events of the previous night. Personal issues had to be subjugated to the development of the practice. In order to be able to stand a chance of getting major jobs they had to build up an effective team (it wasn't just Harry and Freddie, Tariq was there too), they needed to build a reputation among the press and potential clients, and to be able to work together efficiently to win the jobs in the first place.

But Freddie didn't think his quick fumble with Eleanor was that big a deal anyway. If he was to be continually concerned what boyfriends, partners, husbands were going to think of him it would significantly cramp his style and his range of prospects. He knew that Harry had taken it badly and understood his partner's reactions well enough to keep away from the subject. He also knew that Eleanor's father would be deeply upset. And he was bankrolling the firm.

Harry, Freddie and Tariq would endlessly discuss ways in which they could expand the business. Their interests and skills matched so well: Freddie always went for the big picture, Harry the detail, Tariq provide sound business sense and reined in the other two's enthusiasms.

Tariq, unaware of the tensions left over from the night before, was outlining their business strategy: "The economy is just beginning to come out of recession and there should be a lot more work about. Mrs Thatcher is promoting home ownership, the council house building of the last thirty years has all but stopped. There's going to be a lot of private housing to build."

"But who wants to work for private housebuilders?" argued Harry. "They produce crap – Noddy houses peppered across the country. They have no idea of quality. They're only interested in selling their second rate products as quickly as possible and buggering off. We should go in for more competitions. That's where the best projects are. There's a fantastic one in *Building News* this week for the design of a museum in Germany."

"Competitions cost us a lot of money," cautioned Tariq. "We spend a fortune entering them and the chances of winning are just too slim. We've got to have a regular income from other work to be able to afford to enter them."

***

The practice grew, as did the economy. The work started to come in through recommendations and word of mouth. The three never did agree on a business strategy; they took on each job as it came.

***

Freddie announced his engagement to Harriet Foster-Clark soon after the incident with Eleanor. They had met at a drinks party to celebrate the completion of one of the practice's more expensive private houses. She didn't need money, her family owned estates in Northampton and Perthshire and she would come into a substantial inheritance when she was 25. Harriet, attracted to Freddie's edgy working class background, could see he was going places. She was excited by the prospect of pushing him up through the complex layers of English society. Harriet knew exactly what sort of married life she wanted – a fine country house full of children and dogs, stables with horses and ponies and a couple of Norland nannies. But she was enough of a rebel to enjoy the contrast between Freddie and the farmers, bankers and brewers who formed the rest of her social circle.

She wanted Freddie to be working on high profile buildings that her friends would know about. While she had high hopes for Freddie, she also thought that Harry was holding her man back, and she didn't take to Eleanor at all.

"He's such a nerd and she's so awfully loud and spoilt," she complained. "You've got to get rid of him Freddie! You'll do much better on your own."

As the practice got bigger Harry and Freddie started to look after jobs separately; they built up their own teams of designers and tended their own clients. The work of each team started to take on a subtly different character. Harry stuck to his clean, angular style, perfecting the detailing, honing his architecture down to its simplest elements, creating a stark beauty. Freddie's architecture became more flowing, with curves and sculptural elements that Harry found fussy and unnecessary. There were two unmistakeable strands of work emerging from the firm.

They were doing well; they took over the rest of the building in Goodge Street and the flush doors gave way to Marsoni's modular office system that was designed to cope with the mass of wires that spewed out of the new generation of computers and plotters that were taking the place of the drawing boards.

Booming economies are kind to architects. Clients build in booms – often too much. Architects need clients to be able to practice their art. Equally, when the economy slows building projects and budgets are cut and the construction industry crumbles.

***

And thus they continued, not knowing that greater forces would soon create havoc with their comfortable but fundamentally dysfunctional world.

On the morning of Monday, October 19 1987 shares on the Hong Kong Stock Exchange started to fall rapidly, presaging a record collapse in values around the globe.

Black Monday threw the economy into recession and, quite simply, most of SJP's clients stopped commissioning buildings. It became increasingly difficult to get paid for those jobs that were carrying on and a couple of firms that still owed fees went bust.

"We've got to start cutting staff," said Tariq "we just haven't got the work for them to do or the income to pay them."

"I agree" Freddie responded, "we've only got enough cash to keep us going for six more months at this rate and no new jobs in sight."

"We can't do that" Harry stared at them both, "we've spent nearly ten years building up these teams of people. The work will start coming back; the recession can't last that long. We've got to hang on to our employees – they're the key to our success."

Harry wan't going to budge, and Tariq became increasingly frustrated. This was no way to run a business.

Harry felt he was being out-manoeuvred. How could he sack people who had help build up the practice, who had worked together in a creative unit that would take years to replace once it was broken up? He was damned if he would get rid any of the 15 people who formed his team. These were people who understood Harry's approach to his architecture, and who believed in the same design philosophy about what was good and what was bad.

Harry spoke to his father in law. Riccardo was sympathetic of Harry's plight but as a businessman he realised that their business just couldn't last in the present climate.

"You're going to have to take some pretty radical steps, and take them soon" he advised.

Harriet could also read the runes as far the economic outlook of the firm was concerned. Her experience of dealing with her family fortunes, helped by a bevy of top City advisors, had given her a sound understanding of finance. Freddie had told her about Harry's intransigence as far as taking necessary and urgent action was concerned.

"Now's the time to get rid of him! And as for Eleanor, she's just not the right sort of person to have around when you are entertaining important clients. You've got to set up on your own, Freddie, but make bloody sure you take Tariq with you."

***

Riccardo had long planned to replace his ageing factory outside Milan, it wasn't big enough or flexible enough for modern manufacturing techniques and couldn't adapt to meet modern Health and Safety Regulations controlling sawdust, toxic adhesives, fumes and the use of dangerous machinery. He realised that because of the recession the price of building materials was dropping like a stone, while the best labour was easy to find and very cheap.

He mentioned the project to Harry "I'll give you the job, if you set up in practice on your own. The fees will keep you going for a bit – and if they don't I'll support you again." Eleanor had told her father of how Harriet seemed to despise her; Riccardo thought Harriet was a stuck up English cow of the worst kind and he was insulted that she should treat Eleanor in the way she did.

The spilt, when it happened, still managed to shock Harry despite the fact that the disputes and disagreements that had been going on for many months.

The weekly management meeting had started innocuously enough with small talk about which practices had won what jobs that week. Then Freddie suddenly started: "Tariq and I have something to say" he stared at the meeting room table, unable to look at Harry. "We've agreed we are setting up in practice together. We want to dissolve SJP as soon as possible." He stopped as abruptly as he'd begun

Harry didn't answer. He couldn't. The reality of the split, which deep down he had known was inevitable, was much more painful than he had dreamed it would be. He had been proud of the work they had created together; the Harlyn Bay house and the Marsoni furniture range had been great critical successes, but suddenly it all seemed so meaningless. Most hurtful of all was the feeling that Freddie and Tariq had ganged up on him.

Freddie knew Harriet would be happy that he had taken the plunge; Tariq, who didn't have a rich wife, was nervous but glad to get rid of Harry and flattered that Freddie seemed so keen to work with him. Tariq thought that Freddie had the better business brain and sticking with him was a safer bet.

Harry swallowed hard. He couldn't face an argument right then. He stood up.

"I'll ring my lawyer to sort things out," he proffered, and left the room.

He looked straight ahead as he walked grim faced between the row of desks, he didn't want to catch the eye of any of the staff who might lose their job as a result of the meeting. Harry walked across the street to the Cambridge Arms.

"Double vodka" he said to barman.

"And another," Harry said as he put the first shot of many to his lips.

***

Although Harry and Freddie had split as business partners their paths would cross many times over the coming years – they would take part in a titanic struggle as they each clawed their way out of the recession, to come head to head in competition for the top projects around the world – a fight that would reach its climax on the site of the EuroGames in Frampton-on-Tees.

Chapter 4

A year or so after the split, Harry and Freddie attended The Institute of Art Annual Lecture, one of London's most glamorous cultural occasions attended by rich patrons, politicians, celebrities, artists and critics. The lecture was to be given by the Japanese architect Tomo Koji.

When Koji had finished his talk, which had been delivered through a translator and thus took rather longer than expected, the invited VIPs made their way to the grand rooms of the 19th century galleries where pre-dinner drinks were on offer.

"Oh didn't that go on!" said Eleanor as the throng made its way up the stairs.

"That's the problem with translated lectures," Harry added, "they take twice as long as they should and you can only understand half of what it said!"

Keen to get to the long-delayed drinks, the disgruntled assortment of the capital's *beau monde* squeezed into the Baroque Fred Biretta Room, named after the benefactor who had recently paid for the space – with paintings, putti and plaster cartouches smothered with gold leaf – to be restored. It was a noisy and tight knit scrum as people grabbed a glass of champagne and then turned to debate the qualities of Koji's architecture and his lecture. While the Institute's organising team had sensibly designed the dinner table plan so that Harry and Freddie were at either ends of the long table set out in the James Raschenbacker Room next door, during drinks there were no such diplomatic controls.

Bankers in Savile Row suits mingled with tieless architects; the wives of patrons of the arts displayed frocks that cost as much as a Henry Moore print, their taut faces as immobile as the classical artist's busts that were arranged around the four walls of the room. Like bees flitting among the flowers, some moved from group to

44

group pollinating them with gossip and picking up useful tidbits for their own re-use. Freddie, keen to let as many people as possible know his views on Koji's work, moved effortlessly through the throng.

"This minimalist stuff is just dull, dull, dull. Sure there's a certain Zen beauty about his buildings but they're only good for temples or museums."

Freddie always liked to circulate amongst this coterie of the crème de la crème of architecture and its clients. It was important to be noticed. He wanted to know what his competitors were up to, to chat up potential clients and to find out the gossip. He was practised at assessing the room with one quick sweep; who was there, who he should talk to and who he shouldn't bother with. He didn't have a lot of competition from his peers, they mainly only wanted to chat to other architects and soon became engrossed in arcane conversations about Modernism, Post Modernism, Deconstructivism, Prince Charles, the Planning System, English Heritage, sailing, and the Frazer Prize. Some were accompanied by their wives who tended to be more observant of the opportunities the room provided as they nudged their partners (sometimes business partners as well as marital ones). "Isn't that Sid Dixon/ James Sainsbury/Gerald Ronson over there? Go and speak to him!" the recalcitrant spouse would be urged.

Harriet didn't need to convince Freddie to circulate. It was her job to provide a solid back up as he navigated his way through the various groups. She would chat to the wives about frocks and foundations, regularly slipping in positive messages about Freddie. She knew that as Sir Rich Client was being driven home, in the back of the Merc, Lady Rich Client would be singing the praises of Freddie and his work.

Harriet's ambitions for her husband had been given additional edge as the competition between Freddie and Harry had become more intense. At first, the division of spoils seemed remarkably amicable. The fact that both Harry and Freddie had realised the inevitability of it all, that they should go their own ways, meant their initial emotions were one of relief that the dysfunctional relationship was over, mingled with enthusiasm for their new projects.

Harriet had circulated around most of the room when she reached a group that included the developer Sid Dixon and his wife.

"Hello Veronica" she said with her most unctuous smile. Veronica smiled back with a wide grin. She had recently had her teeth veneered and was keen to show them off. She was squeezed into a tight gold dress that matched the gilt swags on the walls and harmonised with her deep coffee tan, her ample bosom squeezed upwards to resemble the buttocks of the cherubs that adorned the room. Harriet thought Veronica Dixon cheap and quite beyond the pale, but knew that Sid, as one of the most active developers in the country, was someone Freddie needed to cultivate.

"Do tell me," Veronica asked eagerly after only a few moments of introductory chat "what's happened to your husband's firm? I hear he and Harry Jamb have split up."

"Yes, they have," answered Harriet "Freddie has set up on his own."

It just so happened that in the moving tide of people Harriet and Eleanor had been thrust together. They were now standing back to back. Eleanor, could hear Harriet's voice quite clearly, but Harriet was unaware of the other's presence.

"It was just no good," continued Harriet, imagining how her conversation would be reported back to Sid in the car home. "Freddie couldn't work with Harry, he had no idea how to run a business and no idea of keeping costs on his buildings under control. And you, of course, know how important that is, particularly in this economic climate!"

Eleanor turned round in a flash. Her eyes blazing. She knew deep down that there was some truth in the comment but she could not bear the smugness with which Harriet had criticised Harry. She was livid.

"You bitch!"

She couldn't stop herself and threw her recently topped-up glass of champagne into Harriet's face.

Her first thought was of regret – not that she had thrown the wine but that it was white wine and not red. It seemed to make such little impression. Harriet stood there imperiously, wine dripping off her nose and onto her dress, yet hardly showing up on the dark fabric. Without a word she turned back to the horrified group of Freddie, Veronica, Sid and a couple of elderly painters who thought it was all rather exciting and just the sort of thing that was supposed to happen in artists' circles. Harriet wiped the wine from her face and smiled again at Veronica.

All eyes were on Eleanor. Before Harry could say anything she shouted "Let's get out of this bloody place" and strode to the door with Harry feeling rather foolish, trailing behind.

***

Some weeks later an interview with Freddie appeared in *Building News* where he was asked about his new practice, Frederick Shaw and Partners (they had talked about calling it Shaw and Shah but that didn't work and anyway Tariq was happy to stay in the background). The article was illustrated with a new portrait of Freddie standing against a white background to accentuate his black and white style; his blond hair was cropped a bit shorter, its slightly ruffled look suggesting that he had taken to using hair gel.

Next to the portrait was a selection of photographs including the Harlyn Bay house, the Hong Kong project and the Marsoni office furniture. Not one of the captions included any reference to FJP or Harry. Eleanor was the first to see the article.

"Look Harry – there's a picture of Harlyn Bay and no mention of you at all."

She remembered well the way the two architects had worked so closely together and so hard to produce the designs for the iconic house. Every element of the plans and elevations had fitted into place like a glove as each brought his own particular sensibilities to the design.

Harry couldn't believe it.

Architectural practices have all the same problems of marriages when they go through a divorce – splitting up the assets, fractured personal relationships, dependents (for children, read staff) and money squabbles. The big difference is the importance the parties place on the accreditation of past work. Who actually designed the buildings? Who could use the photographs to promote their current work? Who should win work that is based on past performance? Why is one architect claiming the credit for a building which was designed totally by his erstwhile partner? Celebrated splits like those of Stirling and Gowan, Farrell and Grimshaw, Foster and Shuttleworth were played out in the press as the former colleagues sought to ensure that they received proper recognition for their contribution to previous success.

Harry and Freddie had spent hours and huge fees with lawyers who thrashed out how the schemes they worked on together should be credited following their split.

"Like any artist, the correct accreditation is fundamental for an architect whose success or failure is judged by the quality of his or her buildings," intoned the £350-an-hour legal eagle. "While profile and personality, wealth and lifestyle may influence the media, clients are interested in the designer's ability to deliver a good building."

"We did that building together. It's impossible to separate out who did what. It makes me look daft among my peers. They'll start to think that Freddie was the brains behind the practice."

"I'll frame a strongly-worded letter advising him not to do it again, Harry, but it probably won't do much good. We can sue him but it won't be worth it and anyway he'll probably blame the magazine. Your best bet is to write a letter to the editor and hope they publish it," said the lawyer.

Harry wrote the letter, telling the magazine's readers the correct attribution; he also sent copies of the letters to other magazine editors in case Freddie tried the same thing on with them. But he didn't like doing it. When the letter was published it seemed as if he was whining, a sort of 'Disgruntled of Clerkenwell'. "Shit" he thought as he opened the letters page of the magazine, "this hasn't done me any good at all." He had corrected the detail but he had came out of it second best.

He was on the back foot. First blood to Freddie. He wouldn't let that happen again.

***

As Britain slowly emerged from the recession in the mid 90s both Harry and Freddie got busier and busier. Freddie had commissions all over the world designing museums, offices, libraries and law courts. They worked in very different ways – Freddie was keen to expand, to become a global firm with offices around the world; Harry wanted to stay fairly small but was happy to work in partnership with other architects from the country he was working in. He had managed to retain his small core team during the downturn, and they made an incredibly effective unit, working well together, they understood exactly what Harry wanted. Harry made six of them partners in the practice and any one of them could confidently present a Harry Jamb Associates scheme to the most demanding client. This meant Harry was able to concentrate on what he saw as the exciting bit of a project – the early design work. For Harry this was when all the ideas came together to generate the main concept of each project – a concept that had to be held onto, that had to be fought for, right to the day the final piece of the building was put into place.

Freddie, in contrast, with Tariq's keen business mind behind him, was building up a global empire. Each time the firm won a major job in a new country they would open up an office there. Freddie found himself flying constantly between the growing offices. He got to know the aircrews on the BA flights so well that they greeted him by his first name. Freddie was the face of the firm and had to be there when the clients asked for him. He stopped designing, sometimes running off a few scribbles in his Moleskine sketch book that would be scanned and emailed back to the office.

He didn't often get home much to Harriet. She stayed happily with the children in their beautiful Arts and Crafts home in the Surrey Hills which had been commissioned in 1890 by Harriet's great grandfather. Freddie, had a pied-a-terre in the Barbican which he used when he was in London. The rest of the time it was a hike from five star hotel room to five star hotel room – the National in Moscow, the Burj in Dubai, the Mandarin in Hong Kong and the Grand Hyatt in Shanghai.

The local office would generally lay on a dinner with clients or local contacts, and include among the guests a suitably attractive partner for Freddie, who could be depended on to agree to accompany him to his room. If Freddie didn't get enough sleep or sex he became edgy and difficult.

But it was not only in the way that they ran their practices that the two former friends took different paths – the style of their architecture had become very different.

"While Harry Jamb is sticking to his perfectly detailed architecture in which the right angle is the defining geometry," wrote Rachael Dove in *The Gazette*, "Frederick Shaw's work is becoming increasingly sensuous, curvy and sculptural. Some suggest that this shift has been accelerated by the hiring of the brilliant young South American architect, Carlos de Souza, who has recently finished at the London Academy of Architecture having won all the prizes there were to be won, including the Earl Grey Medal, the most coveted award of all."

Before he came to Britain, De Souza had worked for the celebrated Brazilian architect Oscar Niemeyer. As a student he had been entranced by the beautiful sculptural forms of Niemeyer's work in Brasilia. Niemeyer had told him "There's no need to draw in a straight line," and frequently referenced his sensuous designs to the female form – volumes and curves of which he had studied in close detail as a young man on the beaches of Rio de Janeiro. While the *maestro* drew his curves in simple Picasso-like pencil lines which looked more like art than architecture, Carlos worked with the most sophisticated computer programmes to generate his forms. De Souza used similar anthropological terminology with Freddie when he explained the development of his designs. It was an approach that Freddie could appreciate through his obsession with the female form. Bringing together his two great loves – women and architecture – seemed to make a lot of sense.

Freddie celebrated his 50th birthday with a quarter bottle of champagne from the mini bar of his room at the Mandarin in Hong Kong. He admired himself in the full length mirror. He looked younger than his years, he kept himself in shape and in spite of his punishing schedule he looked trim and taut.

He also felt good. He was establishing his name independently from Harry, his work was maturing with a recognisable signature. Architecture must be the only profession where you're still 'young' at fifty he thought, but so many great architects have been middle aged before they did their best work – Mies van der Rohe, Le Corbusier, Frank Gehry, James Stirling, Denys Lasdun – you've got to get a bit of experience under your belt to produce a really rounded buildings. He did twenty quick press ups to prove to himself that he could.

"No sweat" he murmured as he stood up and smiled at his reflection.

He had woken at 6.00; the pretty Thai girl who had kept him company for the night slipped silently out of the Chater Road side entrance and Freddie went up to the gym for a workout and sauna. He needed the exercise to stretch his muscles after too many hours in the air. Back in his room he zapped on the TV to catch the news as he tucked into his room service breakfast of fruit and yogurt.

"It is my proud duty to announce that the EuroGames is awarded to the city of . . . Frampton-on-Tees" intoned the EU Minister of Sport on the BBC World News round up.

Freddie tensed. This was the big one and I'm ready for it, he thought.

Just as Harry, a few hours earlier, had instantly recognised the redundant steelyards of Frampton as the field on which their battle would be lost or won, so Freddie saw it as the means to settle once and for all who was the better architect. He grabbed his phone. In London, Tariq would still be in bed, so Freddie sent him a text.

"We shld enter Frampton games comp. Call me at 2pm local time."

He pushed aside the breakfast tray and went out onto the balcony to enjoy the spectacular view. The hotel always gave him one of the north east corner rooms which looked out onto Victoria Harbour and Kowloon on one side, and Statue Square with Harry Seidler's sensuous Hong Kong Club as well as Norman Foster's ground-breaking HSBC Bank building, on the other. Over to his left towered the 400-metre high International Financial Centre by Cesar Pelli, and in the distance on West Kowloon, the ICC building by Kohn Pedersen Fox – which would be even taller – was beginning to take shape.

The morning sun sparkled on the steel and glass towers, highlighting them against the intense blue of the sky. The harbour was already busy with tankers, coasters, junks, launches and the Star Ferries criss crossing the ever-shrinking waterway. Below Freddie could hear the ancient trams clanking along Des Voeux Road and the teeming red taxis that made this one of the most accessible cities in the world.

Freddie loved its compactness, the ease and speed that he could get from meeting to meeting. The buzz, the scale of buildings, the optimism for the future that they represented and their sheer quality as objects excited Freddie every time he stayed in Hong Kong. Looking out from the balcony he felt pumped up for the first meetings of the day.

He slipped quickly into his familiar white shirt and black suit. The humidity was up to 87 per cent, so he was glad he had had half a dozen lightweight linen copies of his suits made at Sam's Tailors in Kowloon especially for use while he was in the Far East. He had five meetings planned for that morning, the first was with the Hong Cho Property company, one of the clients he had continued to work with after the split with Harry. He planned to get back for a leisurely lunch in the China Club and then discuss the EuroGames competitions with Tariq.

Tariq called on the dot of 2.00pm and immediately launched into an obviously prepared response to Freddie's text message.

"Freddie, we need to think long and hard about getting involved with the EuroGames. We have to make sure it doesn't damage our ability to deal with our existing clients and the work we already have in the office. We've got plenty of projects in Moscow, Dubai and China and they need to be looked after. Clients want to see you. These big public projects are fraught with problems and could absorb an awful lot of your time. They can also go horribly wrong and that can rebound on us even though it may not be our fault. Look at what happened to Richard Rogers with the Millennium Dome and with Terminal 5 at Heathrow. They were great buildings but Rogers caught the flak for problems that were way beyond his control."

"If we worried about the way our clients were going to operate our buildings, we'd never take on any projects at all" Freddie managed to interject.

"But these buildings will be designed and built in the full glare of publicity," Tariq countered, "the press will have a field day if they go a penny over the budget. And it's almost inevitable they will because the decisions are controlled by politicians, and they don't know what they want in the first place, demand a cheap price so they can get it through, keep changing their minds and then hang you out to dry when the press get hold of the figures. Remember how Enric Miralles was totally shafted over the Scottish Parliament Building."

"We're rather good at keeping costs under control," insisted Freddie, "we can show them how it ought to be done."

"And I've been doing a bit of homework on Frampton. They've got a go ahead Mayor who knows what he wants and is willing to cut red tape to get it, and he's advised by a very bright Planning Chief called Ed Clutton."

"But the place has got problems" Tariq interjected. "It's never really recovered from the closure of the steel plant in the 70s, there are areas of massive poverty and some vocal and active community groups. And that's not all: one of the biggest problems for us is the Duke of Frampton who's incredibly powerful in the area. He hates modern architecture with a passion and he certainly won't like anything you might design for the Games. He owns a lot of land in Frampton, he funds local charities and he's President of the Frampton Civic Society, which is run by a chap called John Veduty, a very clever guy, who is against anything modern happening in the city. The Duke has already been on the Radio 4's Today Programme calling for a design based on the Coliseum in Rome!"

"He can't be serious!" Freddie blurted, "this is the twenty-first century! What sort of image will that give to the rest of the world?"

"OK – if you want to go for it, get ready for interminable fights with the project managers who will be keeping an eye on every design decision you make. The sorts of buildings that you and Carlos do aren't easy to build and they're not cheap. You are their worst nightmare Freddie."

Freddie was only too aware of the problems that such a project might bring, but he didn't care. "I'm not going to let fucking Harry fucking Jamb win it!" and at that moment Tariq knew he'd lost the argument.

Chapter 5

"The two most prominent buildings in the Games masterplan will be the Swimming Complex and the Main Stadium," Planning Chief Ed Clutton told the Frampton-on-Tees EuroGames Committee. "My team has developed the overall layout; now we have to select world class architects for these buildings and for the rest of the site."

"The 'rest of the site' includes the International Press Facilities, which will have to cope with some 4,000 journalists, TV crews and radio reporters as well as a mass of equipment, satellite dishes and wires, and a range of 'temporary pavilions' for use as ticket offices, cafés and lavatories."

"Most of the old steelworks buildings on the site have been demolished and we are currently decontaminating the ground which is full of a pretty toxic cocktail of chemicals."

He talked fast and always with tremendous enthusiasm. His crumpled grey suit was a nod in the direction of his bureaucratic role, the garish tie and frequent stubble suggested an independent, and mildly rebellious streak. His energy never seemed to flag, the dreams of a better Frampton kept the adrenalin pumping through his hyperactive system.

"Our job now is to find the best designers in the world to give us a set of buildings that will become the icons for the EuroGames. They will be seen by TV audiences around the world, they will promote the international image of Frampton as a twenty first century city."

Ed thought back to his all-expenses-paid, fact-finding trip with Mayor Jarvis. They had travelled together to study how other cities had tackled the problems of putting on a major sports event, and what the long term effects had been for their economies, their image and the physical cities themselves. They had been pretty impressed by Barcelona where the celebrated Mayor Pasqual Marigall used the Olympics to totally change the structure of the city: the individual buildings were good, but the legacy of new housing, new beaches and the redevelopment of the dockland area was the real clincher. At Sydney they discovered the Olympic Park provided a permanent sports venue for locals right in the heart of the city, and a general feeling that the games had been good for the city and for Australia, despite the questionable economic returns. Athens had not fared so well: the chaotic preparation merely confirming in the world's eyes the country's lackadaisical organisational skills. German organisers of the Football World Cup told them of the improvement to Germany's image as a result of the friendly atmosphere surrounding the games. Overnight Germans changed from being seen as efficient and bureaucratic by the rest of world to becoming welcoming and friendly. Beijing was another story: "It's very dramatic but not for us" Ed said to the Mayor as they toured the Bird's Nest. "It used ten times more steel than a comparable stadium. That sort of design just isn't sustainable. It's plain wrong."

Ed returned to the matter in hand: "I have designed the EuroGames masterplan to be an extension of the city – the network of roads on the site is linked in with the existing streets so that when the games are over the spaces around the buildings can be developed with homes, offices and shops," Ed continued. "I just hope the selection committee agrees with me about who are the right architects to complete the plan!"

This barbed plea came from his annoyance that he hadn't been allowed to sit on the Games Committee which would select the architects. The Council's legal department had decided that as a Council Officer this could be seen as a conflict of interests. He found the decision highly frustrating because he saw himself as the most qualified person to make the right choice as to which architects should be selected. Not having a vote, he would have to engineer the right result from the sidelines; he would make sure the Mayor, who chaired the Committee, was briefed about which architects he should be steering the Committee towards.

Ed had to keep a particular eye on the local Councillors – he knew from bitter experience that election to the Council conferred power to confound his best-laid plans, but not the understanding to judge what constituted a good building. He hoped that the representatives from the Royal Institute of British Architects and the Committee for Better Architecture (CofBA) who had been invited to join the Committee would support his view. He wasn't sure what to make of Sir Nigel Frith, the Chancellor of Frampton University, who had commissioned a lot of new buildings for the campus in recent years and was one of the most experienced members of the Games Committee.

A team of expert advisors – engineers, cost consultants and construction experts – had been drafted in to inspect the tendered architects' drawings to make sure the buildings would stand up and wouldn't cost too much – this group was chaired by Joe Porley, the kick-ass American Project Manager whose job it was to deliver the buildings on time and on budget.

To Ed's relief, the Committee had unanimously approved his 'shortlist' of five architectural firms for each of the four main projects – a total of 20 firms. The architects were from France, Germany, the US, Australia and Japan as well the UK. Each was invited to produce designs for a selected building and then the committee would choose the team that had best interpreted their brief as the winner.

***

Ed had made sure he was allocated an office high up in the Council's building when it was refurbished a few years earlier because it gave him a panoramic view over Frampton. Looking out of the arched windows he could see most of the significant sites over which he held sway. He would point out to developers the features that marked the historical development of Frampton, the few remaining parts of the medieval street pattern that he was keen to protect, the swathe cut by the 60s' ring road that he would dearly like to cover over, and the ring of concrete towers that did little to enhance the city skyline and which he would demolish if it wasn't for Frampton's chronic shortage of affordable housing. On the plus

57

side, near the station was an old Post Office depot that would make a brilliant site for some luxury housing, he thought.

It was here, from his office window, that Ed worked on the Mayor, grabbing his arm enthusiastically and steering him to look towards the Games site in the distance.

"We have to make it very clear to everyone that we are looking for the best firm to design the building; we are *not* selecting a finished design" he said emphatically. "If the press think the competition design is fixed we'll have a devil of a job making changes if we need to, and we'll find ourselves continually fighting with the architects if they see their competition entry as their final design."

Ed could see the Mayor needed a run down of the history of architectural competitions to make sure he understood some of the pitfalls of selecting architects by this method.

"President Mitterand got himself in a real pickle over the competition for the Bastille Opera house in Paris," said Ed. "All the entries were anonymous but the jurors thought they recognised the work of the celebrated American architect Richard Meier – he was just the sort of high profile superstar they wanted. But having selected the design they found out it was by an unknown Uruguayan called Carlos Ott!"

"They didn't do much better with the French National Library Competition. Everyone thought that Jan Kaplicky had won it – you know, the guy who did that new curvy white building at Lords cricket ground – but the politicians intervened and Mitterand gave it to a French architect instead with a scheme all of glass. Terrible for books. And they had to redesign it with big wooden shutters all over the place to keep the sunlight out."

"The highest profile disaster of course was the Sydney Opera house," Clutton continued "The designs by Jorn Utzon, chosen by the competition jury, were unbuildable – and as the architect and engineers worked out how to build it, costs rose from just $7million to a massive $100million!"

"They got a great building though," Jarvis interjected "and it's become the icon of Australia. I wouldn't mind a building like that in Frampton."

"But it took sixteen years to complete!" Clutton countered. "The games would long be over before the building was ready. We just cannot afford to have those sorts of delays."

"That's why we've hired Joe Porley as the EuroGames Project Manager. He's worked on some of biggest building sites in the world and he's never been late yet!"

***

On a fine, sunny Monday morning in June, the twenty chosen architects took their reserved seats in First Class on the 8.30 Virgin Pendolino from King's Cross to Frampton-on-Tees. Joe Porley had organised a visit to the city so that the shortlisted teams could see the site, understand its relationship to the city, and get a proper feel of the place.

Harry and Freddie were seated at either end of the carriage. In between there were staff from Frank Gehry's office, Foster's, Rogers's, the US giants Kohn Pedersen Fox and Skidmore Owings and Merrill, and Aussie outsiders DCM.

On the seat opposite Harry was Josh Stern from Associated Architects Partnership – they had got to know each other when Harry worked at AAP after he left the Academy of Architecture.

"Hi Josh," said Harry warmly as they shook hands "Congratulations. I hear you've been made senior partner. I hope you're going to shake the old place up a bit!"

"Yeah! We're celebrating our fortieth anniversary this year," Josh replied "and the old codgers have finally agreed to pass the business on to me and some of the younger architects. They don't really get what we're doing any more. Despite our firm's venerable age we've been giving the younger, trendier firms a run for their

money in the last couple of years. We've picked a lot of awards and even Rowan Moore has given us a couple of good reviews."
The firm had been started in the 1960s by four ex students from the London Academy of Architecture, all committed left wingers. They passionately believed that an architect's *raison d'être* was to serve society, that their design skills could help improve the lot of the working man by delivering affordable and functional accommodation, efficient and safe workplaces, and cities where all were equal.

"I guess our way of working is from another age." Josh continued.

The founders had purposefully avoided using names in the title of the practice and were committed to working cooperatively as a team – individual egos subsumed for the greater good. Much of their work was in the design of council housing and educational buildings, including a couple of new universities as part of the expansion of post war higher education. They refused to design offices.

"They thought property developers were corrupt capitalist thugs!" Josh exclaimed.

"I always thought The Blackbird Lane housing scheme was the best project in the early days of AAP," Harry said. "It had a real influence on me. It such a pity that just because of poor maintenance by the council they're thinking of knocking it down. The Twentieth Century Society's trying to get it listed, but they don't seem to be having much luck."

"Of course I know Frampton pretty well," said Josh "The firm designed the campus and buildings for Frampton-on-Tees University."

"Blimey, are you still working on that?" exclaimed Harry, "I did some early sketches for the new chemistry block when I was at AAP."

The University had been built on a green field site just outside the city. AAP's plan provided individual buildings for each department linked in a crescent by covered walkways and overlooking a landscaped lake that was one of the first uses of heat pumps to reduce energy consumption. The project had started in 1972 and the practice had been working continuously on small and large buildings on the site ever since.

"Yes, it's been a great cash-cow for the practice over the years. And I get on very well with Sir Nigel Frith, who's now the Vice Chancellor. I hope he'll be able to put in a good word for us among the powers-that-be in Frampton."

"I'm sure he will," laughed Harry "you always get clients eating out of your hand, Josh! I wish I could handle clients like you".

But Harry's praise was half hearted; he felt that a willingness to please clients, planning committees and politicians meant that Josh's work lacked the edge that made truly great buildings.

Josh had been a brilliant student, top of his year at the Academy. He came from a single-parent family in the days before that was common. He never knew who his father was, but his mother, who had worked as a cleaner, intimated to him that he had been a toff of some sort, and he had left Josh plenty of money, and so Josh always tired to play the part of a grandee. Thus he dressed in Savile Row suits from Anderson and Shepherd – pin striped, slightly waisted with double vents, worn with starched splayed coloured shirts and bright knitted ties with Windsor knots.

Harry knew that Josh was gay. Josh was very open about it, often commenting on the comeliness of young men in the office. What Josh didn't talk about was his taste for rough trade – the rougher the better. He enjoyed being hurt by men he met on his regular visits to West Heath or one of the public lavatories of north London. The thought of the stark contrast between his upright professional persona and the degradation he experienced at the hands of his temporary and anonymous friends gave him a frisson of excitement.

Urgently texting from the adjacent seat was Amanda Stone, one of the few successful women architects in the country. Amanda first came to notice in the 80s when she won the international competition for a major new museum in the Middle East. Unfortunately the Sheikh who had commissioned the building fell out of favour with the Ruler and the project was halted and Amanda's client put in gaol. However the drawings that Amanda did for the museum showed such brilliant originality, such a command of space and form that her reputation as a bright new star was established. Since then she had produced a steady flow of buildings around the world that had been well received by the architectural critics. However, she had yet to appeal to clients in Britain where she was seen as 'difficult'.

For her part, Amanda was used to a greater respect shown to her by clients in the other countries she worked in and she certainly wasn't going to go asking for work in Britain. But the Frampton Games were different – at least she hoped so.

Like most of the people in the carriage, their bags boasting Platinum Airline membership, Amanda travelled a lot, generally on her own, and her Blackberry had become a great friend. She found it hard to put down, texting friends and business colleagues endlessly. She had just started tweeting and was building up a large group of followers largely of architecture students amongst whom she held heroic status. Amanda understood women architects were a rare breed, and ones at the upper echelons of the profession even rarer. But she could help change that.

Sitting across the aisle was Tomo Koji with Yuki his wife who acted as his interpreter. The couple had flown in from Japan for the visit. Koji sat impassively watching the English countryside rush by as the train reached the cruising speed of 125mph. He was thinking about how he would marry the best of western architecture with Japanese culture into his buildings for the EuroGames.

Koji was highly ambitious. He desperately wanted to win the Royal Gold Medal and each year held a private dinner at Claridges to promote his cause to the great and the good. So far he had met with little success.

Jonny Spon, one of the members of W.I.L.D (Why I Love Design) the Britarch practice run as a co-op, had taken over most of the four seat table for himself; papers, laptop and magazines were spread between the coffee cups and complimentary biscuits. No one was very keen to sit next to him anyway. Jonny revelled in his radical reputation. He enjoyed upsetting the architectural establishment which in his eyes included most of the people in the carriage. His untidy mop of hair, shaven close at the neck and piled high on the top made him look like a mix of Eraserhead and Pedro Almodovar. He wore a Harris Tweed suit and waistcoat with an unbelievably loud Prince of Wales check shirt and workboots which he pointedly rested on the seat in front.

Joe Porley walked up and down the aisle, introducing himself to the architects he didn't already know and generally making small talk. Joe was in charge of the train party and four of the teams would be in his charge for the next four years while the Games buildings reached completion. Joe was loud, tough and very clever. He knew more about architecture than he let on (having worked with the great Bruce Graham at Skidmore Owings and Merrill in Chicago for a number of years). He was driven by a love of organisation as well as a desire to build great buildings. He admired the end products of his architect colleagues, but could never understand why they kept changing their minds and why they found it so difficult to understand what things cost.

As for those on the train Joe got on well with Josh, was wary of Harry and worried about Freddie. He wasn't quite sure what to make of Jonny and didn't think that Koji should have been invited because spoke very little English.

The train pulled into Frampton Station under the huge 20 metre curved spans of the majestic 19th century roof – the simple barrel vaulted arches curved round the tracks, like the inside of whale's rib cage. Along its length the roof was supported by decorated cast iron columns recently repainted in garish, but original, colours. Network Rail's architects had scraped off years of paint to get down to the bottom coats and specially mixed the colours to match.

"Just because it's original, it doesn't mean its good" Josh commented as he and Harry peered out of the carriage window at the clashing hues.

Mayor Jarvis and Ed Clutton greeted the architects as they stepped off the train and led them to the hired coach which was to take them to the site and then on a tour around the area. The day had warmed up and most of the visitors slipped off their jackets as they took their seats on the coach.

"Welcome to Frampton-on-Tees" the Mayor spoke into the microphone tour-guide style. "Frampton is one of Britain's most innovative and exciting cities – and now the host city for the EuroGames. We look to you and your teams to help us create a Frampton for the twenty-first century. Modern architects and planners have not always been kind to this city, but we think that we have on board the talent and the imagination to create buildings that are really memorable and that will provide a new image for the city. This is the greatest regeneration project in Europe and we will be looking for world class architecture."

He sat down to polite applause as the coach made it way through the busy traffic of the city centre.

Jarvis sat at the front in the tour guide's seat with Ed across the aisle in the passenger front seats. Jarvis was happy. Real change was about to come to the city that he loved and *he* was in charge. He was not just any old mayor, he was a city maker, a patron of architecture. He wanted history to see him in the same light as Frampton's City Fathers whose statues decorated the Gothic niches of the Civic Centre.

"I don't want to be seen in the way we look back at those politicians of the 60s who destroyed so much of the heart of Frampton in the name of the car," Jarvis had told Clutton. "They were well meaning, they wanted to improve the city and the lot of its people; but they sucked the life out of the centre."

"But they were only responding to public taste at the time," Ed argued, "you can see from films and photos of the time that there was a romantic image around dual carriageways with speeding Ford Cortinas, Austin Minis and the odd E type Jaguar. They reflected the aspirations of the period; but taste has changed. We now need to create 'sustainable' places that people like and buildings that they feel comfortable with over time. Public spaces they can enjoy. That's the challenge that faces our team of designers."

The scale of their task became clear as the coach made its way through the Conway housing estate that surrounded the Games site. Twenty-storey tower blocks, grey and gaunt in the late morning sun, emerged out of an untidy mixture of nose-to-tail parked cars, scrubby open space with more bare patches than grass and two-storey brick built terraces that looked as though they should be somewhere else. This mess – visual and social – was a result of the Council's attempts in the 80s to put right the mistakes of the 60s. The underground car parks were closed because of vandalism, muggings and drug taking; the parks that had been a part of the vision of the designers of the towers – that the tall buildings released land for play and fresh air – had suffered through lack of maintenance. Then the housing department built over the playgrounds with pitched roofed homes designed for the families with children who were clearly unsuitable occupants of penthouse apartments.

"These are the people who will really benefit from the games," said Ed, pointing to groups of hooded youths lounging about on the low walls that surrounded the estate. The architects peered and pointed their cameras at the group who responded dutifully with V-signs and aggressive Liam Gallagher style stares. "There'll be a lot of jobs in the construction phase and we expect to generate many millions of pounds of investment from companies wanting to move to the city because of the games. Our economics department reckon that they will bring something like 16,000 temporary jobs, 2,500 new permanent ones, £50 million of investment and 300,000 visitors to the town. On top of that it will provide access to heaps of Government and European Union grants."

The coach drew up to the site. Workmen were busily erecting a plywood hoarding around the perimeter to take the place of the wire mesh fence, overgrown with buddleia buzzing with bees and butterflies, that had unsuccessfully attempted to keep the local youths off its muddy expanse. The Mayor had been worried that someone might get hurt and that would not be good publicity for the games. The site was a hazard, deep pools of water had collected around old basements that had not properly filled, and God knows what chemicals and waste had seeped into the land over the last century.

The empty buildings of Frampton Steelworks – once the city's major employer – had been demolished the year before, having lain empty for over twenty years.

"It's huge," said Harry as he and Josh put on heavy site boots before walking into the middle of the open area.

The Kojis were walking close to them. They hadn't spoken to any of the other architects and Harry felt a bit sorry for them.

"Hi, I'm Harry Jamb and this is Josh Stern from AAP. I'm a great admirer of your work."

Koji bowed slightly and shook Harry's proffered hand.

"Very pleased to meet you" was as far as Koji's English would take him before his wife joined in.

"My husband is great admirer of your work too. He likes the Blackbird Lane housing and the Kensal Art Gallery building."

"I went to see your new museum at Saigato earlier this year," said Josh "and I found it a most exquisite building, the beautiful concrete finish was the best I've seen anywhere and the load bearing glass was an inspired choice. But the genius of the building is the way that it fits into the landscape – it is at the same time monumental yet looks as though it has always been there." Koji's wife dutifully translated.

Harry stopped to take some photographs as Josh and Koji continued across the site. There wasn't much point in photographing the muddy site so Harry did a continuous 360 degree panorama. To the south was the housing estate they had passed with the city centre hidden behind it; to the east were lower suburban houses with some of the taller university buildings emerging above their chimney pots; to the north was a strip of woodland that hid the M1 motorway beyond.

On a hill a couple of miles to the west Harry could make out Frampton Hall, the beautiful Palladian home and family seat of the Dukes of Frampton. Ed Clutton saw Harry looking up at the house.

"This site used to be owned by the Framptons until steel was nationalised by the Labour Government in 1949." Clutton said. "The family originally made their money from coal mining. Ironically, the mines run under the house. Some of the tunnels have collapsed and Frampton Hall started to subside a few years ago. The Duke's spent a fortune underpinning it."

"When the steel works closed down, the site was compulsorily purchased by the Council. The Duke wasn't at all pleased and he has made it very clear to us that he's going to be keeping a close eye on the proposals for the Stadium – not just because he wants to protect the views from the house, but also because he hates modern architecture with a passion."

Harry took out the copy of Ed's masterplan and compared it with the site in front of him.

"Ed, I can see how it all fits onto the site, but that building over there doesn't appear on your map at all!" Harry said pointing to a two-storey brick building with a large sign saying 'Ecoplastic Mouldings'.

"That's a bit of a problem," Ed answered, "Ecoplastics have ten year's still to run on their lease and they don't want to move. Sam Spurling, the MD, knows he's got us over a barrel and is driving a very hard bargain. If we can't get him out by the end of the year the whole programme for the Stadium could fly out of the window. You'll probably meet him later at the Civic Reception."

Chapter 6

The Duke of Frampton stood out on the first floor balcony of Frampton House and focused his pair of *Kriegsmarine* binoculars on the old steel works site. He could make out a charabanc parked on the site and figures walking over the muddy expanse.

"The battle begins" he said, partly to himself and partly to his daughter sketching the view of the city below, her long, lanky body leaning against the stone balustrade. Her loose floral pattern cotton dress ruffling in the cooling breeze, and her shock of pre-Raphaelite hair and bare feet were in stark contrast to the suited figure of her father beside her. Petronella Conway – she didn't like using the family name or her titles – was a talented artist and scholar at the Ruskin School of Art in Oxford. She drew exquisite drawings of real and imaginary buildings. Her favourite subject was Frampton Hall.

Her delicate pencil line formed the profile of the eponymous city. The soaring spire of the Cathedral, the bulbous shape of the Frampton FC Stadium, the pointed profile of the Civic Centre and the ghastly slabs of the concrete tower blocks created a well balanced composition. Petronella loved the view much more since the steel works had been demolished; it had been a real eyesore, rusting and dilapidated and useless. The smelting stopped before she was born so she had never seen it in full swing with the belching smoke and steam. Gone was the haunting sound of the factory hooter – once a signal to her forebears that the Frampton-on-Tees coffers were being handsomely topped up by the minute.

The Duke put down the heavy binoculars; his father, an Admiral in the Second World War, had relieved them from a German commander after he had sunk his U-boat during the Battle of the Atlantic in 1942. Peter Conway, the 5th Duke of Frampton, had not joined the forces despite his father's wishes. He was much more interested in farming than fighting, and after Eton had gone to the

Royal Agricultural College at Cirencester so that he could manage the family's substantial estates in England and South Africa.

Rejection of the military did not mean that the Duke had missed out on the Frampton fighting gene. Just the opposite. To prove he wasn't a pushover the Duke seemed always to be looking for a battle whether it was drunken fisticuffs at agricultural college or cantankerous debates in the House of Lords.

He was deeply upset when hereditary peers were removed from the Lords, and since then had thrown himself into every local cause and campaign that he could find.

"The architects for the EuroGames buildings are all in town today" he told his daughter. "That twerp Jarvis wants what he calls 'iconic' buildings. We'll have to keep a close eye on him if you're going to have any sort of view worth drawing in five years time. I've been asked to a reception for them all in the Civic Centre tonight – would you like to come, Pet?"

The Duke liked going to events with his daughter. She was good company, cut a striking figure and had inherited his argumentative streak. The Duchess preferred staying at home; she was active in the local Women's Institute and opened the odd fete. Other than that the Duke thought she was pretty bloody useless.

"Ooh, yes please Daddy!" Petronella knew quite a lot of architecture students and liked them. She found that her fascination with buildings through her drawings created a common ground. She was excited at the thought of meeting a group at the very top of the profession in spite of her father's hatred of their work.

***

"Let's get them back in the bus" the Mayor said to Clutton after the group had been wandering around the site for an hour. Freddie's and Harry's paths had crossed a number of times as they paced out the positions of the various buildings from Ed's masterplan but they studiously ignored each other.

Ed asked the driver to sound the horn and made feverish beckoning gestures to the distant figures who started to stroll back to the bus. Once they were in their seats Ed checked the numbers. He was one short.

"Who's missing?" he called out.

"I think it's Jonny Spon" responded Amanda Stone, "at least, he was sitting next to me on the way here."

"Come on Ed! We've got to get going," said Jarvis, irritated at the delay, "the press conference starts in half an hour."

Clutton peered out of the windows at the site. There was no one to be seen and Jarvis had a short fuse and could be extremely unpleasant when he was angry. One of Clutton's skills was to sense the Mayor's mood and respond accordingly.

Ed found acting as right hand man to such a powerful man both frustrating and uplifting. Jarvis was a bully who frequently used his aggression to get his own way but could also carry out incredible acts of kindness, as Clutton discovered when his wife was diagnosed with cancer. Jarvis could not have been more caring and considerate and sent her a huge bunch of roses when she got the all clear after chemotherapy. She thought he was a pussycat. Sometimes he could be pig headed and obstinate about the most ridiculous things and then at other times he could be visionary and far sighted, delivering the sorts of strategies which Ed believed could turn a city like Frampton around.

Ed couldn't make up his mind if he liked him or not, but he was only too aware that he needed someone like Jarvis if he was to implement the ideas he had about planning and urban design.

"OK let's go" he ordered the driver. The bus bumped off the site and back onto road. The driver turned into the housing estate.

"There he is!" called Amanda as she caught sight of Jonny's distinctive haircut rising above a huddle of hoods.

Spon was in deep conversation with the group of youths they had seen earlier. The driver tooted the horn and Jonny made his way to the bus.

"That's the bit of Frampton you should be looking at!" he said as he sat down. "It's not the big brown site that's important, it's the people!"

Spon's architecture was driven by the community response to projects and not by any fixed idea of style or context. W.I.L.D organised workshops with people who would be using their buildings.

A team of architects lived in the neighbourhood to get to know the place and the people before they designed a thing. Jonny argued with the 'clients', cajoled them and inspired them to express themselves using cardboard models, drawings and videos. The end product was nothing like the people had expected when they started. But they felt an ownership of it – just the opposite to their feeling of alienation towards the environments most of them lived in.

"Next stop is the press conference," announced Clutton, "and we're expecting a good turnout from the nationals. *The Gazette* is doing a special supplement so you should speak to their architecture writer Rachael Dove afterwards. The editor of the *Frampton Times*, Roger Chase, is right behind the games but he has to reflect local opinion so don't expect a totally easy ride. The Civic Society is keeping a very close eye on what is going on. They don't want anything that's too modern. Their president is the Duke of Frampton so they have quite a lot of clout in the city. You'll need to watch out for John Veduty who runs the Society; he's very bright and knows the planning process back to front. If anyone knows how to stop a project in its tracks it's Veduty."

Clutton spoke from experience. The Civic Society had successfully halted a couple of housing schemes that Ed had supported close to the Cathedral. The developers had at first proposed a modern design, but got cold feet after furious reactions from the Society and commissioned a traditional, neo-Georgian scheme instead.

The Frampton-on-Tees Council chamber was decorated with a fine 19th century terracotta wallpaper in the Etruscan style designed with superimposed Gothic tracery picked out in gold leaf. The circular space was topped by a grand dome; pairs of arched windows surrounded its base, while triangular tracery panels curved up to the crown accentuating the structural form. The seating in the chamber was arranged in a horseshoe facing the Mayor's throne and a long table normally occupied by the Town Clerk. The sun cast diagonal beams of light across the space that struck the councillors' carved desks which had been temporarily appropriated by the fourth estate. The architects were ranged along a table beneath the Mayor's throne that dominated the room.

The Gazette's Rachael Dove sat close to the front. Rachael was a sharp dresser, liked bright red lipstick and nails, and sported a Vidal Sassoon 60s style bob accentuated by her dyed black hair cut at an angle across her pale complexion. She had a weakness for famous architects; indeed she was building up a quite a list of names of those she had bedded, Freddie and Jonny among them. Tomo Koji looks interesting she mused, as the Mayor got up to speak.

"Thank you for coming today ladies and gentlemen." Jarvis began. "First, I have an important announcement to make. The Games Committee has decided unanimously that the main stadium should be named after one of the city's most famous sons – Martin Hester, the Olympic Decathlon Gold Medallist in the 1968 Games in Mexico. As you are well aware he is a key member of the "Healthier Britain" campaign to get more people taking up sports activities. He makes the ideal public champion for the Frampton Games. Please welcome Martin Hester!"

Although in his sixties, Hester cut a fine figure as he made his way to the podium. Tall, bronzed (Is that tan real? thought Rachael) with a well-cut navy suit that accentuated his powerful frame he smiled engagingly to the room with the ease of someone who is used to adoring audiences. Only the previous week he had been mobbed by young boys and middle aged women alike when he completed the Great Frampton-on-Tees Marathon in 2 hours 43 minutes.

"I'm glad you could all come to Frampton today to see what a great city it is. I was born in Conway Street just a few hundred metres from where the Games will be held. The back-to-back terrace I was born in was demolished long ago to make way for the new estate. My father was a foundryman and would wash off the soot and sweat from the works in a tub in the kitchen. Those Saturdays with Dad at Frampton FC are my most treasured memories. Especially when the Founders won. And winning is what sport is all about – not just coming in first but helping people win better, healthier lives. Frampton has won the bid for the EuroGames and that gives us a chance to change the city for the good, to bring jobs to the area and to get more people leading healthier lives by running, jumping, cycling and getting involved in the wealth of opportunities that will come our way in the next few years. I am honoured by the decision to have the new Stadium named after me and I will work tirelessly to help make these Games the success that Frampton deserves."

So excited were the three young ladies from the Frampton Public Relations Department that they started clapping; the intern working on the news desk followed; instinctively the architects joined in as Hester stepped down from the lectern.

The journalists sat stony faced, pencils, pads and recorders in hand. They were not there to support the project, they were there to scrape away the PR spin and deliver the truth to their readers. The Games would be a treasure trove of 'truth' – lots of overspending, misuse of public money, safety, risk, arguments and the wisdom of the Duke of Frampton who was always good for a quote.

The Mayor called for questions; hands shot up in unison.

"What's the total budget and what do you say to those who think the Games are a massive waste of ratepayers' money?"

"We expect the costs to be in the region of £1.5 billion, which includes money that will be spent on regenerating run down parts of the city and in improving vital infrastructure which will serve the city into the future. If you look at other games-hosting cities like Seoul, Barcelona or Atlanta, for every £1 million of public investment they generated £2.7 million in economic benefits. That's not a bad rate of return."

"How many hospitals could you build for £1.5 billion?"

"It's not a question of either, or. This is new investment coming into Frampton through Government and EU grants, money from the European Cultural Fund and Sport England. We already have a wonderful hospital, anyway!"

"How much will it add to the Council's Rates of the long suffering citizens of Frampton?"

"There will be a small hike in rates but to balance that we're expecting . . ." Jarvis checked with his notes "additional employment with some 6,000 permanent jobs in the city as a whole as well as 900 temporary jobs during the Games."

"Frampton Hospital was five years late and 40 per cent over budget. What make you think you can deliver the Games buildings on time and on cost?"

"We learnt a lot from building the hospital and we'll make sure we don't get it wrong again. We've hired Joe Porley, one of the top project managers in the business to keep costs under control. I'm sure he'll do a great job."

"What sort of building would you like your name attached to? What do you expect it to look like?" The last question came from Rachael Dove and was directed to Martin Hester.

Hester smiled.

"I'm no architect and I'm happy to leave that decision to them. Ed Clutton tells me we've got some of the best architects in the world in the room – and that's good enough for me."

Jarvis called the meeting to close. He was relieved that there hadn't been more questions on the budget. That seemed to be the only thing the papers were interested in most of the time.

"I hope you'll all be able to join us at the reception in the Grand Hall and feel free to speak to the architects in more detail over a glass of champagne."

***

Local dignitaries, councillors, businessmen as well as the marketing and sponsorship teams from a selected list of corporate sponsors crowded into the hall. The architects and journalists mingled together on one side of the room and the local councillors swapped notes on the other.

There was an audible if brief pause in the hubbub as the Duke of Frampton and his daughter entered through the double storey medieval style doorway. Petronella had changed into a long clinging dark green velvet shift her bra-less nipples prominent against the fabric's sheen. She looked as though she had emerged from a Rosetti painting. The Duke peered around for a moment and then saw the Mayor making his way quickly towards him, followed by John Veduty.

"Evening Jarvis. So you've got the architects for the Games buildings here. Can I speak to 'em?" His tone made it quite clear he wasn't there for the small talk.

"Of course your Grace". Jarvis led the Duke across the room to the group of journalists and designers. Veduty followed.

"May I present His Grace the Duke of Frampton – Harry Jamb, Frederick Shaw (even though it meant standing with Harry, Freddie wasn't going to miss the opportunity to raise his profile a bit) and Jonny Spon – one of our up and coming architects."

The Duke shook each by the hand. His face held in a slightly pained expression as though he was smelling gas.

"Yes, I could see you all at the steel works site this afternoon wandering around like a bunch of ants. I have a very good view from my house and I hope you will bear that in mind when you are designing your buildings. I have never hidden my dislike of modern architecture and the last thing I want to see from my bedroom every morning when I wake up is some bloody great concrete monstrosity. In my view the most suitable material for the Games is stone. I have told Mr Clutton of my view and will be speaking to the Chairman of the Planning Committee about it this evening."

"Well, your Grace" Freddie was determined to get in first. "As architects we respond to the instructions of our client, and it is our job to make sure the buildings are value for money and most importantly in this case will be finished in time for the first race of the Games. I'm not sure that we could commit to building a traditional stone stadium in that time."

"I have been studying the use of large scale structural stonework," Harry sucked up "The use of stone suits my architecture and I would feel very comfortable working in, say, limestone . . ."

"Good, good" said the Duke.

". . . But I do tend to agree with Frederick about the time and the cost."

The Duke swiftly turned to Jonny and silently awaited his response.

None came.

"Well, Mr. . . er . . .er . . . Spon, what do you think?"

"To be frank, that was the biggest load of patrician bullshit I've heard since Prince Charles gave his carbuncle speech."

The architects and journalists stopped talking and turned to listen. The Duke visibly reddened; the gaseous sneer was replaced by a rictus of horror.

"Just because you own half the bloody county it doesn't mean you can dictate everything that goes on here. I don't care a fuck (he paused as in the corner of his eye he saw the journalists scribbling away at their pads for all they were worth, and decided to go for it) I don't care a fuck about the view from your bedroom and if you hadn't fought to stop development of the land further down the valley Frampton wouldn't have housing shortage it has now. I care more about what the people on the Conway Estate think rather than a bunch of toffs on the hill."

By this time the rest of the room had fallen silent. The Duke was dumbstruck and John Veduty ventured to interject.

"I can assure you that it is not just his Grace who wants a more sympathetic style of architecture for the Games, the members of the Civic Society are equally concerned that we do not   get buildings that will wreck the city."

"Thank you Veduty" the Duke managed to say through gritted teeth. "I think it is time to go" and he turned on his heel towards the exit. The first shock of Spon's outburst has given way to barely containable anger. Nobody spoke to the Duke like that, Verduty contained his thoughts, indeed nobody had ever spoken to the Duke like that. Damn' arrogant architects, who did they think they were?

The Duke strode angrily to the exit flanked by Jarvis and Veduty.

"Make sure that little shit doesn't get anywhere near the Games, Jarvis! I'm warning you now!"

He was gone before the Mayor could answer. Jarvis turned back into the reception with a worried look on his face. The Duke's power and influence in the region could not be denied. If you got on the wrong side of him, he could make a Mayor's life very difficult indeed. He supported a lot of good works – the new hospice and the planned public library. There had been a move to design a glass monstrosity, which was going to be called The Knowledge Place, but the Duke put a stop to that by offering to fund a classically-designed building instead designed by the up and coming traditionalist Inigo James. The upper echelons of Frampton-on-Tees's social life were desperate for invitations to the Duke's cocktail parties and balls. Whether Spon liked it or not, thought Jarvis, the aristocracy still retain huge influence. He may have been ousted from the House of Lords, but he was still a power to be reckoned with. And he owned half of the county to boot.

Petronella, who had been chatting with Amanda Stone, ran past the Mayor in bare feet, her mane of hair flowing behind her, her face flushed with excitement, to catch up with her father.

The Mayor signalled Clutton to his side.

"We've got to make sure that little idiot doesn't get anywhere near this job, Ed." He leant into Clutton's ear "Life's going to be difficult keeping the Duke happy as it is, without having some bloody Marxist stirring things up."

***

Veduty returned to the Grand Hall. The Duke's dramatic exit let everyone know what his views of the situation were, but Veduty understood that it was only by getting close to the local politicians that he would be able to change things.

The conservationist made his way towards the group of Councillors who were excitedly debating the events of the evening. Councillor Merton, the Chair of the Planning Committee, was in the centre of the group.

"You see, gentlemen, what we are up against," Veduty announced. "These architects will go to any lengths to pursue their egotistical designs. This way of selecting architects is designed to protect the interests of the modernists. It excludes all those who disagree with the tastes of the architectural establishment. It is essential that you institute a process whereby the people of Frampton have a greater say in what is designed for the Games and that the Civic Society plays a role in that."

"What, do you think you represent the ordinary people of Frampton?" scoffed one of the Labour members, "the Civic Society's made up of toffee nosed, social climbing, middle class pensioners! There's plenty of democracy in the planning system anyway – if you want to use it."

"Order, order" Councillor Merton interjected: "I have every confidence that my committee will take the right decisions, and all representations, including yours Mr Veduty, will be taken into account!"

"I know how you can stop the current plans," came a voice from the back of the group. It was Sam Spurling the MD of Ecoplastics and a leading light in the Frampton-on-Tees Rotary Club. "They can't do a thing while my building is on that site. I can delay things so that they'll have real problems completing the buildings on time. Either that or it's going to cost them a lot of money!"

The Civic Centre catering staff, having been told to look after the visiting architects, had ensured that their champagne glasses were continuously topped up. Tomo Koji, unused to such overbearing hospitality, was beginning to feel rather the worse for wear and was desperate for a pee. He followed the signs to the 'Toilets'. In his befuddled state he missed his directions and wandered, disoriented, through the complex of dark gothic corridors. Seeing a sign for a 'Ladies' he imagined, from his knowledge of building services and drainage, that the 'Gents' must be fairly close. As he stood outside the lavatory, the door opened and Rachael Dove emerged.

"Have you been following me, Tomo?" Rachael said coquettishly, poking her finger playfully into his chest. If the Japanese architect didn't understand the words, he followed the sentiments. He took hold of Rachael's hand and drew her towards him.

"Wait! Someone might come!" she cautioned as she turned to try the door handle of one of the offices with "Treasurer's Department" painted in white serif letters across the oak panelling. The door opened and Rachael pulled the Japanese architect into the room.

Coitus was quickly completed and as Rachael put some papers, which had become dislodged during their energetic fumblings, back onto the desk she read the heading at the top of one of the pages. "EuroGames. Construction Budgets."

Without hesitation, she pushed the sheets into her open blouse.

***

The party of architects returned to London on the last train, Frederick and Harry again seated at opposite ends of the carriage. Koji sat rather dazed and could not look in Rachael's direction. Joe Porley surveyed the rail carriage with a mixture of despair and expectancy, as a gruff Sergeant Major might view a bunch of unruly new recruits who need a bit of square bashing to get them into order, while Rachael tapped out her copy on her laptop for the next day's edition of *The Gazette*.

Chapter 7

The massive front-page headline in *The Gazette* drew on Rachael's steamy research: "Games Stadium costs budgeted to rise to £200 million"

A side story announced "Duke attacks modernist plans for Games"

Richard Jarvis received alerts on his iPhone so that any story with the words 'Frampton Games' was emailed to him every day. Waking at 6 am he checked his emails and immediately rang Ed Clutton.

"How the hell did that bitch get this story? We hadn't told anyone about those new figures. Anyway they're totally dependent on the rate of inflation and may not happen."

"Only half a dozen people had access to those figures," Clutton said blearily. He had made the mistake of going to a bar to swap notes with Joe Porley before he got on the train back to London. Porley was as hard a drinker as he was a manager. "It shouldn't be difficult to track down the culprit."

***

The Deputy Treasurer was devastated.

"I-I-I- just p-popped down to join the party for half an hour. I must have f-f-forgotten to lock the office," he stammered. "I noticed the papers were in a bit of a mess when I got back. It's never happened before."

Jarvis, still livid, fired the unfortunate accountant on the spot. The Mayor realised that normal security measures were not going to be enough now that Frampton was such a focus of interest. He immediately instituted a new security regime which not only would keep the journalists out but also gave Jarvis and Clutton greater control of the flow of information in the Council. In the light of the Duke's threats of the night before, *The Gazette* story had provided an excellent excuse for Mayor Jarvis to tighten his grip of the reins.

***

The architects' presentations to the Selection Committee had been scheduled for October so, after briefing his design team, Harry arranged to spend August with Eleanor and Amelia, now a very attractive and mature 17 year old, in the Scappi family villa in Tuscany. Harry enjoyed these times with his family. He worked hard building up the practice, and it was good to be able to get away from it and spend a bit of time with his daughter. The two enjoyed a very warm relationship. Amelia was lively and headstrong but she wasn't a rebel.

The classical façade of the villa was plastered in faded ochre, crumbling slightly at the edges, with interiors that looked as though they hadn't seen a lick of paint since the *quattrocento*; it was an effect that Harry would never have contemplated in his own architecture. But holidays relaxed ideas of taste as much they did mind and body; just as he was happy to slip on a pair of washed out shorts and a sloppy shirt, so he enjoyed not having to care about moulding the place to his professional taste. The accretions of time were acceptable on holiday; at work he would be inclined to clear them out.

The villa sat on a hill a few miles to the west of Siena overlooking a valley of olive orchards and wheat fields, with views towards the hilltop town of Montepulciano in the distance. An avenue of pencil-sharp cypress trees led up from the road and rows of vines spread out on either side of the driveway.

Eleanor used to spend most of her school holidays at the villa with her mother; Riccardo would come over whenever he could get away from the factory. After her mother died Eleanor didn't like going back and only visited sporadically. Marrying Harry changed that and they stayed there for as much of the summer as they could afford.

Behind the villa was a collection of more rustic stone-walled farm buildings and barns which over the years had been converted into holiday lets and accommodation for family friends. These overlooked the 30-metre swimming pool where all those staying in the Scappi compound would gather to socialise.

Riccardo had bought the villa in the early 60s when land and property prices were dirt-cheap. A 140-hectare estate came with the buildings together with 20 hectares of vines. The estate was run by Victor who had made something of a name for himself as a winemaker producing 300 cases a year of a rich fruity *classico* red marketed under the 'Villa Scappi' label.

Over the August period there was a regular flow of family friends, Riccardo's business contacts and designers, architect and clients and self invited guests usually phoning or emailing (we're going to be in Siena/Florence/Tuscany next month will you be around?), not to mention other English families with second homes in the Tuscan hills. Most received an invitation for lunch or supper. Harry enjoyed the idea of an open house.

While they were up in Frampton, Harry had invited some of the other architects to stay during the week of the Siena Palio, the major highlight of their Tuscan calendar. "Come down for the Palio in August," he had asked them. "These crazy Sicilian jockeys race round the Piazza del Campo. It's one of the most exciting, stirring and elemental events I've ever seen. The animal rights people want it banned but it's been held every year since 1656 and has fanatical support in the town. The locals would go mad if they tried to stop it."

Harry never ceased to be thrilled by the heady mixture of the passion of the people in the local Sienese neighbourhoods, the *contrade*, the danger and drama of the race itself, the celebrations of the winners and the bitter, bitter disappointment of the losing *contrade*. He loved the beauty of the spectacle, the flag waving, the processions, the whole mise en scene: the crowds surrounded by the historic architecture looking onto the Piazza del Campo including the looming Torre del Mangia which formed the focus of the asymmetrical plan.

***

Josh Stern had taken up Harry's invitation and was driving down from London in his silver grey Ferrari F430. He had managed to put his foot down in the early morning hours as he sped south. Josh loved speed, he lived much of his life on the edge; that thin line between the thrill and oblivion – whether in a fast car or at sado-masochistic orgy – was where he overdosed on adrenalin. His architecture reflected his love of mechanics and the imagery of the machine.

"I take great pleasure in honing my building designs so that they are as efficient as they can possibly be," he would say when he lectured to students "just as the engineers at Ferrari worry over every ounce of paint, I want my structures to be calculated so that there is no excess material and no waste. Efficiency creates its own beauty." He would then show a slide of Concord "The sleek beauty formed by the function of supersonic flight is as stirring to me as the Venus de Milo or the spire of Salisbury Cathedral."

Concord was followed by a picture of the great American philosopher and engineer Buckminster Fuller holding a 'tensegrity' mast.

"Bucky developed tensegrity structures by separating out elements in compression from those in tension – so he could build lightweight towers and domes out of wires, which were in tension, and sticks, which were in compression. This is the perfection of a structural idea that I try to emulate in my buildings, every force, every material and its performance, is understood and expressed."

What Josh didn't tell the students about were the problems in making buildings that lived up to his dreams. Buildings had to be approved by planners, to please clients and to be used by people – factors which often led to compromise and an end product that was less than perfect.

It took characters steelier than Josh to deliver dreams unsullied by the pragmatism so redolent of contemporary business culture.

Such concerns seems far away as Josh savoured the pure beauty of the Tuscan landscape. The sun was just appearing above the hills behind Sinalunga as he turned off the road and drove slowly, in consideration of its still sleeping occupants, up to front of the Scappi villa. The scrunching gravel made more noise than the softly throbbing motor. He got out of the car and stretched; he looked out over the rolling hills.

How do they do it? Not one bit of the composition appeared to him out of place; the rich but muted browns of the ripening corn, the sandy Tuscan stone, and the terre verte of the olive leaves harmonised like an Ilse Crawford room set. Hesitating to ring the doorbell at such an early hour Josh walked round to the side of the house overlooking the pool. Already there were two swimmers pounding up and down as they completed their daily fitness regime. He walked to the poolside and watched.

He could recognise the bulky figure of Riccardo Scappi, his tanned body, craggy features, and flowing grey hair (even when plastered flat by the water) were unmistakable. But Josh couldn't make out the second swimmer who was scything through the water at about twice the speed of Riccardo – this clearly annoyed the ageing Italian who at each turn checked his partner's progress and attempted unsuccessfully to keep up. The long slim body was pale but clearly muscled. The swimmer's effortless style was a perfect illustration of the sort of economy and efficiency that Josh so admired.

"Fifty!" called the unknown figure as he reached the end of the pool and in one deft movement pushed himself out of the water to stand as though to attention a few feet from Josh.

Josh swooned. The tight rubber swimming cap accentuated the symmetrical features; the tanned hairless chest sported a discreet nipple ring from which a small diamond sparkled in the morning sun. The taut six pack led Josh's eye to the tight Speedos and bulging crotch.

"Hi! Jason Vent."

"Hello, I'm Josh Stern" Josh took the wet proffered hand. The grip was like steel. Josh liked working out, but this guy was serious.

"You're on the shortlist for the Frampton EuroGames job aren't you?"

"Yes, but we don't stand much chance. Those guys are looking for younger, trendier practices. Our name doesn't fit with the fashion for novelty. We're not good at icons."

"I've just been appointed to design all the branding for the Games," said Jason. "Eleanor thought it might be useful if I met some of you architects so she invited me down for the week."

Eleanor had been doing some work in Harry's office, helping with the marketing and public relations and had met Jason at the press conference to announce his appointment. Jason headed the global brand consultancy Ican C 4 Miles and had also been commissioned to art direct the grand Opening Ceremony. Eleanor knew that Harry would have strong views on the sorts of logos which – if he won – would be plastered all over his building.

Harry came out of the main house and walked down to the poolside.

"Hi Josh, really glad you could make it. Riccardo will look after you, I'm just off to Florence airport to pick up Amanda Stone and Jonny Spon, they're arriving on the same plane."

***

Harry returned with the airport party three hours later. Amanda emerged from Harry's beaten up Land Rover, looking cool in a floaty white cotton dress, closely followed by Emily Boudin, the senior design architect in her office. The two had had a close working relationship and an on-off personal relationship for several years. Their falling outs generally centred around Emily's jealousy that Amanda got all the credit for the work coming out of the office, despite the fact that Amanda frequently had very little personal involvement in a project. Emily also resented her own dependence on Amanda, whose brilliance she feared she could never match on her own. When she was off Amanda, she frequently contemplated setting up in practice by herself, but could never quite take the plunge.

Almost as an afterthought Jonny Spon, in worn jeans and a bleu de travail jacket, clambered out of the back of the Land Rover carrying a single holdall.

"I'll show you to your rooms and then in an hour or so we can all have lunch in the olive orchard," said Harry as he pointed to a protected spot on the hill behind the house where a long table was being laid by Maria, cook and housemaid to the Scappi family for over twenty years. He looked down to the pool to spot his other guests and saw that Josh and Jason were already oiled up and sun bathing side by side on the loungers.

***

Harry loved the lunches around the long table set out in the shade of the olive trees, drinking the rich red Scappi wine and eating food produced on the estate, living out some imaginary Fellini film. Just as in his work he liked to be surrounded by a familiar and supportive team, he received great satisfaction from entertaining and feeding the sort of extended family who had gathered there that summer.

Eleanor had been in Tuscany for three weeks with Amelia before Harry managed to get there. Amelia was the image of her mother, elegant and olive skinned, she was outgoing and mixed freely with the older guests. Over the years Eleanor had built up a network of other British families with children of the same age who spent their holidays in the region. Amelia had recently passed her driving test and for the first time was enjoying the freedom of visiting her friends unencumbered with parents.

That day Amelia was off to meet friends in Siena and waved gaily to the group assembling in the orchard as she drove off in her vintage Cinquecento. The tiny car had sat unused and rusting for years in one of the stables and Riccardo had had it beautifully restored. He'd presented it to Amelia when she passed her driving test – on the strict understanding that the car stayed in Italy. Although much of his life and business was in England and his children and grandchildren were more English than Italian, he was keen that they should retain roots in his homeland.

Harry sat one end of the table; Riccardo the other, Josh grabbed a seat directly opposite Jason, keen to get to know him better; Amanda and Emily, clearly in one of their 'on' periods, sat together. The group tucked into wine and bread as Maria, in white workcoat, served a plateful of pasta to each of them.

The weather was hot, up in the thirties, but it was pleasant beneath the trees; a gentle breeze through the valley rustled the grey green leaves as the dappled light danced on the laden table. Many years before Riccardo had cut a flatter area into the sloping hillside to accommodate the rustic dinning table; he had positioned it so that as he looked down its length he had a perfectly composed view of the valley, framed by the house on one side and the small copse of Umbrella pines on the other. Through the haze he could make out the conical form of Montepulciano, its stone houses perched vertiginously atop the distant hills.

Eleanor started the conversation.

"Do you know Tuscany well, Jonny?"

'Not really. I cycled round Europe when I was a student and visited Siena and Florence, but I haven't been back since. I'd forgotten how exquisite it is. Every view is a photo opportunity."

"Yes, it's beautiful, although this time of year the towns are so crowded you can't really go into them . . . Siena, San Gimignano, Florence, all packed to the gills with tourists."

"What is interesting about Tuscany," Riccardo joined in "is that it's so popular with architects when there's not a new building to be seen for miles. Do they come here so they aren't reminded of their work or do they deep down hate the sight of modern architecture?"

"They certainly wouldn't want to come here to work," said Harry. "Planning in Tuscany makes even the system in Britain look a paragon of efficiency. It took us nearly five years to do the alterations to the farm buildings, and a fortune in fees and back handers. Everything takes absolutely ages and is incredibly restrictive."

"So it should be, this is just the most wonderful theatrical backdrop." Jason waved his hand across the panorama of the valley below "Modern things seem totally out of context against the timeless feel of the natural landscape and the indigenous buildings – which look like they're made from stone dug out of the ground they sit on."

Amanda nodded: "But it's not the real world. It's protected from the realities of life by tourism. When they do new stuff its just as grim as anywhere else. Look at that horrid big hospital outside Siena. It sticks out like a sore thumb."

"Not like Frampton, where there are so many sore thumbs, a few more won't be noticed!" Jonny joked and everyone laughed.

"And they have their games every year – not once in a lifetime" Eleanor added. "If the Frampton Games are half as exciting as the *Palio* tomorrow then it will have done well."

"And that's why I've invited you here this week," interjected Harry, " because I thought you'd all find the Palio a fascinating lesson in the organization of sports events. And it breaks all the rules. Nobody seems to have heard about Health and Safety down here, and if they have they ignore it."

"A good thing too." Josh added, excited by the very idea of physical risk; he hated the suffocating restraints created by more and more regulations at a personal and professional level. "Risk keeps you alive – all these rules and controls are a conspiracy between the insurance companies and the lawyers who make fortunes out of them."

"You'll see plenty of risk tomorrow," Riccardo remarked; he had lost count of the number of Palios that he watched, but not the thrill: "The jockeys are fearless, horses crash horrifically into the barriers, crazy supporters run onto the track before the horses have stopped, and the crowd are packed like sardines in the middle of the square – it could never happen in England."

Luckily, back in the 50s Riccardo had bought a debenture for the use of the balcony on one of the palazzi close to the tricky southeast corner of the course. It hadn't cost him much then. Siena had yet to become the popular tourist honey pot it was today and the Italian economy was still recovering from the Second World War. It gave a grandstand view of the spectacle.

"*Salute!*" he raised his glass "*al cavallo vincente!* – the winning horse!"

***

The Scappi party parked on the edge of the town and walked into the Piazza del Campo. They had planned to arrive in time for a light lunch laid out in the front room of the palazzo. The race itself wasn't due to start until 7 o'clock and would last no longer than 90 seconds; it formed the climax of a slow build up of tension as the square gradually filled with spectators and the *Corteo Storico*, the grand parade of historic figures and flag throwers sporting the standards of the seventeen *contrade*, the districts of the city that competed for the Palio.

Amelia had wanted to arrive early so that she could reserve a ringside spot in the middle of the square where thousands of spectators would be penned in once the celebrations started. She and her friends thought this gave them a much more visceral experience than that of their parents in the luxury of their reserved boxes.

The Piazza del Campo is one of the great public spaces of the world. Surrounded by the grand palaces of the Italian aristocracy – the *palazzi signorii* – the asymmetrical square, paved with bricks and radiating lines of travertine marble, slopes down to the Palazzo

Pubblico with its tall brick tower stone battlements. For the Palio, a track of packed earth and sand is laid, protected by a stout wooden fence.

"They've always been very tough on planning here," said Harry as he stood with Amanda and Josh by the high French windows that led out onto the balcony. "The heights of the palaces around the Campo are all the same and that's one of the reasons it's such a great space. Previously the aristocrats had built defensive towers like at San Gimignano and Bologna. Here the planners kept them well and truly under control."

Amanda moved out onto the timber balcony and pointed to the Palazzo Pubblico on the south side of the square "But then the line is broken by the tower. That makes it the real focus of the space. Without the campanile of the Duomo, the space would be really boring."

"It makes a great stadium." Josh added, "The atmosphere is electric. It's a big space but feels very intimate. It's a good lesson for all of us working on the Games."

"The problem is that it's the wrong way round! Most of the people are in the middle and the race goes round them!" laughed Harry "We'd never get away with that!"

The square already seemed full but more and more people continued to crowd in – a mixture of tourists and groups of locals, the latter pushing through the melée lustily singing songs supporting their *contrade*. Every now and then Eleanor caught glimpses of Amelia and her friends among the crush, some of whom Eleanor recognised from parties they had held at the villa. Then she noticed Amelia talking to a tall boy who looked familiar but who she couldn't place.

"Harry, who's that talking to Amelia?" she pulled his arm and pointed into the crowd. But their daughter had once again been absorbed into the shifting sea of heads and Harry couldn't pick her out.

Bugles and drums announced the start of the historic parade that preceded the race. Dressed in medieval costumes the pages, knights and flag wavers marched in slow formation around the track. Pairs of flag-wavers in jerkins and tights performed a delicate duet, sweeping the colourful fluttering cloths across the ground, around their heads, behind their backs, and then finishing by throwing the banners high into the air and effortlessly catching them.

Jason was entranced "Wow, these guys are amazing. Heraldry on speed!"

Scallops in red and blue, shards of white and red, flames of black and white, dragons, eagles, goats passed in a colourful blur. Jason snapped away with his camera. This had the perfect level of drama and syncopation that he needed to capture for the EuroGames' ceremonies. If he could find a contemporary interpretation which allowed the timeless quality of the spectacle – the colour, the beat of the drums, the clarion call of the bugles, the emotion, the passion – he would set the Frampton Games alight.

He leaned into Josh's ear "This is it! This is what I'm going to do for the opening ceremony. Give it a modern twist of course, but all the right ingredients are here!"

The sun was dropping in the west, but the heat was still intense. Eleanor noticed distastefully that Jonny's blue jacket was darkening with sweat, large saddlebag patches spreading from his armpits. She looked away to catch a glimpse of Amelia and the tall boy, his arm protectively around her shoulders in the heaving mass of spectators.

The parade ended with a trundling cart carrying the Palio flag, which would be presented to the winning *contrade*, pulled slowly by four white oxen. Their stately procession in stark contrast to the mayhem to come. It was time for the Palio proper to begin.

To massive cheers, the horses and their riders emerged onto the track. Harry got out a pair of binoculars to take a closer look. The Scappi balcony was on the opposite side of the track from the start and it was hard to make out what was going on. Bareback jockeys jostled each other; horses circled and pranced in front of the starter's rope. One horse, set some way behind the others, was kicked into a gallop, the rope dropped and the race was on. The crowd went wild as the ten riders came round the first corner and down the slope, past Harry and his party, and then into the sharp bend of San Martino, protected by heavy padding outside the Palazzo Pubblico. The two first riders made it through, then in the blur of man and beast that could only be understood in slo-mo analysis, a horse slammed into the padded wall, two others were tripped and fell and were skirted by the following mounts. The fallen horses got up to continue the race riderless, leaving one jockey lying still on the sandy track. He was unceremoniously scooped up and removed from the scene before the thundering group of survivors came round for the second lap.

"They look like they're wearing pyjamas," Amanda shouted. The loose suits in yellow and red, green and orange, striped and quarters and helmets of a cinquecento soldier certainly lacked the style of modern jockeys, but there was no doubting their skill as, without saddle or stirrups, the rest of the field mastered the San Martino corner at breakneck speed. It looked like a grey horse with rider in green and white was a clear winner, but as the pair turned the final corner they hit a hefty timber post. The jockey went flying, the horse stumbled and a rider in black and white stripes raced past.

Gunshots announced the end of the race as the momentum carried the horses and riders into the crowd which had already flooded onto the track. Riderless horses galloped on, mowing down spectators. Josh watched as one man was knocked to the ground hitting his face hard on the sandy track. He got up, clearly concussed only to be knocked down again by another loose horse. Blood poured from the man's face. Josh found the raw violence of the event strangely satisfying.

The winning horse was grabbed by his supporters, the jockey all but pulled from his mount as grateful hands tore at his clothes, men dragged him down to kiss him passionately, his head sank into the crush, to momentarily reappear as though taking breath in a stormy sea, he raised his fist triumphantly to the crowd only to sink again beneath the waves of hands and heaving bodies. A lone *caribinieri* gave up his vain attempt to protect the horse and rider from his admirers.

Amelia and her friends were dragged along with the crowd as it spilled out onto the track. The tall boy continued to stand close to Amelia, protecting her from the crush of celebrating flag wavers and disgruntled members of losing *contrade*. He pulled her to him as the victorious horse paraded past, the jockey visible in his white vest, his colourful shirt and army helmet ripped from him by the desperate fans.

"Thanks Ben. Let's go over to find my parents. I can see they're still up on the balcony."

"Is that a good idea?" Ben Shaw was Freddie's son. He knew of the problems between his parents and Amelia's, and that his mother would not like him meeting up with the Jambs. They hadn't spoken to each other since the break up of the practice when Ben was three. He had met up with Amelia by accident when the Shaws were staying at Lucca with another family of architects whose children hung out with Amelia's group of friends.

"Don't worry. They'll be cool about it. The break up wasn't our fault."

Amelia was right. Harry and Eleanor didn't mind. Harry shook hands with Ben.

"I saw you in the crowd with Amelia" exclaimed Eleanor, "and knew you looked familiar, but I couldn't quite make it out."

"Yes, everyone says I look just like my Dad."

"Are your parents in Tuscany?" Harry asked.

"Yes, they're staying with the Johnsons up in Lucca. They should be here somewhere. We were planning to meet up in the Campo

94

after the race. They're with Martin Hester. Do you know him – the Olympic Gold Medalist who's working on the Frampton Games?"

"We all met him on our site visit" Jonny butted in, his shirt now back to its standard blue. "Your Dad doesn't miss a trick does he? Holidaying with the home team."
Ben blushed.

Harry rose to the defence: "Take no notice Ben. We're very pleased to meet you again."

"You were just a babe in arms last time we saw you" said Eleanor pensively.

"I think I should ring my parents."

He tapped his father's number on his iPhone.

"I'm on a balcony overlooking the square with the Jamb family," he replied to his father's question as to his whereabouts. Eleanor could hear that Freddie had raised his voice and was clearly upset at what Ben had told him. "Where are you?" asked Ben unwilling to respond to his comments in front of Eleanor. Freddie was clearly close by. "Look up at the palazzo near the corner where all the horses crashed. I'll wave."

Harry saw them walking towards the palazzo. Freddie in his usual white collarless shirt and black trousers; he had forgone the jacket but was wearing a Panama hat, Harriet marched next to him in flower-patterned frock.

"I-I I'd better go down" Ben said hesitantly." It was nice to meet you," and he shook hands with Eleanor and put out his hand to Harry.

"I'll go with you." Harry put his arm round the young man's shoulder as they walked down the marble stairs and into the dusk of the square still busy with celebrating supporters, tourists and street cleaners. Harriet stopped in her tracks as soon as she saw Harry with Ben. Freddie walked on.

"Hello Harry," he said frostily "Hi Ben, time to go home."

Harry offered his hand to his former partner. He thought their dispute had gone on long enough; a handshake might start to mend the relationship. Freddie hesitated, glanced over to where Harriet was standing and then quickly took Ben by the arm. They walked off into the thinning crowd.

Harry was stunned. Did Freddie not see his hand? It was a small gesture, why couldn't he bring himself to reciprocate? They had got on so well once upon a time; surely the fundamental interests and aspirations that created that first bond were still there despite what had happened. Surely Freddie could bury the hatchet as Harry felt he had? Harry was sure that without the looming presence of Harriet, Freddie would have reacted differently. He walked slowly back up to the first floor of the palazzo as the others were collecting their things to return to the villa.

"Daddy, did you speak to Ben's parents?" Amelia approached him enthusiastically "He's so-oo nice! We're going to meet up when we get back to London."

Harry didn't say much as he drove the group back to the villa. He didn't feel like joining in the excited conversation going on behind him.

"That was one of the most intense experiences I've had for ages" Josh had thrilled to the wiry nut-brown bodies of the jockeys, and the whole thundering spectacle. He pictured the bloody face of the celebrating *contradaiolo* who had been violently knocked to the floor by a riderless horse, yet had got back up to continue shouting and punching the air. Pain and ecstasy. Josh loved that.

Jonny had been more moved by the social impact of the Palio "It's fantastic how an event like that can be used to bring the community together. Did you see the tables laid out in the streets ready for the *contrade* supper? We don't do that sort of thing anymore, which is a shame. I'm going to organise a huge street party just like that in Frampton if I win the competition."

"It's just like football teams – Liverpool, Everton, Sunderland, Celtic, do just the same sort of thing. If you want to do anything you should get Frampton City up there in the Premier League." Jason laughed.

They chatted on, Amanda about the beautiful arena formed by the 14th century buildings, Jason about the flag throwers and Jonny about the architect's responsibility to the community. Harry's phone rang.

"Hello, is that Harry? It's Martin Hester here."

"Hi Martin, good to hear from you."

"I'm staying up in Lucca at the moment and was driving down past your place tomorrow and thought I might drop by."

"Of course. Do come for lunch. Get here at midday and you'll have time for a dip in the pool before we eat."

***

Hester's Porsche 997 crunched up the cypress-lined driveway to the Villa Scappi. He walked down to join the rest of the party around the pool slipping into the shower room to change into his trunks. Harry had built the little pavilion a few summers before out of stone that had been dug up around the estate. He had built it without any mortar as a spiral wall with no roof, the centre of the spiral forming a mini spire. It had a rustic, timeless feel and looked as though the artists Richard Long or Andy Goldsworthy might have had a hand in it. Harry hadn't bothered to get planning permission thinking that it could easily be taken down again, but the simple form sat so comfortably in the landscape that Harry felt as though it had always been there.

Hester cut a fine figure as he emerged from Harry's stone shelter. He had been preparing for the summer in his own Hester Health Club tanning studio in Frampton, and his body still retained much of the muscle and shape of his sporting days.

He dived cleanly into the pool and scythed through ten lengths as all the others looked on in awe. Josh had always thought of himself as a good swimmer, but the speed and style of a professional like Hester, even a retired one, was in a very different league.

Hester vaulted out of the water to be greeted by Eleanor handing him a towel.

"Lunch is ready." Eleanor thought he didn't look as though he ate much, as she admired his six-pack stomach and rippling shoulders. There wasn't an ounce of fat on him anywhere.

Harry pulled out a fat 6B pencil and started drawing on the tablecloth. He was sitting at one end of the table with Jonny, Amanda and Josh. They were discussing the layout of the Masterplan for the Frampton Games. Amelia had driven into Siena in her Cinquecento to meet up with Ben and given Jason a lift as he'd wanted to buy lots of contrada flags to take back to London.

Hester and Eleanor sat together; excluded from the architects' discussions they talked at length about his sporting career, his ex-wives, his love of Frampton and his pride at having the city's most significant modern building named after him. Eleanor found herself more and more absorbed in his conversation as well as in his enveloping masculine presence – something that Harry, so wrapped up in his architectural world, didn't even raise half a glance to.

Part 2 – Designs

Chapter 8

The winning architects for the Frampton EuroGames' buildings were to be selected by a special committee made up of Sir Nigel Frith, the Chancellor of Frampton-on-Tees University, Astrid Sollet, the spiky, glamorous Chair of the Committee for Better Architecture (CofBA), Sid Dixon the leading developer, together with Mayor Jarvis and Ed Clutton his planning chief.

"The problem with Nigel Frith" Sid Dixon said to his wife Veronica when he received the letter inviting him to join the Committee "is that he believes it's high time he was made Lord Frith. He's a pompous old twat. He's been involved with a lot of building projects at the University. He uses Josh Stern a lot because AAP Architects designed the original buildings in the 60s; so he's not very adventurous. I can see we're in for some fun and games!"

Tall and patrician, Frith walked with a slight stoop, his shock of grey hair gave him a professorial air, but his grey suit marked him as a bureaucrat. He was a stickler for procedures. In contrast Dixon was short, energetic, stylish and one of the leading figures among a new breed of developers who used cutting edge architects to design striking buildings that appealed to a young, metropolitan audience. He was the antithesis of Frith.

Sid worked closely with Veronica who he had met when she was the top sales assistant of the first development he had ever done. Bouffant and brassy, Veronica had been key to the success of Dixon Developments and was now the firm's International Sales Director. She and Sid were often seen out together but that was more a marketing exercise than a sign of true love. Their marriage had been 'open' for years, Sid, just turned 50, preferred his partners in bed to be half his age, or less.

"The Committee's first task" announced Sir Nigel at their first meeting "is to visit the offices of each of the architects to ensure that they are able to cope with the job. While the majority of the firms are located in London, there will also be visits to Manchester, Dublin, Paris, Rotterdam and Tokyo. In order to speed up the task I propose that the Committee split up the overseas visits, two members visiting each of the offices and writing a report for the Committee. We will all visit the London offices together."

Thus the group found themselves, one bright October morning, standing outside the Marylebone offices of Frederick Shaw and Partners. There was a slight autumnal chill in the air, but London had been enjoying a glorious Indian summer that year and no one had yet needed to don their winter coats.

Astrid felt strangely nervous as she walked into Freddie's office. She had worked with Freddie soon after she left university and when he was still in partnership with Harry. They had enjoyed a brief fling together which had ended perfectly amicably. Although she frequently bumped into Freddie at social occasions, this was different. The effect that winning would have on the successful practice would be immense and she was well aware that the competition for the Games was seen by the architectural community as a battle between the two former partners. It had briefly crossed her mind that she should have declared her affair with Freddie when she had filled out the form that asked whether she had any interest that might affect her decision making as an assessor.

"Astrid! How lovely to see you!"

Freddie, together with Carlos de Souza his design associate, had been looking out for the arrival of the judging party and greeted them all as they entered the reception area. He gave Astrid a gentle but noticeable squeeze as he kissed her on both cheeks before shaking hands with the rest of the party.

"This is Carlos de Souza my senior designer." Carlos smiled and bowed deferentially to the group. It always annoyed him when Freddie introduced him as 'my designer'; he was *the* designer. The games proposal was *his* building based on ideas he had been working on since he was a student. Freddie had made a few comments when he looked over his shoulder in the studio, but that was about all he had had to do with the development of the dramatic forms of the design.

The large reception area with its bright primary coloured walls and dimpled rubber tile floor, doubled up as an exhibition space for work by the practice – large perspex cases enclosed a Lilliputian version of Freddie's vision for the world.

Along one wall were the framed certificates of the many awards the practice had won – the RIBA Award, the Civic Trust Award, the Steel Construction Award, the Concrete Society Award – there were more awards than could fit on the wall and a stack of recent ones leant against the skirting. Freddie entered all the awards he could – not only did he like receiving them but he found them a very effective way of promotion. They helped to provide the oxygen of publicity so vital to architectural firms and they gave clients confidence.

Freddie led the party through into the main studio. A former upholstery workshop, it had been extended at the rear and the architect had inserted a mezzanine floor into the roof to provide extra space. A wide stair led down to the basement workspace.

"We have 150 staff working here," said Carlos. Designers looked up briefly from their screens as the groups walked past. They all seemed tremendously young, thought Astrid. And multicultural too. There were Chinese, Asian, Latin American. She walked past a group holding a team meeting. Australians, she thought, or were they New Zealanders?

"Working for Freddie looks great on a CV," one of Astrid's old colleagues who still worked with Freddie had told her over a drink. "Kids come from all over the world and get paid a pittance. They're very bright, they work all hours of the day and night, and they can go home and get a really good job. It's win win."

"Sounds more like slave labour to me."

101

"You won't get shown down to the basement when you visit" said the friend. "That's where all the secret stuff goes on. The practice generally loses money on its high profile jobs. Freddie and Carlos spend too much time getting the design right. They're our loss leaders. They get into all the design and architecture magazines and make our reputation. Down in the basement they're churning out designs for big industrial estates in the Midlands and whole cities in the Far East – but you'll never see our name linked with them. Tariq set the whole thing up. It keeps the practice profitable."

Astrid had not seen Tariq Shah since she left the office of Shaw and Jamb nearly 15 years ago. He stood behind Freddie in the boardroom as Carlos described the practice and how it worked. Tariq was still reserved and polite, in the background, but he exuded a confidence Astrid did not remember from the days they worked together.

He was wearing an expensive well cut suit, sober tie, gold cufflinks (not flashy) and highly polished shoes. He wasn't saying much, but he's in control, thought Astrid. While Freddie talked through their approach to the Games project, Carlos sketched endlessly with a 6B pencil on long rolls of yellow tracing paper to explain an idea, a concept, a form. Astrid was full of admiration for the way that Freddie had developed his firm.

"Three people. A trinity." Astrid thought.

Many of the most successful firms of architects have been threesomes. Skidmore Owings & Merrill, Kohn Pedersen Fox, Ahrends Burton and Koralek, Yorke Rosenberg & Mardall, Howell, Killick, Partridge. Scott Brownrigg & Turner. One partner is the front man, the public face, the work getter, one is the designer and one makes sure the office can deliver the work. Even single name practices, if they're going to grow, have these guys in the background.

"We've got a fantastic team here of the most talented designers from around the world" Freddie told the Committee as he waved his arms to the rows of architects peering intently at their computer screens visible through the glazed partition wall of the meeting room.

The group returned to their mini bus.

"They're a pretty impressive bunch," said Ed Clutton "They can certainly take on a job of this size."

"I didn't take to the South American chap at all," grumbled Mayor Jarvis "far too big for his boots. I can see fireworks ahead if he's on the project."

Sid laughed "It's his Latin passion that makes their work exciting. Before he came along Freddie was really boring. If you want great buildings, Richard, you're going to have plenty of fights on your hands."

The Mayor had had plenty of fights in his time and generally enjoyed them. As he rose up the ranks of his local party he had built up a reputation as a bit of a bruiser. However this was different. He knew it was important that the Games buildings were striking examples of modern architecture, but he wasn't sure what that was. He didn't like many of the buildings he'd seen in Freddie's office, but all the others seemed very impressed. In matters of taste he felt out of his depth – an unusual feeling for him – and relied heavily on Ed Clutton's advice.

"It all looked very expensive to build," Jarvis finally countered: "how are we going to make sure they stick to the budget? As far a the voters are concerned you can have the most beautiful bloody buildings in the world but if the rates go up they won't thank us."

"Joe Porley is one of the best project managers in the business," replied Ed "if anyone can keep costs on track he can."

"Yes but you've got to be careful," Astrid interjected, "cost cutting – or value engineering as Joe would call it – can so easily rip all the quality out of the design." Astrid had seen it happen so many times. CofBA would approve a scheme in its early stages, only to find that had changed materials and simplified details so that the final building was but a shadow of the architect's renderings.

***

Harry's office in Clerkenwell was a simple open space, lined on three sides with large arched windows, painted white, with a polished timber floor. The practice was smaller than Freddie's with around 50 architects. Harry had never wanted to get too big; he liked to be able to keep a close eye on every job and had built up a strong and trusted team of senior directors and assistants.

Astrid recognised the woman who greeted the group as they arrived. Jenny had stayed working for Harry as the Office Manager after the split with Freddie. She looked after Harry's every whim. She was meticulously efficient and dressed the part with drawn back hair, heavy rimmed glasses, four-inch heels, and pencil thin skirt with a suggestive slit that Sid could not take his eyes off. Jenny had been in love with Harry since she first joined Shaw, Jamb and Partners.

But Harry seemed blissfully unaware of the reason for her unswerving devotion to her job.

Jenny led the way to the meeting room, her heels clacking sharply on the timber floor, followed closely by Sid. She pushed open the frosted glass door and ushered the group in to where Harry and two of his design team were waiting. After the usual introductions they all sat down in the comfortable black leather chairs.

"I love the photos" Astrid broke the ice as people studied the room, "they're taken by Alex La Touche aren't they?"

Alex La Touche was one of best, and the most expensive, architectural photographers in the world. He had trained as an architect before taking to the camera, so he understood the way his clients' minds worked. He photographed their creations the way that they saw them in their mind's eye. He took the best angles, he cropped out the grotty surrounding and he always waited for the best light conditions.

Harry always chose Alex to photograph his buildings because he found good pictures were generally more important than good buildings when it came to getting work published in the magazines.

"What's so great about them?" Jarvis leant across to Ed and said in a low voice that all could hear "there's no bloody people in any of 'em"

Ed cringed. There were times when the Mayor lost his characteristic optimism and upbeat manner and sank into a bullying and curmudgeonly gloom. He hoped it wasn't going to last all day.

Harry had heard the remark and thought it best to take it head on.

"We see our architecture as the backdrop before which the drama of daily life is played out. Our buildings are not designed to overpower the user, but to empower them. We don't go in for fashionable forms and so-called sexy shapes. Our architecture is timeless and beautiful, based on rules of proportion, immaculate detailing and sympathetic materials."

Jenny, who was helping serve coffees to the party, wanted to clap. Harry was so good in front of an audience. He became totally authoritative, totally convincing. She knew it was a skill he was going to need to draw on extensively in the next couple of years – providing they won this job.

Ed wasn't sure the Mayor got the message, but Harry's firm and elegant riposte certainly settled him down and the rest of presentation ran smoothly.

***

The next visit was to Jonny Spon's studio in Shoreditch. Ed's secretary had arranged lunch for the party in a local and highly fashionable Chinese restaurant recommended by Spon's office, without letting on that the interior had been designed by Jonny himself.

The Mayor was met by the effusive owner who led the team of assessors into a private room designed like a giant fish tank. Jonny had based the design on a theme of water – walls of water, rippling streams under a raised glass floor, falling streams in plastic ducts tumbling from the ceiling and Perspex table tops encapsulating moving water bubbles. The owner's plan was to roll out the brand once the Shoreditch site had established itself.

Astrid had wanted just a light lunch. A salad would have done. But the dishes kept coming, fine soups with tasty prawn ravioli, lobsters, deep-fried soft shell crabs, black cod, hardly touched, followed by sweetmeats and exotic fruits. It was a major feast. The Mayor was looking at his watch, the food was fantastic but they had a tight schedule to meet.

"Better get the bill, Ed" he said to Clutton.

"There's nothing to pay" said the owner "compliments of Mr Spon."

"That just won't do!" Nigel Frith exploded "we will have to pay. We cannot be seen to be taking favours from one of the competitors."

Ed Clutton could see through the watery wall the owner and his maître d' excitedly discussing the bill. After some delay and several impatient waves from the Mayor, the owner delivered the bill on a salver. Jarvis's face was one of undisguised horror. In Frampton a Chinese meal cost no more than a tenner. In Shoreditch it was more than ten times that amount. How could he put this on his expenses? Some bloody journalist would dig it up and use it against him. He could just see the headlines now. He couldn't let Spon pay or Frith would kick up a fuss.

"This one's on me" Sid cheerily, noticing the Mayor's discomfort, and took the bill.

"I told you that bloody Spon would be trouble" Jarvis spat into Ed Clutton's ear.

***

"You can almost tell the age of an architectural practice by how far east it is" Astrid said as group entered Spon's scruffy warehouse building. "In the 80s rents started to drive younger architects from Fitzrovia to Clerkenwell, in the 90s they moved on to Shoreditch and now you can find them in Deptford and Bow."

Concrete stairs. No lift. The Mayor led the way; Nigel Frith, slowed down by painful arthritis, struggled up to the fourth floor. Jarvis pushed through the double doors and entered the large high ceiling space. A dozen Brompton folding bicycles in a variety of colours were ranged along one side of the door. A single, wide table stretched the length of the room. A dozen or so faces turned from their screens to look at the newcomers. Brown leather armchairs were grouped informally along one side of the table. More like a living room than an office, thought the Mayor. On the other side two jean-clad figures played table football.

"Let me show you round" offered Jonny and he walked the group up and down the table describing the projects each of the architects was working on. Few of the designers were asked to contribute to the conversation. Astrid was surprised that there were so many architects, she had read in *Building News* that Jonny had had to lay a number of people off when he lost a big housing commission in Holland.

At the end of the room a row of recycled cinema seats was lined up in front of a large floor to ceiling screen. Jonny signalled the group to sit down; as they did so the room darkened and *Paradise City* by Guns 'n' Roses boomed out from mammoth speakers on either side of the screen. Computer generated images of buildings flew through the air, boxes stacked up upon each other were blown apart in simulated explosions and re-stacked to illustrate different configurations.

"This was done for us by Abstract, they're the best on computer graphics." Jonny enthused as the boxes turned to pencil lines and the anonymous shapes became recognisable building forms with Lowry-like figures moving around the spaces in between. The movie cut to a group of people sitting around a table covered in paper and coloured pencils.

"We work with local communities to come up with ideas that inspire them and that they feel they own." Huge coloured shapes spun across the screen and morphed into exotic building forms.

As the group drove back to their hotel in the minibus the Mayor was the first to break the silence.

"I didn't understand that – he did all those workshops and ended up with something that was just like the stuff he always does. Shouldn't that sort of process mean you end up with something different?"

"You can call it inspiration – or brilliant salesmanship. He convinces people of the rightness of his ideas." Clutton responded "Yes, he adjusts his designs to take on board specific comments but he pushes people to accept ideas that you would have never imagined they would at the start of the process."

"I look forward to him trying to do that to his mates on the Conway Estate." The Mayor had singularly failed a few years earlier to push through a new housing scheme next to the estate in the face of major protests from local residents

***

In total, fifteen offices were visited by the committee. The final inspection was Tomo Koji's Tokyo office with just two members of the team – Sid and Astrid

Sid lobbied Clutton hard to agree for him to go. He was a great Japanophile. He loved the elegance of the people and the architecture. He loved the food, the trains and the women. The contrast of samurai, ninjas, Iwo Jima and Hiroshima and the hectic, crowded city life with the quietude of interior spaces of shoji screens, tatami mats and tokobashira mirrored something of the way Sid viewed his own internal conflicts. He loved the contemplative spaces of the grounds of Shinto temples, the exquisite peace of buildings like Tadao Ando's Naoshima Art Museum and his Church of the Light, and the Japanese fascination with the perfection of arrangement – whether of flowers, pebbles or shop windows. He had come a long way from the used car plot he started with soon after leaving school at 16. He had wanted to get out fast and did a few things, involving baseball bats and hard drugs, that he wouldn't want to own up to now.

The two assessors arrived at Koji's office which was located in a residential area just outside the centre of Tokyo.

"*Arigato!*" Sid practised his phrase book Japanese as the driver automatically opened the cab door.

"He's the only one of the candidates who has actually built his own office" remarked Astrid as they looked up at the minimal four-storey concrete cube that nestled against the traditional-style houses of the neighbourhood.

Inside, the cube opened up into a grand top-lit atrium ringed with shelf-like floors. As they walked into the ground floor space Astrid and Sid could see the whole Koji office hard at work. Some of the architects peered into computer screens, some were building models of buildings or large scale details, others were grouped in meetings. A restrained buzz filled the space. Every single employee was dressed in black.

The two visitors introduced themselves to the receptionist sitting behind a large concrete desk; the young girl smiled and bowed. But as Sid started to introduce himself the smile disappeared. An angry voice could be heard coming from a frosted glass box sitting in the middle of the space. The meetings stopped talking, the computer keyboards fell silent, as the voice got louder, its rants linked by the same muffled apologetic reply.

Suddenly the shouting stopped and a few moments later a small black-clad figure emerged from the glazed office, his monochrome appearance marred by the crimson stain spreading across the small towel held up to his nose.

"Blimey" said Sid. He'd heard stories of Koji's temper but he hadn't expected such a dramatic display of it. "One chap who worked here told me that Koji keeps a bamboo cane and if they weren't working hard enough he's beat them across the shoulders!" he whispered to a Astrid who was quite shocked by what she had just seen.

"He said there are bunk beds for staff to sleep on because they work such long hours they don't have time to go home!"

The receptionist led the pair towards the glass office: she stopped by the side of the door and signalled for them to enter, bowing as they did so.

The architect was sitting at his desk drawing intently as though nothing had happened. An assistant stood next to him holding a tray of coloured pencils which he proffered to the maestro on command, as a nurse might hand an implement to a surgeon during an operation. Koji didn't look up for several minutes. Astrid watched fascinatedly as he sketched out the form of a building with the confidence of a draughtsman trained in the flowing line of Japanese calligraphy. Sid was becoming increasingly irritated. He wasn't used to being ignored like this – especially by architects who were normally all over him like a rash, eager to get a job off him.

With a flourish Koji signed the drawing with kanji symbols. He picked up the heavy handmade paper with both hands, pushed back his chair and walked round the desk to where Sid was standing. Without saying anything he bowed and proferred the drawing to the diminutive developer.

"*Domo arigato gozaimasu*! *Koji San*" enthused the immediately mollified Sid. This must be worth several grand, he thought, as he gave a bow to match the Japanese architect.

The crayon carrier then introduced himself as Tak, the Office Director at Tomo Koji and Partners.

"You speak really good English" Astrid remarked.

"Yes, I studied at GSD Harvard and worked in New York before returning to Japan. A lot of our staff here have worked in Australia and the US – so language won't be a problem if we are selected to work on the Games."

"Mr Koji has asked me to say that he wishes to work together with the AAP practice to deliver the Frampton Games project. He had a meeting with Mr Josh Stern when he was last in England and they came to an agreement. He thinks that AAP are a very efficient firm and Mr Stern understands the requirements of our architectural approach."

Koji said nothing during the visit. Tak had explained that his boss could speak no English, but his reactions to certain points of interest made Astrid think that he understood more than he let on.

But Koji's thoughts had turned elsewhere as the discussions about Frampton and the chiaroscura of Rachael Dove's cleavage took him back to the treasurer's office in the town hall. As he relived the daring adventure he pondered the possibility of a repeat performance next time he was in Britain.

"I look forward to seeing you next month when you present your designs," said Sid to the silent Koji, and they both bowed as they said goodbye. "And thank you for this wonderful drawing."

Tak shook hands with Astrid and leant towards her: "Perhaps you could enlighten Mr Dixon that the translation of the inscription on the drawing says 'A gift to the people of Frampton-on-Tees'."

Chapter 9

For the next stage of the competition the architects had to present their designs to the Selection Committee.

Koji was very concerned that his drawings for the Media Centre would get lost en route so Tak flew to London from Tokyo to deliver them in person. It would also give him a chance to meet up with Josh Stern to show him their ideas and prepare him for the final presentation to the assessment panel.

Tak arrived at Joe Porley's office with a half a day to spare.

"You're the first one to arrive," said Porley's PA as the Japanese architect handed over the heavy box of drawings, bound reports and CDs.

The deadline for delivery of schemes was 5.00 pm and it was not until after 3.00 that the taxis started to arrive with the rest of the architects' submissions. Office assistants with portfolios, some expensively branded with especially designed logos, others no-nonsense corrugated plastic holders and wire-o binding. Models were carefully juggled out of the back of black cabs, while Shaw and Partners needed a pantechnicon to transport their large scale mini-building complete with its bespoke aluminium flight case.

***

A few weeks later – once Joe Porley's technical team had studied the submissions to check the drawings, to make sure the proposed buildings wouldn't fall down or cost too much – the rival teams, supported by their engineers and cost consultants – travelled to Frampton to formally present their designs to the Selection Panel. The original long list of twenty teams had been reduced to twelve – three for each of the main schemes: the Stadium, the Swimming

Centre, the Media Space and the Temporary Pavilions. The interviews lasted three whole days.

It was an arduous task but one which Astrid relished. She was fascinated to watch some of the top names in architecture performing in this highly charged, theatrical environment. Normally confident designers mumbled incoherently, their words stuck like dry toast in their trembling throats while laser pointers zig zagged across the power point screen as speakers desperately tried to mask their shaking hands. Others were put off their stride when they couldn't get their computers to work – losing valuable time as they struggled to download their images or to get their Apple Macs to speak to the conference room's PC.

Astrid was appalled that only eight of the teams had women members and only one was led by a woman – Amanda Stone.

Some of the presentations were brilliant. As Astrid expected, Harry came over beautifully. He was relaxed, very clear in his vision for the stadium and looked attractive to the assembled assessors. She noticed Jarvis looked up from his blackberry and listened when Harry started talking, others leaned forward in their seats.

Harry's design for the Hester Stadium was clean, crisp and minimal with a wafer thin oval roof suspended effortlessly above the banked seating.

"The building is a beautiful backdrop" Harry told the assessors; "although large, it is essentially modest, it accentuates the colour and the drama of the Games that will take place within, rather than snatching all the attention for itself."

Freddie was equally captivating but in a different way – he gave a brilliant sales pitch for the practice before handing over to Carlos to explain their designs for the Swimming Centre. The South American's passion was infectious as he described the thinking behind his giant glass bubble sitting in the centre of a lake.

"The lake is reflected in the building and vice versa; the façade shimmers with light even on a dull day." He stroked the fluid form of the metre-long model as he spoke. "The soft shape represents the form of a giant drop of water; it is a building which speaks to the observer who, by entering the building is immersed in the concept of water. It is about love: love of people, love of space, love of water."

His eyes welled with emotion as he sat down and handed over to the cost consultant and engineer to explain how on earth they were going to build the exotic structure within the tight budget and immoveable deadline.

Koji, accompanied by Tak and Josh Stern, processed into the room, with four assistants supporting at each corner a model of a large spiralling tower, like Shinto priests carrying a sacred palanquin. The three architects were dressed in black with collarless shirts and aligned themselves along the end of the table. Tak and Koji bowed deeply. Top marks for theatricality, Astrid thought.

"Good morning" said Koji unsmilingly. They were the only words he uttered throughout the whole presentation.

Tak described the tower in his fluent New England drawl.

"We decided to propose a tower for the Media Centre to differentiate the building from the inevitably lower buildings of the Stadium and Swimming Centre. We provided the large press conference and social spaces at the lower levels while providing efficient and accessible recording studios and offices within the tower."

"It's a big building," added Josh "we felt the alternative of a big box would be very intrusive on the site."

"Quite right" nodded Nigel Frith. The other contestants in this category had both produced lower buildings which were totally wrong for the site. Frith liked Josh Stern's no nonsense approach – linking up with Koji had been a good idea. This looked like it would be one the best buildings AAP had done.

***

"Where the hell are they, Ed?" said the Mayor, irritated. After Koji and his team had left, the assessors had had time to make a few notes, check on their emails and txts, pour themselves a fresh cup of coffee and then sit expectantly around the table.

"The office says they're on their way but Amanda's not answering her mobile."

As he spoke the doors burst open and half a dozen twenty-something architects strode into the room carrying large boards of drawings, easels and a series of plastic models. The group was followed by the elegant and imperious figure of Amanda Stone in slim fitting black trousers, high collared bolero jacket and white blouse upon which rested a striking geometric solid silver necklace, part of a collection she had designed for Astley's the Bond Street jewellers. She was closely followed by Emily Boudin.

The two sat down and the team of assistants disappeared as quickly as they had arrived leaving one of their number standing stiffly by the easels.

Jarvis waited for an apology, but none came.

"We have allocated one hour for each team to present their scheme. I am afraid we have already lost twenty minutes of that time and thus you will have just forty minutes for the presentation and questions," he announced rather stiffly.

"But it's just not possible to explain a scheme of this complexity in that amount of time." Amanda retorted.

"I'm sorry but we have a tight schedule and I cannot permit you any more time."

It seemed to Astrid that Amanda was about to stand up – was she about to walk out? It would not be the first time. But Emily held Amanda by the arm and spoke quietly in her ear.

Without any further comment Amanda signalled brusquely to the assistant by the easels and, as he placed the first drawing in front of the jury, Amanda set out the thinking behind her scheme and the complex forms and patterns it generated. It was an impressive if somewhat theoretical explanation of the proposals; the practical elements were filled in by Emily.

"Very interesting" interrupted the Mayor clearly still irritated "but we must move on to questions as we only have a few minutes left. You haven't mentioned anything about cost. Can you tell us how you have met the budget?"

"A full report from Nevis, our cost consultants, is included in the report we have sent you." Amanda responded coolly.

"And does it meet the budget?"

"We do not feel that cost is the most important issue here. Too much concern with cost restrains the designer's imagination; the building must be what it is. We want to deliver the best building possible for this site and that is not done by penny pinching and value engineering."

Jarvis could hardly believe his ears. "But we set a budget for this building at £500 million – can you build your designs for that amount or not?"

"The costs proposed by Nevis show a total cost of £650 million. We feel this is still good value for money."

"Value for money!" Jarvis exploded. "Don't you realise we haven't got an extra £150 million to spend?"

"You can find it if you want it." Amanda stood up and walked out of the room. Emily smiled apologetically and beat a hasty retreat.

***

Jonny Spon's presentation for the temporary pavilions that would house ticket booths, corporate entertaining and public lavatories could not have been more different. Astrid was expecting a rebel but once Spon started describing his ideas he came alive; eyes wide, tousle headed, dressed in jeans and loud check shirt, gesticulating wildly he paced up and down in front of the astonished assessors. Every now and then he would grasp his head and close his eyes as though seeking inspiration. A well-timed pause ensured attention for his next scatter-gun delivery. His enthusiasm was contagious. Even Joe Porley was impressed.

"We've come up with a range of ideas to show you how we work but which won't be fixed until we have a chance to present them to the local community. If we get this job we will want to set up workshops with people living around the site, to involve them in the design process, and come up with buildings that they feel some ownership of. And vitally, when the Games are over we want to leave buildings can be re used."

"How can we choose Spon if he hasn't told us what he's going to do?" complained Jarvis as the assessors were clearly moving towards selecting the radical young designer for the temporary buildings. "All the others came up with complete designs."

"I like his approach" Clutton responded, "We can really get people in the town involved in the planning for the Games. We're going to have to push through the big buildings, but the temporary buildings are the last parts of the programme so we've got time to give Spon his head."

The Mayor still wasn't sure, and he hadn't forgotten the architect's outburst in front of the Duke. But he decided to go along with the rest of the assessors. As the process of choosing the architects had gone on, Jarvis had been impressed with a lot of what he had seen and by the explanations that the architects had given for their decisions. He had always been conscious of the power of great buildings but never fully understood the complexity of the decision-making, nor the processes that were involved in a major building project from the foundations – and this Games site sat on top of one of the biggest coalmines in the area – to the finishes on the façades.

Jarvis had also been impressed by the calibre of his fellow assessors: Sid Dixon with his experience in the cut and thrust of

117

commercial development had given valuable advice about how to keep architects, who were always trying to push the boundaries of what they could do, under control but without destroying the quality of their architecture. Nigel Frith had commissioned a lot of new buildings for the Frampton-on-Tees University campus over the years – one of his bugbears was the cost of maintenance and he had regularly quizzed the designers about the longevity of their proposals. Astrid was looking for a building that would work, but would make a statement about contemporary architecture, that would be a stunning form creating beautiful spaces.

"Frederick Shaw and Partners' design with the large sphere sitting on the lake will be very difficult to build" Joe Porley told the panel, "but the effect will be stunning. Structurally it's quite tricky – we will have to look very carefully at the calculations at the base where the bending movements will be at the greatest. The engineers have said that the cantilever where the seating rows spring from the circulation routes could be a real safety issue."

Little was Joe to know how big a problem this critical junction was going to be.

"His design was by far the most striking," said Astrid "he really answered the brief to design an iconic building that could become a symbol for the Games."

The panel analysed the three proposals they had received for each of the four main buildings. As they got to the end of the process the final decision was made with a surprising level of agreement.

"It's important we make clear when we announce the winners that we are choosing a team not a design. Once we get into detailed design we will need to make changes and I don't want either the architects or the press to complain when that happens." Ed Clutton was also concerned about the way the three large buildings would relate to each other; now he'd seen the designs, he wanted to make changes to his Masterplan.

***

The Frampton Council Press Office, assisted at great expense by Loftus Global the London-based public relations agency, issued a press release announcing the winners.

"Richard Jarvis, the Mayor of Frampton-on-Tees, today announced the selected architects for the major buildings for the Frampton Games. They are :

Main Stadium	Harry Jamb Associates
Swimming Complex	Frederick Shaw and Partners
Media Centre	Tomo Koji Architects with Josh Stern and AAP
Temporary Pavilions	WILD Architects"

***

The headlines on the *Building News* website took a different line. Its headline screamed: "Amanda Stone snubbed in Games competition" and followed with a story that claimed that Amanda should have been selected to design the Swimming Complex. Her project was preferred by all the jurors but had been rejected by the technical panel on the grounds of its complexity. A source close to Amanda was quoted as saying:

"This is a complete nonsense. The Stone design is perfectly buildable; it was just too radical for the boring little people who believe that cost cutting is an art form."

And Amanda herself was reported to have said:

"I'm getting pretty used to this sort of thing now. I have major projects all around the world but none in Britain. Architecture in this country is in the hands of the project managers with no taste and no vision. No wonder the general quality is so poor."

The national press focused on photos of Freddie's Swimming Complex. The powerful spherical form dominated the front pages of all of the broadsheets but the headlines varied. "Duke attacks Modernist stadia," lead *The Daily Telegraph.* "Budget alert for Games" ran *The Guardian* quoting an anonymous cost consultant that the designs could never be built for the proposed budget. "A new icon for Frampton" said *The Times* while inside the architectural critic Tim Tickle reviewed Freddie's work and career.

The *Frampton Times* ran a double page spread with a large photograph of Martin Hester standing next to a model of the stadium that would bear his name. "A fitting tribute to a local hero" ran the headline.

"This is a beautiful building" Hester was quoted as saying (a quotation lifted verbatim from the Frampton Council press release). "Harry Jamb has created a Stadium that reflects the inspiration and excitement of the EuroGames but also provides a legacy to the young people of Frampton for whom it will be a wonderful facility for the future. I am very proud that my name is connected with the building and will work tirelessly to ensure that it becomes a magnificent showcase for the track and field events but also that it helps to deliver health and fitness to the local community."

A few days after the announcement Astrid was invited to attend a Crit at the London Academy of Architecture. The students had been set a project to design a building based on the brief for the Frampton Games. One of the best schemes was designed by a young Asian – tall, thin and elegant – who Astrid recognised. He produced a striking scheme for the temporary pavilions. Where had she seen him before? It annoyed her that she couldn't place him. After his presentation she went over to where he was removing his drawings from the wall.

"Haven't we met somewhere?"

"You spoke to me when you were visiting WILD's offices for the Games competition."

Astrid recalled the stylish youth sitting at the long desk that ran down the centre of Spon's office.

"So that's why you produced such a good scheme! How do you manage to have a job and keep up with your school work?"

"Oh, I don't work at WILD. They texted a few friends to ask if they could send over some students to make it look as though the office was busy. They didn't have any work, and Jonny thought it would look pretty bad if the office was empty. He was on the verge of shutting up shop, but he's OK now."

Astrid didn't know how to respond to the student's openness and lack of guile. The assessors' decision had saved a very good architect from closing down, but he had bent the rules. If *Building News* got wind of this there would be more critical press and calls to review the result from the thwarted contestants. Busy office or not, WILD had come up with the best proposal.

She decided to say nothing and walked away as the student rolled up his drawings. She had a sneaking admiration for Spon's chutzpah but worried that a carefully structured selection process might be derailed if too much bad press leaked out.

Thankfully a distraction was at hand: Jason Vent was about to take some of the pressure off the architects. Loftus Global advised that this would be the ideal time to launch Jason's branding for the Frampton Games.

Ever since the Palio in Siena Jason had become obsessed with flags and the exotic heraldry of the *contrade*. He had taken the patterns and figures of the *quattrocento* and given them a twenty-first century twist. Rich red became vicious pinks; royal blue became cyan and gold, lemon.

"I want flags! Flags! Flags!" Jason thrilled as he unveiled his designs to the world's press at a reception at the Design Museum in East London overlooking the River Thames.

"Flags on the stadium, flags on the streets, flags all over the city! I have been inspired by one of the world's oldest and greatest sporting competitions – the Palio in Siena. Inspired by the drama of the event itself, by the preparations leading up to the events and most of all by the involvement of the citizens of Siena in the whole event!"

As he finished his introduction the doors that led onto the riverside walk opened. A group of androgynous figures clad from head to toe in multicoloured skin tight lycra leapt forward; they tapped on the row of black discs set out in front of them. The electronic drums produced a convincing snare sound to accompany the group of Frampton Comprehensive School children who then marched across the riverside stage each waving a brightly coloured flag decorated with Jason's powerful graphic derivations of heraldic patterns.

Imitating the Sienese flag throwers, the kids swept their banners across the ground, across their bodies, around their heads, before tossing them high into the air, catching them with well-rehearsed finesse to enthusiastic applause from the Mayor and his party.

A small figure emerged from the melée holding a square banner and carried it ceremoniously to where Jason Vent stood. The designer grabbed the flag and held it so that the assembled press, and photographers, could clearly see the graphic device printed on it. The drummers produced an expectant roll.

"Ladies and gentlemen! – I give you the logo for the Frampton EuroGames!"

There was a deathly hush.

"What the hell has medieval Italy got to do with post-industrial Frampton-on-Tees?" murmured the feature writer from *Blueprint* to the news reporter from *The Daily Telegraph*. The *Telegraph* man thought his readers would like the heraldic references, but not the colours.

"That didn't go well," Ed Clutton said to Jason as they waited for a taxi outside the Design Museum. Ed was surprised how cheerful the designer was after his mauling in the press conference.

"Don't worry about it Ed. It's always the same. People hate it. They complain about how much it costs. Then they get used to it and they moan like hell if you ever try to change it. Wait and see."

***

The Duke of Frampton was apoplectic. He could just about come to terms with the Hester Stadium – controlled in its form and classical in it proportions if not in its details. But Freddie's spherical Swimming Complex icon was too much.

"It looks like a testicle sitting on a petri dish" he complained to Petronella as they looked through the press cuttings "and on the grounds of decency I shall desist in commenting on the anthropomorphic comparisons one could make to the Japanese tower except to say it is an erection too far!"

"I think the tower is rather nice, actually. A bit like origami. I wouldn't mind seeing that in the distance." Petronella knew her comments would be like a red rag to a bull but she wanted her father to understand that she didn't want to be drawn into the battle that was about to commence.

She had always supported him in the past. Because her mother had little interest in the Duke's architectural campaigns, he had depended on his daughter to accompany him to meetings, help him write articles, and produce damning drawings of proposed modernist carbuncles. This time, she had decided, she wasn't going to get involved.

The Duke was surprised at the positive reaction the building proposals had received in the press and he was depressed that he didn't have his daughter's support. He had found in the past that a few well-chosen words thrown into a speech would be enough to scupper major building projects he didn't like. The Games were different. Too much delay would be disastrous – if the city couldn't deliver the buildings on time it could say good-bye to the sort of outside investment that the Games would attract. But he could not stand by and see these monstrosities constructed almost literally in his backyard. What an insult! What a victory for his adversaries!

The Duke drew a sheet of writing paper from the drawer of the carved escritoire which his great Grandfather had purchased at the

Great Exhibition in 1851. Underneath the embossed arms of his ancestors he wrote to the Mayor:

"CONFIDENTIAL

Dear Jarvis

I am appalled to see the designs you have selected for the Frampton-on-Tees Games buildings. They are utterly out of context and will be a blot on the city for generations to come. You have selected architects from a particular modernist clique and seem to have ignored the many talented architects we have in this country who are following more timeless forms of building.

You will be aware that the Frampton Family Trust is currently providing the major part of the funding for the new Frampton Library. I would wish you to be aware that should you decide to proceed with the Games' designs as published, we shall have no option but to withdraw our support for the new library.

Yours etc

Frampton"

The new city library had been designed by the traditionalist architect Inigo James. James's father had been an assistant to Lutyens – his middle name was Edwin – and he had been schooled in the benefits of Classical architecture from an early age. He ran a highly successful practice from a converted barn outside Newbury; most of his workload was made up of designing second, third or fourth homes for hedge fund managers and Russian oligarchs. Enormous Palladian country houses in England, pedimented bungalows in Barbados or timber-columned hunting lodges in the Caucasus – James was in such demand that he had a client waiting list of three years. But, when Frampton announced plans for a new library, he had been willing to delay all his luxury jobs for a chance of designing a major public building in Britain.

He didn't normally go in for competitions.

"The problem with architecture in England today" he would tell anyone willing to listen "is that it is a modernist monopoly. It is controlled by the followers of Le Corbusier whose rigorous censorship of taste is as complete as any political dictatorship. Designers like me who look for their inspiration to the tried and tested architecture of the past are totally neglected by the Establishment."

But he knew he stood a good chance in the Frampton Library competition since the Duke had put up most of the money for its construction and was chair of the judging panel. The announcement that he had won the prestigious commission caused a furore in the architectural press. The Library Committee was attacked for its 'nostalgia'.

"We cannot ignore the fact that we live in the twenty-first century" ran the arguments "we must design buildings that reflect social and technological progress. The selected design is a pastiche, a hollow copy of the architecture of a bygone age."

The designs however had the full support of the Frampton Civic Society and a poll among the readers of the *Frampton Times* showed that 80 per cent of respondents liked the scheme.

The Duke invited Inigo James to lunch at the Hall to inform him of his protest and warn him of his threat to the funding of the Library. He also wanted to garner his support for the campaign to stop the proposals for the Swimming Complex.

James cut a tall and aquiline figure as the butler ushered him into the grand hall. He was wearing a lightweight Harris Tweed suit with a high-buttoned waistcoat and heavy brown walking shoes. He carried a roll of drawings under his arm. He shook hands with the Duke and kissed Petronella who the Duke had invited to join them.

Although the architect was quite a bit older than his daughter, the Duke thought they might make a good match. They had a lot of interests in common, but Petronella never seemed very interested in young men.

"I had to do something to put the fear of God into that fellow Jarvis," explained the Duke as they tucked into estate-shot pheasant. "The design of the swimming pool is just so bloody awful, it has to be stopped."

"Jarvis has been brainwashed by his sidekick, Clutton, the planning chief. He's bought the modernist conspiracy hook, line and sinker – totally ignoring the tastes of the majority of the population who much prefer traditional architecture. There weren't any traditionalists even on the shortlists for the Games buildings."

"So how do we stop them James?"

"Well Sir, maybe we should put forward an alternative design, show people that a modern building can work inside a traditional skin. I put together a few ideas. . ."

He reached for his roll of drawings and spread them across the spacious dining table. The Duke could clearly see, drawn in James's distinctive pen and ink style, a building of tiered arches, a veritable coliseum.

"We can fit the pools in the middle very easily; all the support accommodation goes under the seating banks. The tension structure roof I have drawn is based on what we know of the *velarium* – the canvas system used on the Coliseum in Rome – but using the most up to date technology."

"Brilliant! Brilliant!" said the Duke rubbing his hands "this will spike their guns."

***

"A coliseum in our backyard!" Petronella said to her father as Inigo James drove off down the drive and they looked out over the valley towards the Games site. "Wouldn't that be pretty?"

"I must call that girl from *The Gazette*. This is front page stuff!" What a clever chap! Don't y'think Petronella? He's just the sort you should get hitched up with."

"He's nice enough, but just not my cup of tea." She paused. "Daddy, there's something I need to tell you. . ."

"He'll make a name for himself – just imagine, a grand Classical Library to match the Civic Hall and then the Frampton Coliseum. Great grandfather would be proud of us. What was it you wanted to say?"

"Never mind, it can wait." She couldn't spoil his day. He had been very depressed ever since the announcement of the designs for the Games. In the past the thought of a fight put him on his mettle, but this time the odds seemed stacked against him. The Games would be a great benefit to Frampton and opposition to the building projects could delay and damage the image of the city and its ability to deliver. But an alternative scheme that could be built in time and provide the sort of traditional buildings he liked – that might just work. He was more cheerful than he's been for months.

Petronella kissed her father lightly on the cheek and got into her car to drive back to London.

Chapter 10

Harry walked unsteadily out of the St John Restaurant in Clerkenwell. He hadn't been so drunk in the afternoon for years. Frank Cummins, who had now retired to a rather spectacular house near Montpelier, was making one of his rare appearances in London and had invited his former student to join him for lunch.

Even at the age of 80, Frank could down a bottle of claret and a couple of brandies over lunch without seemingly any ill effects. Harry couldn't keep up and was slurring his words even before they had finished their mains of chitterlings and greens.

"How do you do it Frank?" Harry asked "This amount of drink killed off all your bar companions years ago. Jim Bragg was a wreck at 60; he couldn't finish his book and was totally paranoid by the end, thinking all his students were ganging up on him – which I suppose they were because his lectures became so unintelligible."

"You need a strong liver and a non-addictive personality, but most importantly you have to see drink as something to be enjoyed – wine is a gift of the gods to be studied and savoured – not a drug to anaesthetise you against the injustices of the world! Use it as a crutch and you're finished. . ."

They were words that would come to haunt Harry in the coming months as he was sucked deeper and deeper into the whirlpool of intrigue, competition and confrontation that became his daily diet as the Games's buildings progressed.

***

"We should hold an exhibition on current British architecture which will focus specifically on the work of Harry Jamb and Frederick Shaw," suggested Sheranie Philips the Programme

Director at the prestigious Institute of Art to the gallery's Exhibitions Committee. "Their projects for the Frampton Games are giving them international press coverage, and interest in their work will continue to grow as the buildings come out of the ground. It will be a very popular show. I think we should go for it."

"Hang on, hang on," Sir Richard Frank, Chairman of the Exhibition Committee, complained, "this is just showbiz architecture. If you want to do something on current British architecture it needs to be a much wider survey. There's plenty of good stuff out there." Frank was annoyed that Philips hadn't included any of his work in the proposed show.

"I just don't think that sort of exhibition would bring in the numbers of visitors we'd need to make it worthwhile. Shaw and Jamb are in the press all the time, people know who they are." Sheranie didn't add that few people outside the architectural profession had a clue who Richard Frank was. He had designed several half decent college buildings at Oxford and Cambridge and done some worthy work on Government committees, but his staid output was hardly a crowd puller.

"I suggest we take a vote."

"Those in favour?"

Sheranie counted the raised hands. It was a close run thing with a handful of the committee members – as miffed as Sir Richard at not being included in the show – keeping their hands firmly under the table.

"Carried."

***

The detailed design of the Hester Stadium proved to be the toughest job Harry had ever done. He was getting a lot of grief from Joe Porley over the costs of the building.

"You've got to bring this in under £500 million Harry. That was the budget you were given and that's what we've got to spend."

"But you know as well as I do Joe that those figures were set deliberately low to keep the politicians happy. It just can't be done for that price."

"I can show you half a dozen stadia of this size that came in cheaper."

"Of course you can, but they're all rubbish. There's a lot at stake at Frampton and we've got to deliver a very special building."

His faithful team of designers were working twelve to fourteen hours a day as well as weekends. Harry was getting hardly any sleep at all. When the rest of the office went home he continued to worry over the progress of the design, the schedule, the budget and about his next battle with Joe Porley.

One night after some of the architects had been celebrating a colleague's birthday, Harry picked up what he thought was a glass of water which had been left on his desk. He took a swig. The neat vodka hit the back of his throat like a jackhammer.

The warm glow that followed settled Harry down. After that, the work seemed to go that little bit easier. Since his days at the Academy Harry had kept his drinking under control. More units than was healthy, but nothing that he couldn't handle. Without thinking he refilled the vodka glass.

The next night, as his enthusiasm for reworking the basement plan for the third time started to fade, he sent one of the assistants out to the office for a fresh bottle. It helped. A shot of vodka became a regular pick me up as the tension of the project increased. Harry felt rather pleased he'd found a way of making the process of designing the Stadium more bearable. It was a temporary stimulant – as soon as the building was on site things would ease off and, he told himself, he'd ease off on the booze.

***

Eleanor spent three days a week working in the office on public relations and marketing for Harry's firm. She took control of the communications team – two arts graduates who prepared press releases, presentations and organised photographs of finished projects. She realised that the firm needed a much more proactive marketing campaign if it was to make the best use of the publicity that surrounded the Games and to make sure that Harry got the appropriate credit for his work. Freddie had a team of eight people in his office burnishing his image; he had also commissioned Loftus Global to provide additional strategic advice.

"We've always had good publicity, our books have always been a good way of attracting clients, I don't know why we have to go down the same route as Freddie," Harry was sceptical about the value of public relations, "the buildings will speak for themselves."

"That may have worked up until now" countered Eleanor, "but things are different. We're moving into a different league, Harry. It's not just about publicity any more, it's getting the right publicity. The papers are always looking out for any scandals, cost overruns, structural problems or design mistakes and we've got to know how to react. This project is going to put Harry Jamb Associates into a whole new international orbit and we've got to make the most of it."

"The Stadium's connection with Hester is great for publicity" Eleanor continued, "he's got a high international profile and the press turn out for him more readily than they do for any architect."

So Eleanor arranged a series of events for editors of magazines where Hester was the guest of honour and Harry was there to talk about the design of the Stadium. Breakfast at the Wolseley, lunch at the Caprice, dinner at The Ivy . . . the journalists turned out to meet Hester and ended up writing about Harry.

At the height of the design programme Harry would often go back to the office after supper to see how the team was getting on. He made sure the office fridge was well stocked with chilled vodka. After a liberal dose of Stolichnaya, on top of the bottle of claret at dinner, he was little help to the design team. Sometimes he would sleep it off on the couch in his office to be woken by Jenny who was invariably the first in. She made sure there was a clean shirt and pressed suit so that no one on the office was aware that Harry's drinking was getting out of hand.

Meanwhile Eleanor was enjoying Hester's celebrity lifestyle, she loved the attention and the recognition that went with his fame. And Hester liked having her around. She was the life and soul of any party and she looked good.

Hester, with his mature-but-muscular looks, was an attractive and amusing companion, but that was about it. He was twenty years Eleanor's senior, almost a father figure, she was a busy working mother. So it came as a surprise when he made his move.

In London Hester lived in a new block of flats overlooking the Thames – a flashy monstrosity that Harry would invariably rail about whenever they drove past.

"The river is London's best piece of open space, how can they allow such rubbish? You see the same sort of crap all the way from Canary Wharf to Chelsea – you wouldn't think we had a planning system at all."

On Bonfire Night Hester was driving Eleanor home in his new Aston Martin. The sky flashed and sparkled as coloured rockets rose and exploded above the tree line.

"Let's go over to my flat – you get great views of the displays all around London from there."

Hester's penthouse was located on the bend of the river with spectacular views of the Houses of Parliament. Deep balconies rose up the front of the white rendered building culminating in a setback the size of a tennis court. A row of silver birch trees emerged above the top of the parapet.

"Evening Mr Hester" the uniformed porter saluted with a friendly smile as the two entered the marbled reception. Mr Hester was regularly accompanied by younger women when he arrived at his London *pied à terre*, but not often as classy as this one.

"Wow!" Eleanor exclaimed with genuine excitement as she walked into Hester's double height living space. It had floor to ceiling glass on three sides with panoramic view across the capital. Below, the dark water of the River Thames glistened menacingly, its threatening demeanour alleviated by the star-like illuminations on the filigree structure of the nineteenth century Chelsea Bridge. As Hester had promised the horizon was lit up with sporadic and spectacular displays of bursting colour.

Martin pressed the remote control and the windows slid silently apart. Eleanor noticed that it was surprisingly warm on the wide terrace; the infrared heaters had clearly been on for some time in preparation for visitors.

It was a clear night and the Houses of Parliament loomed large as the river snaked eastwards. Eleanor soaked in the spectacular backdrop of the unmistakable curved profile of Norman Foster's Gherkin, Renzo Piano's Shard and the floodlit façades of Canary Wharf formed a suitably dramatic backdrop to what was about to take place, as the ageing athlete set in train a series of events that would have dramatic and disastrous consequences for Harry, Eleanor and Hester himself.

"Earth has not anything to show more fair." Eleanor recited, a school performance of Wordsworth's ode suddenly coming to mind with a surprising clarity. "Dull would he be who could pass by, A sight so touching in its majesty."

"Champagne?" Martin was unmoved by the poetry as he moved into action. He had even put the Krug on ice ready for their arrival. Eleanor knew what was coming and she didn't mind. He was charming, good looking, well kept. A bit fatherly, maybe, but she was finding that rather reassuring as the stress of the Stadium build up was taking its toll on her relationship with Harry. He was hardly ever at home and when she was, and if he was, he was no good for anything. They hadn't had sex for months.

"Why not?" she thought, "Why fucking not!!" She took the fluted glass of Champagne from Martin.

"Cheers!" she said quietly. She looked up, her full red lips apart, wide eyed and supplicatory; his chiselled features, flickered red, green and blue as the spectacular Hurlingham Club fireworks display burst into the sky.

She didn't have time to take a sip. Martin's muscular arm swept around her waist and effortlessly lifted her off the ground. The crystal champagne flute fell silently onto the fake grass carpet as he pressed his lips to hers. Eleanor had never experienced such strength. Martin was gentle, but every movement, every muscle was incredibly firm. He knew just how hard to press in all the places he needed to press. It was the control of someone who had spent their life training their muscles to do precisely what he wanted them to do.

Even as she abandoned her emotions and body to his firm hold, her thoughts momentarily strayed to the architectural brief for the accommodation for the Athlete's Village. Behind the formal wording about the arrangement of rooms it was clear that the organisers were conscious of the need to design specifically for the testosterone-fuelled activities of hundreds of muscular, toned and virile sports men and women. Now she understood why.

***

It was about a week later that the Institute of Art held the private view for their exhibition "**** it – Britart Reaches Middle Age" curated by the eccentric critic Ned Stein.

Harry rang Eleanor to say that he was stuck at the office and wouldn't get there till late, so he would meet her there.

"I'm coming with Martin" Eleanor said openly as though nothing had changed in the past week, "there will be lots of press there – you and he should be photographed together." She surprised herself how easily she shifted into professional mode.

She was right about the photographers. As the driver Martin had hired for the evening dropped them off at the entrance to the Institute the flashbulbs started popping. Martin held the door open as Eleanor got out of the back seat of the Merc. She was wearing a short skirt that slid up her long and still tanned thighs; as she leant forward she provided the throng of photographers with a perfect composition of décolletage and naked flesh framed by Martin's muscular form.

The art celebs were all there: Eleanor spotted Tracey Emin, Anish Kapoor, Neil Tennant, David Furnish, Donatella Flick and Lord Palumbo even as she walked up the curving classical staircase that led to the galleries.

Eleanor had seen most of the work before – Hirst's cow shorn in two, Emin's bed and Ofili's elephant dung, but for Martin it was a first. He'd read the headlines but never seen it in the flesh.

"I still can't get my head round why people pay money, big money, for this stuff."

"Martin, there's more to art than Jack Vettriano" Eleanor riposted. She had a long term plan to upgrade Hester's views on art and architecture – if only so that he could properly appreciate the Stadium building that would bear his name. "Art's function is to reveal things to us about ourselves and our place in the world. Hirst does that dramatically. He's told us more about our relationship with death than any artist since Goya."

He had never thought much about art and architecture but found Eleanor a persuasive teacher, particularly so since his success between the sheets. He was enthused. She was twenty years his junior, vivacious, beautiful and bright. She made him feel good. She made him feel young. He wanted to make sure this was more than a one-night stand.

Eleanor reminded him he was about to have one of the most important new buildings in the country named after him, the least he could do was to understand something about architecture. Martin agreed it was time he caught up on those artistic appreciation classes that he had always skipped at school so he could get onto the sports field. The irony that he was screwing the wife of the architect of the eponymous structure had not yet occurred to him.

Eleanor told him about Goya's Black Paintings, the Disasters of War and the Chapman Brothers as they stood sipping champagne in a corner of the gallery. They were about to move on when Harry arrived.

Making his way unsteadily towards them he sensed something amiss about the way they stood together, the way they were looking at each other. Even in his drunken slur, Harry wasn't blind to the fact that Eleanor had been seeing an awful lot of Hester over the last couple of months, albeit on the basis that it was all a part of her role in the office dealing with 'external relations'.

Harry decided to tackle Eleanor in the taxi home.

"I'm getting fed up with having Hester hanging around all the time. I think we should change our PR strategy."

"But we're getting lots of publicity. *The Gazette* want to do an interview with you both in their 'How we met' series and *Elle Deco* want to photograph Martin in one of your interiors. We'd never get that sort of coverage if it was just you on your own."

"I just don't like it. You and he seem to be getting very friendly; why can't he just go back to Frampton."

He wasn't ready for her sudden response: "Well, at least he provides me a bit of company. You're never around, you're always at the bloody office, you never see the kids, and when you do come home you're pissed." She delivered the rebuke as she got out of the taxi and slammed the door. Harry fumbled with his wallet to pay the sympathetic cabbie.

"Blimey mate. I wouldn't want to be in your shoes. None of my business I know but there's a nice little hotel round the corner I can drive you to if you like."

"No thanks. I'll survive," he said with a hollow laugh; he was beginning to wonder if he would.

***

The CofBA Review Committee studied all the schemes for the EuroGames in detail and published their comments. They gave a clean bill of health to Freddie and Carlos's design for the Swimming Centre and suggested a few minor changes to the Stadium. But they were unhappy with the Media Centre. They criticised the tower for being too bulky and Koji's minimalist design was felt to be out of keeping with the surrounding buildings.

They heaped praise on WILD's Temporary Pavilions. "These smaller insertions into the Games's site have the ability to significantly enhance the visitor experience during the event. The exemplary way that WILD have developed their design in partnership with the local community is an approach that we commend and would like to see followed elsewhere," ran the Committee's letter to the Mayor.

"Bloody hell" said Richard Jarvis as he read the CofBA's fulsome praise "and I thought he was a right twerp."

"You may find that Spon's contribution to Frampton is more important than all the big buildings put together" Ed Clutton replied. "Have you seen the projects that the schools around the Conway Estate have been doing about the Games? They've all been working with the WILD guys and produced some really interesting ideas for Frampton after the Games. Politically I think it might be a good idea if you kept a closer eye on Mr Spon. He's got a lot to offer."

"When he had that confrontation with the Duke at the Civic Reception, I thought he was finished. The Duke warned me to get rid of him or, if I didn't, he would. But the boot's on the other foot now. There are too many votes in the Conway Estate. Anyway, with all this talk about localism, and communities getting involved in what happens to their neighbourhood, maybe Spon is onto a good thing."

***

The Duke of Frampton and John Veduty travelled to London for a council of war at the head office of the Conservation Society to discuss strategies for fighting the Games' buildings proposals.

As the meeting went on the Duke became more and more frustrated.

"There's not a lot we can do," explained Dame Judy Featherstone, the Chair of the Society. "It's a brownfield site, it doesn't involve the demolition of any listed buildings, and the proposed buildings have been approved by the CofBA and would be viewed by any planning inspector as 'good design'. And as far as I can ascertain the proposals are popular with the local community."

"But views of the town will be destroyed with that huge tower by the Japanese chap."

"With all due respect, Your Grace, the impact on the view from your house may not be seen as a material planning issue."

"Mine may be a narrow view, but it is a historic one, and worth protecting. C'mon Veduty" He stood up and stalked out of the Society's office followed by its local representative. His elegant 1947 Rolls Royce Silver Wraith, maroon with black mudguards, was parked on a double yellow outside the office. The uniformed chauffeur immediately broke off his argument with the traffic warden to open the rear door for the Duke and Veduty, slid into the driving seat, adjusted his cap and saluted the parking official as the Rolls purred into the London traffic.

"If there's no way we can stop them giving the buildings planning permission, we'll watch every step they take – one mistake and we'll go for a judicial review," the Duke continued.

"But Duke, I think we're on a losing wicket here. Dame Judy was very clear that she wouldn't support us. The local people are getting right behind the Games including many members of the Frampton Society. We'll just be seen as a bunch of fuddy-duddies.

I suggest we concentrate on getting the Inigo James Library built to show what good traditional architecture can do rather than fight a war we cannot win."

The Duke didn't answer. He had told no one of the threat he made to Mayor Jarvis to withdraw funding from the library if the buildings went through without amendment. Jarvis had ignored his attempt at blackmail and hoisted the Duke on his own petard. If he carried out his threat then doubtless the Mayor would substitute James's grand classical façade with its columns and pilasters, ionic capitals and carved pediment, with some modern monstrosity.

The two sat in silence for the next hour. Both men stared straight ahead. The Duke did not like being contradicted. He had spent most of his life surrounded by people who agreed with him. Even the normally resilient would defer to his view: sometimes because they knew which side their bread was buttered on and sometimes because of the rabbit-in-headlights hypnotic effect the aristocracy still had on large swathes of British society. Veduty could stand the silence no longer. The car turned off the motorway and coasted along the heather strewn moors, all owned by the Duke, and a sight that told them there was at least another twenty minutes' drive to Frampton.

"I'm afraid to say, Sir, it is a lost cause. We have fought a good fight but the public, and even the experts aren't behind us. Jarvis and Clutton have the support of the press and, you have to admit, have hardly put a foot wrong in selecting high quality architects, whether you like their buildings or not. And that chap Spon, who you hate so much, has got all the people around the Conway Estate eating out of his hand. They love what he is doing and they make up a not insignificant number of members of the Civic Society. I'm sorry Duke, but we're going to have to change tack."

The Duke continued to stare ahead. Veduty looked across the seat at the aristocratic profile. The muscles in the Duke's cheek clenched and unclenched but that was the only outward sign of his discomfort. He held his head high as befitted his class and, without turning to Veduty, barked "If that's how you feel then we have nothing more to discuss. James! Stop the car!"

The chauffeur slowed to a halt on the empty road, walked round to the passenger side and opened the door. He knew what was coming. The Duke had done this once before when one of his stewards had asked for a rise.

"Good day, Veduty" the Duke barked. The bemused conservationist hesitated, it was starting to rain, they were miles from anywhere. It hadn't occurred to him to take an umbrella. But it was clear his audience was over. He stepped silently onto the soggy verge.

"If he's not with us, he's against us," grumbled the Duke as the chauffeur resumed their comfortable drive to Frampton.

***

Mayor Jarvis's spies in the Frampton Society soon let him know of the falling out between Veduty and the Duke. It was clear the conservationist lobby was going to prove less of a problem than he had feared.

"Thank God for that," he said to Ed Clutton as the two of them reviewed the programme chart that stretched the length of Joe Porley's office. The Duke could have held things up long enough to cause us real problems. Let's hope he doesn't go for a judicial review."

"That's always going to be a problem" Joe answered. "Even if there's no real reason, he can use it to slow things down. I know we're on a tight programme but we've got to make sure we do everything by the book." The judicial review process was designed to make sure public bodies carried out the correct processes, but even when there was little cause to complain, the more aggressive conservationists had been known to use the system to hold building projects up. "We're not out of the woods yet."

"So where have we got to?"

Joe went over to the huge chart and pointed to a red triangle about a third of the way along. "We're here. We've selected our teams; we've got pretty detailed designs and I've got a couple of van loads of application documents which I'm just about to deliver to the Planning Department. I hope you've got enough people to deal with them. There's a hell of a lot of reading."

"We've just shipped in a boatload of Aussie planners. They know fuck all about Frampton but they should be able to handle it" Ed countered.

"The only thing that is likely to delay us at the moment is this." Joe's finger moved to a black square captioned "Ecoplastics".

"Sam Spurling is refusing to move. We've offered to buy the building at its market value, but he says we'll have to pay for his lost production if he moves and he's quoting ridiculous figures. His building is in the first phase, and if we go down the compulsory purchase route were going to be delayed. He knows he's got us over a barrel."

"Why don't we offer him one of the units on the Majestic Park Estate at a really cheap rent?"

Majestic Park was a joint development with the United Land property company – a public/private partnership where Frampton gave the land and United gave the money. But they were having difficulty leasing the units.

United Land were happy to have Ecoplastics on their site, especially as Ed Clutton had promised to make good any losses on the deal. They had a plan to encourage green industries and Ecoplastics would be a good start. So a few weeks later Sam Spurling signed a lease for a spanking new factory on Majestic Park. He wouldn't have to pay any rent for two years and United Land were going to cover all his moving costs as long as he moved immediately. He was mightily chuffed. It was a brilliant deal.

"You're a very lucky man, Mr Spurling," said the City Solicitor when the lease was signed. "If I'd had my way you would never have got such a good deal. I'd have compulsory purchased your building and moved you out at a fraction of this cost, but I was under strict orders not to be too aggressive. The Mayor knew you had the ear of a number of difficult councillors and the last thing he wanted was to be seen to running roughshod over local businesses. So for political reasons, and political reasons alone you have pocketed a small fortune."

"Don't worry about it, old chap!" Spurling laughed "just put it down as a bit of public investment in new skills and employment. Frampton desperately needs investment in manufacturing and what I do – recycling, sustainability, green products – is the industry of the future. You're right, I'm a very lucky man and the EuroGames are going to make me a very rich man indeed! But it's good for Frampton too, don't forget that!"

***

The letter came in a heavy cream envelope with the Institute of Art's familiar coat of arms embossed in red on the flap. Harry thought at first that it was a formal invitation to a private view and didn't bother to open it for a couple of days. When he did, he was flattered but worried.

Dear Harry,

We are planning a series of exhibitions on leading British architects and wish to begin with a show of your work paired with that of Frederick Shaw. The exhibition is scheduled to open six months prior to the opening of the Frampton Games, at a time when public attention will be focused on your buildings. For that reason we intend to allocate the whole of the main galleries to the show and would hope to include some large scale installations as well as models, drawings and photographs.

The exhibition will be curated by Rachael Dove, the Architecture Correspondent of *The Gazette*, who of course you know.

I would be glad to hear as soon as possible whether you are willing to accept this offer so that we can start planning the show, which I am sure will be a great success.

Yours truly,

Sheranie Philips
Programme Director.

Harry called Sheranie straight away.

"Thanks very much for inviting me but I have to tell you that I would find it very hard to work on a show with Frederick Shaw. We haven't spoken for years. I've tried a couple of times to break the ice but he just blanks me."

"Don't worry Harry. The committee are aware of the problems between you, but we feel that since you would each be in separate parts of the gallery there shouldn't be too much of a problem. Rachael Dove can deal with any overlap. The only time you'll have to be in the same room as Frederick will be at the first night opening and the press conference."

Harry was well aware of the impact a successful show at the Institute of Art would have. Both he and Freddie were well enough known in the rather incestuous world of architectural magazines and critics and the more sophisticated clients, but this would bring international recognition. They would get their name on the lists for all the plum jobs around the world – the museums, the opera houses, the government buildings, the iconic skyscrapers. Clients for those sorts of jobs always had lists drawn up by special advisors from which they selected their designers; they didn't want any old designers, they wanted brands – names that reassured them that they had made the right choice; names that would establish their cultural credentials.

Harry agreed to take part in the show. Sheranie had hardly put the phone down when her PA called across the office

"It's Frederick Shaw on the line, do you want to speak to him?"

"Put him through. . . Frederick, how are you? I guess you've received my letter?"

"I'm very grateful for the chance to show my work, but why does it have to be a joint show? You don't do joint shows for artists – Manet and van Gogh, Picasso and Braque, Hurst and Emin, do you? We have been planning a one-man show with specially made models and computer fly through which would fit well into your main galleries. And I have a sponsor who'll pay for the whole thing."

"The Committee discussed the idea of one man shows but decided a comparative exhibition was preferable and would be more relevant to any discussion of contemporary architecture," Sheranie said firmly.

The committee had discussed the topic at great length and Sir Richard Frank had vetoed the idea – he had been particularly incensed at the idea of a Frederick Shaw show, with good reason.

Sir Richard had been one of a number of architects working on the huge Braveheart Business Park on the outskirts of Glasgow. Frederick Shaw and Partners was also on the team. Freddie wasn't keen on the work the others were doing, and he didn't like sharing, so he secretly developed his own Masterplan for the site and presented it to the board of National Land.

He convinced them to fire all the other architects and take him on as 'master planner' and designer of all of the buildings. Sir Richard had never forgiven Frederick for his duplicity. "The man should have been fired from the fucking RIBA!" Sir Richard bellowed at one of the Exhibition Committee discussions, "what he did contravened the Code of Practice."

"Either you accept the two man show Frederick," Sheranie insisted "or we'll ask someone else. Amanda Stone is only too keen to take your place."

"OK. But I don't want to meet up with Harry Jamb. We don't get on."

144

"Don't worry we've planned for that; you won't have to be in the same room as Harry until the first night opening and the press conference."

"Ah, yes. The press conference." Freddie smiled to himself, a plan instantly started to gel in his mind. He had to make sure it was Freddie the world's press noticed, not his erstwhile partner.

"Bye, Sheranie" he put the phone down and immediately redialled the number of Loftus Global Public Relations.

Chapter 11

"Not another effing change!!" Joe Porley stared in disbelief at the drawings Carlos de Souza had rolled out across the meeting table. "I thought we had agreed to fix the design at our last meeting! We've got to get the planning application into Frampton Council in two weeks and we're already over budget. This is going to make things worse."

Carlos stood one side of the table with Tariq Shah, on the other sat Joe with a team of technical consultants.

"I think it is a small change, but very important. If we use titanium instead of steel for the cladding on the lower half it makes the whole structure seem much lighter." Carlos smiled to the group. It was a road he'd been down many times before. Best to start in placatory mode, sometimes his charm would win over the more susceptible clients, before moving on to the angry defence. His final ploy was to play the passionate Latin card, but he didn't like using that one too often, it was easily devalued.

But his charm was having no impact on the grim faces opposite. He'd better move to phase two.

"It is essential we change the materials; they won't just look better, they'll be easier and quicker to install, they'll lighten the structure and they'll have a much longer life."

"Look, buddy" Porley intervened "I don't care a shit how much longer this material lasts, I'm only interested in something that will last long enough for us to have paid off the costs of the building and the steel will do that. I'm not changing anything!"

"This is ridiculous!" Carlos's voice rose. "We're talking about one of the country's most important buildings and you're fussing about a few hundred thousand pounds. In a few years' time everyone will have forgotten about the costs, we'll be stuck with a crap building for generations. If we don't get it right now we never will."

Joe sighed, and smiled. He'd seen it all before, these bloody architects can never make up their minds, they keep on changing designs just for the hell of it. Give them an inch and they take a mile.

"Don't patronise me!" Carlos was angry now; his negotiating strategy was out of the window. "You and your ridiculous 'value engineering' – it's just another word for cost cutting – there's no value in it at all. You just make everything worse!"

Tariq, could see things was getting out of hand. Carlos's temper was legendary. It was bad enough in the office when he started ranting, in front of the clients' representatives it was unacceptable. He had been getting quite unpredictable and volatile recently, probably due to overwork. It was time for Tariq to intervene.

"Look Joe, if you'll agree to this final change, I'll make sure there aren't any more. There are some savings we can make on the structure that will reduce the impact on the budget." He sketched on the drawing in front of him. "We can lighten the structure here and place a series of bolted connections along the back of the seating bleachers."

It made sense to Joe; the engineer nodded. It appeared to be a simple change, but one that was to have dramatic consequences. "Just make fucking sure that everything's ready for the end of next week," said Joe as he got up and strode out of the room.

Joe had hired a large white van to take the Planning Application documents up to the Frampton Council offices. The boxes of drawings and documents – all decorated with Jason Vent's games logo – almost filled the vehicle. The photographer from the *Frampton Times* snapped the council porters as they transferred the boxes to the Planning Department.

"Game Plans Come to Frampton" ran the headline.

The story described how a team of planners and consultants would spend the next three months studying the documents before the Development Control Department submitted their report to the Planning Committee. Roger Chase, the Editor of the *Frampton Times* wrote a special editorial under the heading 'The Voice of Frampton'.

"The Frampton Times has always been a great supporter of the Games and we agree with much of Mayor Jarvis's vision for the city. The designs for the Stadium and the Swimming Complex will be great additions to the Frampton environment and will play a huge part in the future regeneration of the city, creating dramatic, recognisable landmarks that will bring visitors from far and wide.

The development of designs for the Temporary Pavilions for the Games, which have been carried out in close cooperation with local community groups will be a great success we are sure. The Pavilions will provide facilities for local people after the Games have gone.

However we have grave doubts about the design for the Media Centre. The tower proposed by Mr Koji is out of scale with the rest of the site and with the city. The minimalist design will create a blot on the skyline as great as any of the housing blunders of the 60s.

We would urge the authorities to look again at this design as we are sure it is unacceptable to the majority of people of Frampton."

The volume of letters that appeared in the newspaper in the ensuing weeks confirmed that there were many in the city with similar views to the editor. Judicious selection of the letters received ensured that the anti-Koji brigade were always in the majority.

The Duke sent several letters which were duly published, but the Civic Society was unusually silent. John Veduty had resigned after his spat with the Duke in the Rolls but had, for other reasons, become even more closely involved in the debate about the tower.

Veduty was a regular visitor to the Black Cat in Frampton, a discreet gay bar located in the decorated Victorian arches that ran along one side of the rail station. One night a tall, slight guy, dressed in a well-cut suit and longish hair caught Veduty's attention. He wondered where he had seen him before. He was sitting by the bar watching a pair of boys prancing around a cage suspended from the high ceilinged space. The man came up to the bar.

"Hi I'm John, I haven't seen you here before."

"My name's Josh. I'm not local. I'm up here working on the Games buildings. I'm an architect."

"I thought I recognised you. I used to run the local Civic Society, but I fell out with the Duke of Frampton. You're working on the Media Centre aren't you? I'm afraid that hasn't gone down too well with the locals."

"It's not my design, I'm from AAP architects and we're helping Tomo Koji build it because he doesn't have an office over here. I'd have done something very different left to my own devices. Does the Duke know you're gay by the way? I would imagine he was homophobic."

"I never told him. When I applied for the job the only reference he took was from a mutual friend. 'What sort of family is he from?' was the Duke's only question. If he'd told the truth: that I'm gay and a bastard – I haven't a clue who my father was – *and* into S&M – would I have got the job?"

"Well we have two things in common at least" said Josh as he eyed two leather-clad figures emerging from a door at the back of the bar. "Let's go and have a look in there."

John Veduty knew his way around the dungeons of the Black Cat and Josh had soon exchanged his city suit for an outfit of straps, chains and studded spanking paddle. The harder he hit the erstwhile conservationist the more he complied with Josh's orders. Josh had at last found someone who liked the same sort of things that he did. And someone he could talk to as well. The rough trade he normally ended up were exciting enough for a one night stand but when he saw them in the cold light of day he felt repulsed by them and by himself.

"Let's do this again" John said as they walked uncomfortably out of the Black Cat, "there's a group of us who meet up regularly. You'd be surprised at some of the local bigwigs who turn up. You might recognise a couple of them when they're out of their masks!"

***

The Frampton Planning Committee, with Councillor Merton in the chair, had a mammoth meeting to review the plans for each of the buildings. Joe Porley was relieved to see that although the public seats were full, there was little sign of the protests he had feared. The Duke sat in the front row accompanied by his daughter whose mass of flowing hair and brightly coloured clothes stood out against the rows of more muted Framptonians. Joe was concerned about the construction programme. The English planning system is famously unpredictable – if the Committee, made up of people who knew little about architecture, decided to reject the three main buildings then his carefully planned schedule would be shot to pieces.

But as the discussions went on, Joe was pleased to find that on this occasion the Committee seemed well informed. Ed Clutton, on Mayor Jarvis's instructions had made sure that every Committee member understood the proposals and more importantly, understood the impact of any delays. Not only would it be bad for the Games, it would be a bad advertisement for Frampton as a place for investment.

The Stadium and the Swimming Complex were passed unanimously before discussion began on the Media Centre. From the first speech Joe realised things weren't going to plan. A Councillor who rarely intervened in meetings kicked off the discussion

"Chairman, how can we possibly allow this monstrous carbuncle, as Prince Charles would say, to deface our city? It is too tall, too bulky and its façade lacks any architectural interest at all. We have recently completed a programme demolishing the ugly towers of the 60s, why are we repeating the same mistakes forty years later? I understand the consequences of delay, but we owe a responsibility to our children and grandchildren who will have to live with this eyesore. As you will have read in the *Frampton Times* the people of the city almost unanimously oppose this monstrosity "

Fellow Councillors were nodding in agreement. Something had gone wrong with Clutton's briefing, Joe thought. No one spoke in the building's favour.

"Those in favour?" the Chairman asked. Two hands were raised.

"Those against?" six hands went up. "Permission refused!"

There was polite clapping from the public seats. The Duke stood up and surveyed the room, a triumphant smile played on his lips.

Joe put his head in his hands and started to plan what he would do to avoid total disaster – a Games without the press might as well not exist. Mayor Jarvis seemed surprisingly chirpy as he discussed the evening's proceedings with the members of the Committee.

Roger Chase of the *Frampton Times* went over to talk to Jarvis. "How do you feel Mayor? That was pretty comprehensive defeat."

"Oh, we'll find ways to deal with the Media Centre" he responded lightly. "It's the positive things that I want to concentrate on tonight. We've just given permission for two of the greatest buildings Frampton has ever seen. They will put the city on the international map for the next hundred years. Just look at Sydney and the Opera House, just look at Bilbao and the Guggenheim."

"But don't you see the rejection of the Media Centre as a personal defeat?"

"It's democracy" the Mayor shrugged. If only you knew what democracy is all about, Jarvis thought to himself, then you'd have a real story!

The horse trading that Jarvis had been forced to undertake to get the project this far had tested even his political skills. The public antagonism to Koji's tower as revealed by *The Gazette's* poll had given his enemies on the Planning Committee just the lever they needed to extract promises from Jarvis for their own personal and political ends. Some were easy to comply with, like Councillor Merton's wish to be in the next New Year Honours list, others were trickier. He was forced to abandon plans to put a special 'Games Only' traffic lane through the affluent suburbs at Boroughs End; he agreed on a major funding package for the improvement of flats on the Conway Estate, as well as a series of expensive deals in wards around the city that would ensure the popularity and re-election of the members concerned.

He agreed to sacrifice the Koji building on the promise that the Councillors would support the Stadium and Swimming Complex.

With the plans approved, the London office of Frederick Shaw and Partners was stretched to the limit to produce the final drawings for the Swimming Complex. Tariq's little changes had required a rejig of the main structure; on top of that Freddie was busier than he had ever been, the firm's overseas offices were doing well and he had to keep an eye on them. The press were hounding him for interviews about the Games and Rachael Dove was chasing him about the Institute of Art exhibition.

The design of the Swimming Complex had been well received in the press; the huge sphere floating in its reflective pool had caught the imagination of the picture editors and the cartoonists. So when Sid Dixon was looking for an architect for a new apartment block in the middle of Frampton, Freddie was the obvious choice.

Sid realised that the Games would attract rich overseas investors to Frampton; if they were going to put their money into local businesses they would have to have somewhere to live and there was no top end – 'super prime' his agents called it – residential accommodation in the heart of the city.

Sid had made his reputation by commissioning good quality architecture. Architects liked working for him because his buildings came out at the end of the process in the way they had imagined them. So often developers would take the architects' designs and change details and materials so that the purity of the design was utterly destroyed. But Sid liked to get full value from his architects. He would go through schemes in intricate detail, even questioning the selection of taps and door handles; and he wanted to deal with the senior partner. "Your fees are fucking well high enough – I don't want to be palmed off with the office boy."

Sid called a meeting on the site in Frampton – a prime piece of real estate close to the central square and overlooking the 18th century George Street, a row of fine Grade 2 listed buildings. Sid spent his weekends at his country house in the Peak District and drove across to Frampton for the meeting which had been fixed for ten o'clock to give Freddie time to get up from London. The developer parked his Aston on the edge of the muddy site. He pulled on his site boots, hi-viz jacket and helmet. The site was flat but the demolition contractors were still tidying up and Health and Safety Laws had to be adhered to.

"Sorry Mr Dixon, you'll have to put on the protective glasses and gloves too" said the security guard as Sid signed the visitors' book.

"But it's an empty fucking site!"

"Regulations, Mr Dixon."

Health and Safety Regulations always rankled with Sid. He knew building sites were dangerous places but the bureaucrats had taken over. They added to costs, delayed projects and removed personal responsibility – and they were a sartorial nightmare too.

It was a chilly morning and he was wearing a Prada fur lined jacket that had set him back nearly two grand, now it was hidden under a fluorescent jerkin. He had imagined himself standing in the middle of the site, master of all he surveyed, stylish, cool and in command. Now he just looked like a navvy.

So he stood in the middle of the site anyway. It was brilliant site, good location, good transport; smart neighbours and he'd bought it before the Games had started to push prices up. He'd sell all the apartments off plan and make a killing. He stood there dreaming for all of fifteen minutes when his phone rang. It was it his PA.

"I've just picked up a message from Frederick Shaw. He's not going to be able to make it today. He's got a panic on with his Swimming Pool Complex he says."

"I don't care a fuck what problems he's got on someone else's job" Sid shouted. "He's sure as hell got a problem on this site! Who do these architects think they are! You make them, you pay them, you wipe their bloody arses and this is how they treat you!"

He went back to the car, threw off his protective gear and phoned Ned Jackson the MD of his residential development company.

"Fire Freddie Shaw!" he barked.

"OK boss. But who shall we get to design the building?" Ned asked.

"I think we should try Amanda Stone. She's got a good reputation overseas; she'll attract rich Russians and footballers."

"But she's even harder to handle than Freddie"

"I'm sure I can cope. She's difficult but she designs bloody good buildings."

***

As things turned out, Amanda was a pussycat. She and Sid got on like house on fire: he understood the positive impact that a top quality Amanda Stone design would have on the brand of the project and gave her freedoms she rarely found with clients in the

UK. She knew that Sid could build the sort of scheme she envisaged and she was happy to let him get on with it without continually interfering, as she was often wont to do.

As a result she produced one of her best designs, based on series of beautifully detailed interlocking cubes. The elegant proposal, in spite of the fact that it would be the tallest building in Frampton, sailed through the Planning Committee.

"Now we get on with the marketing," Sid announced "We'll launch it at the Abita Property Show in Cannes. I've asked Jason Vent to come up with some branding ideas."

Jason duly presented his concepts to Sid. With a set of Foamex boards he went through a complex analysis of the market, the competition and his strategy for presenting the individual apartments. As he came to the last board he paused for dramatic effect:

"But the most important thing is to find the right name. I have decided we should call the building. . . The Infini T Tower !" he exclaimed proudly holding up a board with a series of squares and the word set in bold type.

"And I paid you fifty grand for that?!" Sid said only half in jest. It was a simple idea but he could immediately see it on the site hoarding, on the web site, on the adverts in the property pages – even on the uniform of the porter who would be sitting in the huge reception space.

"I like it!"

***

The Abita Property Convention was held each year in Cannes on the French Riviera. It was the biggest gathering of real estate professionals in the world – agents, investors and developers, and a host of others who depend on them for jobs – lawyers, architects and planners. Property people work hard and they play hard; and there was plenty of playing at Abita. More champagne was drunk in the four days of Abita than in ten days of the more famous Cannes Film Festival; it was served from 8.00 in morning by leggy Russian hookers in micro skirts promoting resorts on the Black Sea and big towers in St Petersburg; the scrum of leasing agents that surrounded the bar in The Martinez at 4.00 o'clock in the morning would have made Martin Johnson blanch; in the small hours the Croisette was littered with comatose suits sleeping off a day's consumption of Moet while the girlie bars did their best business of the year, their rohypnol-spiked drinks allowing them to relieve the unsuspecting 'tricks' of their generous expenses allowance. The general air of seediness was reinforced by the transvestite hookers who sat suggestively in their cars parked at each junction, their black stockinged legs with suspenders stretched out of the open doors, adding to the obstacles faced by punters weaving their drunken way back to their hotels.

Sid flew Amanda down in his Hawker 800XP jet. Cannes Private Airport was packed. They saw Norman Foster and his wife arriving – Norman in his jet from London, Elena in her prop-driven plane from Madrid.

The black tinted-window limo swept them up to Mougins, the town on the hills above Cannes where the smart villas were. This was where the grandees of the property world congregated, rarely deigning to descend to sea level and the scrum in the Palais des Festivals. Sid did, however, have to check out The Infini T Tower stand to make sure his sales team were pumped up and that Jason had created a striking display.

The limo swept Sid down to the Palais where the contractors were finishing off the row after row of exotic installations – fake Irish pubs, Formula 1 games, huge city models, massive video screens, bars and reception desks with give away peppermints. The French *pompiers* – even tougher than the Health and Safety guys on site in England – patrolled the halls, strutting around incongruously in braces and turned down wellies, rejecting any installations that had failed to get the appropriate fire certificates. Plastic was being peeled from the factory-fresh corridor carpets, the noise of last minute hoovering filled low-ceilinged halls while designers primped into place their gaudy displays.

The team who were to man The Infini T Tower stand were being briefed by Ned Jackson. Four hostesses listened attentively as Ned went through the sales patter. Sid looked on in awe.

Each one of them was at least six foot, they were clad in skin hugging latex – in Jason Vent's selected sky blue brand colour – which displayed every ripple of their gym-toned bodies, the dresses ended as close as was legally possible to their crotches and their four inch Laboutins were already beginning to skewer holes in the newly laid carpet. Three of them were blondes, their hair tumbling over their toned shoulders – but Sid's fancy was taken by the darker skinned one with smouldering eyes, shorter black hair and full red lips.

Ned introduced the girls to the "boss". The dark one's name was Tracey.

"Make sure Tracey comes to the Carlton tonight, but tell her to dress down a bit." Sid instructed as he admired the taut curves beneath Tracey's skimpy rubber frock.

***

Sid spent the rest of the day by the pool at the villa. The Riviera spring sunshine was pleasantly warm. Hardly tanning weather but a nice change from the chilly wetness of London in March. The office had organised a series of meetings with investors, bankers, Government Ministers, Regional Developments Agencies and agents, all who were keen to do business with Sid who needed to raise a couple of hundred million for new projects – including The Infini T Tower.

The visitors were welcomed in Sid's easy and informal manner. He in bare feet, towelling bathrobe and garish trunks; most of them in suits and ties, the ones from the Middle East in long white dishdashas . All were plied with glasses of Vintage Krug and delicate canapés by white coated, black tied waiters.

At the end of the day Sid was feeling in a proper party mood. He had managed to get agreement for a big chunk of the money he needed. He showered, shaved, slipped into jeans and white open necked shirt and called the chauffeur.

"Take me to the Carlton, Max, *s'il vous plait*." The Carlton was the ritziest hotel on the Riviera; when the fairs and festivals were held in Cannes – the Film Festival, the Advertising Show, the Porn Video Fair – all the most senior executives stayed there. Its white wedding cake façade, topped with two mammarian cupolas dominated The Croisette. The entrance was a 24 hour *bouchon* of Porsches, Rolls and Maybachs. By day during the Abita showcase,, the lobby, with its huge white classical columns and highly-polished honey-coloured marble floors was a haven of calm and quiet luxury as attentive staff fawned over their high-tipping guests; at night it heaved with partying property people who, after a day of downing champagne, needed to continue topping up their alcohol intake just to stay awake.

Sid walked purposefully to the Carlton Club, situated at the back of the hotel at the end of long Aubusson-carpeted corridors. He passed the queue of hopeful entrants whose credentials were under close inspections by security and was waved through by the black man mountain who filled most of the doorway blocking the way to the heaving hedonists within.

Ali, the Moroccan barman, recognised Sid and without instruction poured him a chilled neat vodka which the diminutive developer took with nod and downed in one. Then he looked around the room. Nervous architects who knew the Carlton Club was the best networking place in town looked beyond their companions to check out who might be better to talk to; they smiled at Sid hoping for a glint of recognition, but Sid was practised at avoiding the imploring gaze of the many people who wanted to work for him. Through the crush he caught sight of Rachael Dove, her blond hair piled high, a gash of bright red lipstick and unusually revealing décolletage. He needed to talk to her about The Infini T Tower, but had a feeling this bit of networking might well turn out to be a nice mix of business with pleasure.

The Gazette writer was talking to Wallace Ho, from the Chinese developer Hong Cho, who was building the Ho Tower – the tallest residential building in the world. Attractive women – indeed any sort of woman – were few and far between in the world of property, a shortage that brought to the fore the alpha male behaviour of the real estate developer, a species well used to the mores of the jungle and hardened by a life of high risk and the potential of instant ruin if a deal didn't come off.

Ho thought he had it made. Rachael had seemed very enthusiastic about a trip to the top of his tower, but almost as soon as Sid butted in to their conversation he realised he'd need to find someone else to accompany him back to the yacht that night.

Rachael had been looking out for Sid all day. She knew he was about to launch the new designs for The Infini T Tower and she wanted to get the pictures as an exclusive for *The Gazette*. The trip to Ho's tower could wait.

Sid couldn't believe his luck. They were jostled closer by a guest passing with a handful of drinks. Sid ordered another vodka and a martini for Rachael. And then another. But the keen reporter kept her wits.

"I got the invitation to the launch of the new designs for The Infini T Tower. Is it worth coming to? " she asked coolly.

"Absolutely, Rachael. It's a stunning scheme. It's by Britain's best woman architect and with all the interest in Frampton-on-Tees at the moment it's going to make the front pages. I've got a model in my suite upstairs – I'll show you if you like."

Rachael was now pretty tipsy as the Martinis kicked in; she felt a flood of excitement. She quite fancied a one night stand with Sid, but fancied even more seeing her byline on the front page of *The Gazette*.

"Ready when you are" she responded.

Sid took her arm and guided her through the networking throng, many of them worse for wear, who took little notice of the pair.

As they walked past the queue still attempting entry Sid caught sight of the girl from the stand that he's seen in the morning.

"Hello, Tracey. We're jus' going upstairs." he slurred. Tracey smiled knowingly at Rachael and followed them down the hundred-metre corridor. She had changed into a long silk dress that hugged her taut body like a wet teeshirt. The queue watched open mouthed and envious as Sid escorted the pair towards the lift to the suites on the seventh floor.

The suite was huge; its décor an unfashionable mish-mash of upholstered chairs, circular glass tables, thick pile carpet and a flashy black plasma screen and media centre. In the corner of the room was a large aluminium flight case with 'Fragile' and 'This side up' stickers across it. A silver bucket with champagne and three flutes sat on the central glass table next to an engraved cigarette box.

Rachael realised Sid had planned his evening escapade with care – but had he planned that it would be with her? Or could it have been anybody? She was too pissed to care. She flopped onto a six person sofa with a grotesque silver and black print; Tracey, strangely quiet for someone of her obvious physical exuberance sat primly on the edge of the heavy cushion.

"God she's beautiful!" thought Rachael as she studied the other girl's flawless olive skin back.

Sid popped open the champagne and unsteadily poured a glass for each of them. He then sat down and pulled a chair up to the table and flipping open the silver cigarette box tipped the monogrammed block of cocaine onto the glass.

The two girls watched as Sid efficiently created three lines with a razor blade before handing them each a silver tube.

After that, Rachael's recollection of the next few hours became somewhat hazy. She could recall images of Tracey's exquisite slim body, Sid's surprisingly toned physique, his stamina, his preference for exotic positions and the fact that she had totally forgotten to get any information out of him about The Infini T Tower.

She looked at her watch. Half past eight. The rest of the ultra-king size bed was empty. She got unsteadily to her feet and went through to the sitting room. Bright sun flooded into through the French windows that opened onto the private terrace, a clear cyan sky filled the view. In place of the cigarette case and champagne was a note from Sid.

"We've had to go to our Stand. Thanks for a fantastic night. See you at the press conference." Beneath the note was the invitation to the world's media to attend the lunchtime launch of The Infini T Tower – "modern living in an iconic building designed by one of the world's most important architects – Amanda Stone."

Rachael cursed. There was no way she was going to get a story in advance of the rest of the pack now. The flight case in the corner was gone – she couldn't even take a peek at the model.

She went out onto the terrace where a table was laid for breakfast, plates of bright sliced fruits, piles of croissants and a thoughtfully insulated coffee pot. She poured herself a strong black coffee and stood looking out over the Bay of Cannes where lighters were still plying backwards and forwards from the Carlton pier to the various yachts anchored in the mirrored sea.

She wondered if their parties had been as wild as Sid's. The extravagant entertaining on the yachts of the Tchenguiz brothers, of Candy and Candy and Igor Chermayeff, the Russian developer, was the talk of town every year. Journalists eagerly responded to the invitations in the hope they could track down useful contacts or convince some tipsy guest to spill the beans.

The hacks liked to see how the other half lived, downing the vintage champagne, caviar and *foie gras*, as though to the manner born before slinking back to their two star hotels on the outskirts of Nice. Rachael had got pissed, sniffed a ton of coke, screwed a developer, kissed a woman for the first time and still hadn't got her story.

At midday some 30 journalists gathered in a specially constructed marquee on the beach. In the centre of the tent stood the metre high model of The Infini T Tower atop a mirrored base. Surrounding the model were piles of caviar interspersed with mountains of oysters. The hacks were soon eagerly spooning and slurping, slowing only when Sid started to introduce the project.

"With the EuroGames coming up we believe that Frampton-on-Tees will become a focus for new investment and there will be a demand for inner city accommodation for high net worth individuals. The Infini T Tower will provide luxury living in the heart of Frampton. We have commissioned Amanda Stone to produce a spectacular design which we think will raise the bar as far as the standard of new housing in the city is concerned."

Following a brief presentation by Amanda and the handing out of a fat press pack which included all the information they had just heard, the hacks returned to the trough. Rachael felt too ill to join in and anyway she hated oysters.

At around five o'clock that afternoon as he was about to send his copy off to his paper, the architectural correspondent of the *New York Tribune* doubled up with excruciating stomach cramp. He just managed to reach his hotel room lavatory before vomiting his luxury lunch in a hideous explosion of grey gobbits across the marbled floor. The diarrhoea followed in seconds and he lay stretched between washbasin and WC, unable to move, for the rest of the evening. Similar events were taking place across Cannes and one by one the various papers' deadlines passed.

The only paper with the full story was *The Gazette* which ran a picture of Sid standing next to The Infini T Tower model on the front page with Rachael Dove's by-line.

Chapter 12

"Good evening Mr Jamb, Mrs Jamb" the Vice President of The Incorporation of Architects greeted Harry and Eleanor as they entered the grand classical portals of the architects' official club.

Harry had been invited to present the prizes to that year's crop of top students. The ceremony took place in the high ceilinged Foster Hall; around the panelled walls hung the winning series of projects: to Harry their titles seemed bizarre and highly affected: "The Aggressive City", "Walking on Glass Quietly", "Horizontality and the Green Interface". In his day projects were entitled "Primary School in Wales", "Leisure Centre" or "City Block".

"This meaningless archi-speak makes me cross," he said to Eleanor, "they should teach these students plain English."

He started to read one of the descriptions:

"The 'Energy Giro interface' is conceived as an interactive architectonic intervention, providing sensory stimulation through dynamic material systems that could enable new forms of interactive environment. Architecture is conceptualised as an embodied interface where the user learns to interact with their environment through an intuitive process, engaging the physical presence of inhabitants and forming spatial narratives."

The writing was rubbish, but the drawings were beautiful: elegant pencil drawings of delicate light and shade; spectacular computer renderings of repetitive structures creating forms of previous unbuildability, images of awesome photographic reality and forms of refreshing simplicity and originality. Harry noted down a few names. Some of these students could bring a bit of fresh thinking into the studio, Harry mused.

Black waistcoated waiters handed out cava and canapés on black slate trays (the evening was sponsored by the Welsh Slate

Promotion Board) to a motley mix of architecture students from around the country who had come down to London to party, and members of the architectural establishment who were keen to offer jobs to the brightest and best. Harry gave a short and rousing speech, presented the prizes and started to circulate among the assembled guests.

He frowned when he saw Martin Hester talking to a group of students on the other side of the room. He was getting sick of the sight of the man, and he didn't like the way that Eleanor was spending so much time with him. She told him it was good to keep in with someone with Hester's profile and contacts – it helped with the press and with the people in Frampton, but Harry didn't like it. He sensed something was going on but couldn't bring himself to believe that Eleanor would be unfaithful with a man twenty years older than her. There had been signals – she arrived home one day, her face red and flushed; it reminded Harry of the days when he and Eleanor had kissed long and passionately, raising the colour on her sensitive skin into little pink blotches. Then he found them delightful, now he suspected the blotches were marks of perfidy. A few days previously he thought he smelled male sweat as he kissed her when she got home late one night. Just the faintest whiff, but it unsettled him. There were few more potent, primeval triggers to stir Harry's submerged passions than the musk of another on his mate.

Harry congratulated the winning students and gave them his card suggesting they contact the office when they were looking for jobs. After half an hour or so of swapping news and notes with some of the other architects, he'd had enough and looked round for Eleanor. He couldn't see her in the Foster Hall so he went downstairs where the obsequious Vice President was now bidding guests good bye.

"Have you seen my wife?" Harry asked brusquely.

"Why yes, she left half an hour a go with Mr Hester."

"Yes of course, thanks so much" Harry tried to make it seem like the most normal thing in the world, but inside something snapped, red mist blurred his vision as he pushed through the revolving doors and exited into a wet and miserable night.

As soon as he arrived home Harry got out the bottle of vodka that he kept hidden behind the files in his study. Eleanor had been nagging him about his drinking and he preferred subterfuge to confrontation. He sat in the darkened room staring out of the window. He had enough problems just dealing with his work, the last thing he needed was a bloody great row, but he had no option. He watched the street and waited. He had no idea what he would do when Eleanor got back, but he knew he couldn't let it lie any longer.

At midnight Harry heard the door latch open quietly and someone stumble on the dark stairs. He leapt up and switched on the lights. It was Amelia.

"Daddy! You gave me a fright! Are you all right? You look awful!"

"I'm fine, just a bit fed up, thank you darling. Hard day at the office. Where have you been?"

"Oh just out with friends." she said as casually as she could. She desperately wanted to tell her father where she had been and who she had been with, but she could see that now was not the time.

"Where's Mummy?"

"She's coming back with Martin Hester, we've all been to a do at the Institute of Art. She should be back soon."

"G'night dad," as Amelia passed him Harry gave her a hug and kissed her goodnight. The hug was unusually hard.

Amelia was worried as she walked up to bed. She had been aware for some time of the effect the pressure of the Stadium project was having on her father, he was moody and often came home the worse for wear. She found the ongoing presence of Martin Hester pretty creepy but had no inkling of anything untoward between the ageing athlete and her mother.

Harry returned to the comforting familiarity of his study lit only by the street lamp outside. In the gloom he watched the hands of his Braun alarm clock slowly circuit Dieter Ram's beautiful square faced design, the white numerals as simple and clear as they could possibly be. No fuss, no artifice, every detail thought through to perfection. In his distraught state Harry could gain some solace from the genius of its design.

The smaller hand moved towards the number '2'. Harry noted how precisely it brushed the base of the numeral so that legibility was unimpaired. His critical analysis of Teutonic genius was interrupted by the sound of a car as it drew up in the street. He looked out. It was Hester's Mercedes. He waited for Eleanor to open the door but nothing happened. It was hard to see in the gloom as he looked down on the car; he could make out his wife's profile as she sat in the passenger seat and gasped as it merged with another's. He didn't need to check whose.

He leapt from his desk and ran down the stairs two at a time, it was pitch dark but, despite the vodka, Harry was surefooted and fast and surged with adrenalin. He bounded down the steps of the house and out to where the steamed up car was parked: he threw open the door.

Eleanor screamed as Harry grabbed her arm and Hester lifted his head in surprise from her exposed breast.

"That's enough! Come inside!"

"For God's sake Harry! Leave me alone!" Eleanor tried to wrench her arm away. "Just grow up!"

Lights were beginning to appear in bedrooms along the street as the shouting continued.

"I'm not coming in Harry. You're pissed. I'm going back with Martin! I'm leaving you!" she screamed just as Amelia appeared at the door of the house.

"No! Mummy, you can't!" Amelia added to the hubbub.

"For God's sake have your row indoors!" shouted the art dealer next door as he looked down on a scene that reminded him of Delacroix's *Liberty Leading the People*. Eleanor was now almost completely topless as Harry dragged at her coat and her unbuttoned blouse pulled open. With her free hand she swung at Harry, gashing his cheek with her diamond ring.

Hester walked calmly round the car.

"I think we should all go inside," he said firmly with the authority of one who was able to handle himself in the face of tough physical confrontation.

Harry, holding his cheek as blood dripped onto his shirt, Eleanor, pulling her coat around herself, and Amelia, in floods of tears, duly shuffled in.

"It's no good Harry, we can't go on like this! You're never here, and whenever I do see you you're drunk. Martin has helped me deal with it and he's not a fucking architect! Buildings! Buildings! Buildings! All day and all night. You can't talk about anything else. You're not interested in anything else! I can't stand it anymore! I'm sorry but that's how it is." Eleanor said, as Amelia sobbed in disbelief.

Harry had no reply. She was right. His drinking was out of hand and he was working on the Stadium eighteen hours a day most days of the week. Deep down he couldn't blame her – but to see her going off with that fake-tanned muscle man was too much to bear.

How bloody ironic! What a fucking joke! He had sacrificed his marriage and threatened his health to design and build a stadium that was to be erected in honour of the man who was about to run off with his wife! He felt utterly, utterly crushed. She was right. His work consumed his life.

He got up. He couldn't look at Eleanor or Hester. "I'd better go". He hugged Amelia. "I'll ring you," he whispered.

Harry walked out into the night. He wanted to go to the office; in spite of all the current problems, that was where he felt most grounded: the sketches, the drawings, the models, the photographs of his buildings, all these defined him as a man and his relationship with the world.

As he often did when he was unhappy, when he wanted to think, he walked through the silent streets, his downhill path followed the route of the ancient River Fleet, now in culverts deep beneath his feet, but through history it had shaped the city. House, offices, shops, old buildings, new buildings, renovated buildings stood along it banks. Physical. Reassuring. Harry saw the city as a symbiotic mechanism that when it functioned properly produced a perfect relationship between permanence and renewal, between memory and aspiration until disrupted by catastrophic events like fires, bombs or over eager planners. He read each street like a book, absorbing its story and delighting in its prose. People come, people go but the indomitable spirit of the city continued. Like a painter delicately dabbing at his canvas, it was on the city that Harry made his mark; he was a part of its change but also of its permanence.

Harry blocked out the traumas of that night with such ruminations but was jerked back to reality when he arrived at his office.

There was the faintest glimmer of dawn behind the towers of the City as his fob clicked open his office's glass doors and he switched off the alarm. The movement activated ceiling lights flickered into life and he made his way to his desk.

The yellow post-it note was stuck in the centre of his computer screen so there was no chance he could miss it "Ring Joe Porley first thing – he's not happy with the cladding we've chosen for the Stadium exterior. He wants to change it. Jenny."

Harry groaned. Perhaps he didn't feel so great in his office after all. Almost without thinking he pulled open the file drawer on his desk and felt for the bottle he had filed under 'Future Projects'. He took a swig. And then another.

***

Jenny was the first to arrive in the office that morning to find Harry slumped across his desk, bottle in hand and drawings of the Stadium cladding on his computer. She didn't want any of the staff to see Harry like this and desperately tried to drag her sodden boss to the cyclists' shower where he could sober himself up.

"Harry!" she shouted as loud as she could. There was no one else to hear. She pushed him hard in the ribs. He stood up unsteadily and she guided him between the desks, his arm across her shoulder.

Harry suddenly felt horribly sick and before he could do anything about he vomited all over the front of Jenny's neat office suit. His gastric convulsions brought him to with a jolt.

"I'm, I'm s-s-s- so sorry Jenny. This is just awful." He was surprised she seemed so unconcerned, she continued to steer him towards the showers.

"Don't worry Harry I'll clear it up later." She seemed so matter-of-fact. More like a nurse than a secretary. More like a saint, Harry thought as he removed his stained clothing.

Jenny liked it when Harry really, really depended on her and she knew that now he did. She had looked after his appointments and his work schedule, his clean shirts and his family presents, his wins and his losses for over a decade, but that had never seemed enough.

She had seen the effect the strains of the Stadium were having and worried about his drinking. The electrician had recently found a stash of empty vodka bottles hidden in the suspended ceiling in the gents loo – everyone wondered who's they were. Jenny knew.

And she knew his judgment was being clouded in an alcoholic haze: one evening, at a private view at the Blore Gallery which had an internal courtyard of mirrored glass, Harry, in his cups, had relieved himself against the glazing, blissfully unaware that his micturations could be seen by all those inside.

Jenny realised she had to do something before things got totally out of hand. When Harry told her about Eleanor, she realised her time had come. The plans she had dreamed of for years, could now be put into action.

The next day she found a flat for Harry not far from her own in Camden Town. She organised their first meeting of the day there so that she got him breakfast, she accompanied him to the office in the taxi, kept a close eye on him all day and then took him back to Camden in the evening.

She went with him to evening receptions and dinners, keeping a close eye on his drinking. She removed the stash of vodka from the office. Harry, focused on his work, was relieved to have the rest of his life taken care of. The drinking slowed down and his mental state returned to some sort of equilibrium. He didn't miss Eleanor as much as he thought he would, even though Jenny kept her distance physically. She'd been waiting for ten years; there was no need to rush things.

Amelia moved out of the family house. She couldn't stomach Martin Hester's regular visits. She was due to start at the Slade School of Art in the Autumn and found a flat in Hoxton to share with a friend. But she didn't tell either of her parents who the friend was.

Eleanor had no desire to move to Frampton, so Martin had to drive up and down to London a couple of times a week; he needed to keep an eye on his businesses in the town but he was also keen to spend as much time with Eleanor as he could.

He didn't mind the driving. He had changed the Merc for an Aston Martin V12 Vantage which ate up the miles and was a luxury to drive. Late at night on the M40, when he had made sure there were no police cars in his mirror, he would coax the 6-litre engine up to its 190 mph max. As an athlete speed had always been his goal. It gave him a thrill like no other. *Citius, altius, fortius.* Faster, stronger, higher. He loved pushing the sleek thoroughbred to the limit.

***

Nobody was sure what happened, but the shocked lorry driver on the northbound carriage swore that the Aston was flying at cab height as it flipped across the motorway in front of him. The police found the athlete crumpled in the rear seat of the unrecognisable car which had nose-dived into a ploughed field. At first they thought he was dead, but they found faint signs of a pulse and called up the HEMS helicopter to get him to hospital as quickly as possible.

***

Eleanor had been sitting in the run-down waiting room outside the Trauma Unit operating theatre at the Royal London Hospital for nearly four hours when a figure in green scrubs pushed through the swing doors. The young surgeon pulled off her mask as she walked over to Eleanor, her kindly but serious expression did not bode well. Eleanor was struck by how beautiful she was.

"I believe you are Martin Hester's partner?" Eleanor nodded. The medic sat down beside and held her hand. "I'm afraid things aren't good. We've done what we can. Martin has suffered a complete spinal injury. The possibility of a full recovery is very remote. It means that he will have no movement at all below the area of damage. He will be a tetraplegic and will need a lot of looking after. I'll get someone from the hospital support team to come and let you know what assistance we can give you, but he's going to be very poorly for a long time."

Eleanor was too shocked to respond. The surgeon was stroking her arm as though to restore some life in the motionless body. But Eleanor was thinking. Hard. She had been attracted to Martin by his physicality not by his intellect. She enjoyed his celebrity lifestyle; twenty-four hour care did not have the same appeal. She started her affair with Hester to escape from Harry's obsession with work, architecture and alcohol. She was not about to swap one prison for another. There might be little left of the Hester she knew, she thought, or at least fancied. Sex with the athlete had been the best she had ever had, but that hardly prepared her for a career as nursemaid for the rest of his days.

171

"Thank you" she said in a daze to the sympathetic surgeon. She got up and walked out of the hospital. Photographers were gathering outside the hospital as news spread of the accident.

"That's his girlfriend, Eleanor Jamb! Eleanor! Eleanor!" she looked fleetingly towards the pack as they flashed away before turning and walking down Whitechapel High Street.

She desperately wanted to speak to Harry but couldn't face telling him what she had done. She was ashamed of her reaction to Martin's terrible predicament but she wasn't cut out for a life of looking after someone who could do nothing for themselves. She had left Harry for Martin because he offered an exciting life in the limelight and a proud and powerful physical presence. She could not accept that she would be a prisoner of his disabilities. Martin was not such a part of her soul that she felt she had no alternative than to make that sacrifice.

She just wanted to disappear. It seemed simple enough. She went back to the house, logged on to lastminute.com and clicked on 'last second deals' for the first available flight out of Heathrow. Marrakech £172. She took it, and five hours later was looking down at Richard Rogers' Terminal 5 building, blurred through her tears, as the Air Maroc Boeing 737 rose into the night sky.

The next day the front page of *The Gazette* ran the story "Hester will be in wheelchair for life, say surgeons"; next to it was the haunting photograph of Eleanor as she left the hospital with the caption "Police are concerned as to the whereabouts of Martin Hester's girlfriend, Eleanor Jamb, the wife of architect Harry Jamb."

"Nobody's going to blame you for this, Harry" said Riccardo Scappi when he telephoned his son in law the next day. "Least of all me. I love my daughter dearly, but she has done a bad thing. Don't let this get in the way of our relationship. We must think of Amelia."

Riccardo was also thinking of the new Jamb Range of furniture that was in prototype stage at the factory. He'd invested a lot of money in the project which was due to be launched at the start of the Frampton Games. The stadium's VIP suite would be the centrepiece of the international publicity campaign. . . and he wasn't about to jeopardise that.

Part 3 - Topping out

Chapter 13

"Never mix business with pleasure," had always been Freddie's maxim as far as his sexual peccadilloes were concerned. But he broke his own rule when he started a passionate affair with April Sims, wife of one of the associates in his practice.

April had joined her husband at the firm's annual outing to the fashionable East Beach Café at Littlehampton. Her minuscule bikini, bouncing breasts and smouldering looks had immediately attracted Freddie's attention and he ensured the lunchtime *placement* was altered so that they were sitting together.

It was clear to everyone around the table that Freddie and April were more interested in each other than the excellent *moules marinières* or the battered hake. The staff tried to hide the pair's soulful looks from her husband, John Sims, who was conveniently located at the other end of the café. Freddie couldn't understand how such a staid and boring chap had managed to bag such a bubbly beauty.

As the lunch broke up, some people went to sunbathe, others to swim or kite surf. Freddie could not contain himself.

"I'm staying at Bailiffscourt Hotel – it's only five minutes away. Come with me."

A quick look to make sure her husband was otherwise engaged was all April needed. She slipped into the passenger seat and Freddie drove urgently to the secluded hotel. It turned out to be the most expensive sex that Freddie had ever had.

***

"Well done Harry," said an uncharacteristically affable Joe Porley.

They were sitting in Harry's office looking through the latest interim report from the Stadium's cost consultants. The design was now on budget and they could see no reason why there should be any delays. Harry's design could be delivered on time and on budget.

"It's been a hard slog but worth it, now I've got to go and concentrate on Carlos's sexy curves and see if we can get those to work!" Joe said as he left the meeting room.

Harry punched the air "Yes! Yes! Yes!" he yelled when the Project Manager was out of earshot. "I couldn't have done it without you, Jenny. Thanks for putting up with me," he went to hug her, he wrapped his arms round her slim body and in an instant they were in a passionate embrace, his lips pressed hard on hers as he felt the soft fullness of her breasts against his body. With one hand he pushed the meeting room door closed and flicked the lock before urgently ripping away her blouse. She cried out as he caressed her breasts and he pressed her against the white Vitra Citterio-designed sideboard.

Jenny's moans got louder and louder. The glass walls of the meeting room provided limited acoustic insulation and her cries of passion could be clearly heard around the office.

"About bloody time too!" announced Alex, who had been working with Harry since the Shaw and Jamb days, as the rest of the office pretended to concentrate on the work on their screens.

A somewhat bedraggled Jenny and Harry emerged from the meeting room. "Joe Porley's given the Stadium a clean bill of health," Harry announced. He felt he had to say something to cover his embarrassment. "We're good to go!"

Everyone in the office started clapping, partly at the news of the stadium, but more from relief that Harry's self destructive phase seemed to have passed. They were all well aware of Jenny's long-term commitment to Harry and there was palpable relief that at last Harry had noticed.

"Let's have a party!" called Alex and he sent one of the year out students to get some champagne from the supermarket. They were a close knit team; they had the same belief in what made good architecture, they suffered together the pressures of producing quality design in the face of insensitive clients, and over complex planning processes and tight cost constraints. They had won a battle but the war continued. Tonight they could celebrate: the high ground had been gained and the way forward seemed more clear.

Harry felt happier than he had for months, but there was one blot on his horizon. Amelia had been very upset by Eleanor's disappearance and had been acting very strangely. She rarely answered her phone and wouldn't give Harry the address of her flat. Shacking up with Jenny would be unlikely to improve the situation. But he forgot those worries as he chatted animatedly to his staff around the 1:250 scale model of the Stadium.

"That'll win the Frazer Prize, you mark my words" Alex looked admiringly at their joint handiwork. The Frazer was the most sought after award of all among architects. "It's going to be a bloody good building."

While the two main buildings were shaping up nicely the Media Centre was still a problem.

"We can't get any agreement on the design of the bloody thing and we don't know what we're going to do with it afterwards." Mayor Jarvis complained to his planning chief.

Josh Stern was getting very frustrated too. He couldn't understand why Tomo Koji wouldn't take on board the criticisms and amend his design. But the Japanese architect stubbornly refused.

"This is the design I have done. If they don't like what I have done then they must find another architect."

176

Josh was beginning to agree with the latter statement. AAP were designing a new masterplan for Frampton-on-Tees University which required the provision of a new digital library and innovation centre. It hadn't taken Josh long to work out that with a few modifications the university could take over the Media Centre building after the EuroGames and house the new centre there, thus saving themselves millions. He presented his ideas to Sir Nigel Frith and Frampton University Buildings Committee who enthusiastically endorsed the idea.

"The only problem is, you will have to get rid of Tomo Koji as the architect; he isn't prepared to alter his design and you will need to make substantial changes if my plan is to succeed."

"Would you take the job on?" Frith asked.

"I couldn't possibly comment, Sir Nigel" Josh said with a wry smile, "that would mean supplanting another architect. Kojo would have to resign first."

***

Following their tryst at the Frederick Shaw and Partners annual outing, April Sims had fallen hopelessly in love with Freddie but could not accept that the architect did not reciprocate. She wanted to move in with him. Freddie had no intention of spoiling his comfortable marriage with Harriet, and disrupting his family life. He was happy to entertain her in his Barbican flat, but April was a bit on the side – a very nice bit on the side, but nothing more.

One morning in the office John Sims asked to speak to Freddie privately.

"April has told me what's been going on" he said blankly. "I've told her to move out of the house. She's taking her stuff over to your Barbican flat now. She's expecting to move in with you."

"Bloody hell! She can't do that! This has got ridiculously out of hand. I fancied her. But I didn't expect her to take it all so seriously."

"You should have thought about that before you screwed her! You are such a shit Freddie! I've worked here for so long, being paid a pittance, because I believe in the work we have been doing. But after this I can't go on. I'm resigning"

He handed Freddie a sealed envelope and slammed the meeting room door hard to reinforce his indignation.

"Damn!" Freddie thought. " And she's got a key to the flat."

He ran out of the office and hailed a cab. The traffic was heavy and it took him nearly half an hour to get to the Barbican. He ran up the stairs to the pedestrian deck, grazing his knuckles on a rough concrete column as he slid to a halt at the entrance to his block.

The unforgiving finishes of the massive Barbican estate gave it a strength and solidity rare among British housing. No wonder it's called Brutalism, Harry mused as got into the lift. Its detractors used it as a form of abuse, its fans as praise. 'Brutal' referred to the rough concrete – *beton brut* in French – not to the heartlessness of which so much architecture of the period was accused. Freddie loved the sculptural force of the towers, the pointed balconies, the curved concrete forms and the beautifully detailed interiors.

As he got to his floor he could see the door was ajar, there were cases in the corridor. April was moving in.

"You can't stay here! I've got a wife and family. You're a very lovely girl, but there's no way you can move in with me! I've had a really great time with you, but it's over!" He had told her before that she should not expect a permanent relationship, but she hadn't believed him. Now he needed to be brutal. "You've got to go back to John."

"I can't do that!" She broke down in tears. "I love you so much Freddie."

As she looked around the luxurious furniture of Freddie's spacious pied a terre she was only too aware of the pokey little flat she had just left. She and her husband had a couple of Alvar Aalto stools they bought at Habitat; Freddie had two original Paimio armchairs and a properly worn Eames Lounge Chair and Ottoman; on their walls April and John had hung a selection of elegant screen prints but Freddie had paintings that could have come straight out of Tate Britain – a Gary Hume, Howard Hodgkin, Bruce McLean and a Hockney etching for good measure. This catholic collection of design sat appropriately against stunning views of the London skyline. This was the sort of life she had always dreamed of. She wasn't going to give it up without a fight.

Freddie found beautiful women in tears irresistible. April looked up him with her smudged make up and doleful expression.

"You can't do this to me Freddie," she sobbed.

Freddie could not contain himself. He kissed her hard on the lips and urgently pulled away at her clothes as they sank onto the grey and blue rectangles of the Eileen Grey rug he had recently bought from Aram in Covent Garden.

It was quick and it was a mistake. As his concupiscence waned, Freddie swore at himself – as he had done many times before.

"Shit! Shit! Shit! I'll never get rid of her now. How could I be so stupid?"

He had to do something fast. Harriet would be coming up to London at the weekend as they had tickets for *The Rake's Progress* at the Royal Opera House. Harriet had long accepted Freddie's sexual peccadilloes, but live-in mistress was another thing entirely. They had a fine understanding and he wasn't prepared to spoil it. What if April starts kicking up a fuss? Freddie was increasingly in the public eye and very conscious of his public image. His PR team would not be happy having to handle stories about a spurned lover. He certainly didn't want the sort of publicity Harry had received when Eleanor's affair with Hester hit the headlines.

He had to get April back to her husband. Freddie had got on well with John Sims in the past, they had had a very fruitful working relationship. Although until recently Freddie had known little of his life outside the office, Freddie thought he could talk to him man to man.

***

Sheranie Philips calls an emergency meeting about the planned Institute of Art Exhibition. Neither Freddie nor Harry would agree to attend if the other was there, so they each sent a representative. Tariq went on behalf of Frederick Shaw and Partners and Alex Rich on behalf of Harry Jamb Associates. Also in attendance was the graphic designer Humphrey Bell whose job it was to coordinate the design of the installations and the graphics, and to liaise with the contractors who would build the show.

"We have just over six months to go to the opening of our 'two man' exhibition and we have a number of serious problems." Melanie began firmly. "With its art shows the Institute is used to knowing at least nine months in advance exactly what is going to be in each of the galleries. With this show we still don't have any decision of what buildings you are going to put in! The estimates to build models of your projects are way over budget, the catalogue has to go to press in four weeks time and Humphrey is tearing his hair out – every time he fixes on a layout you change your minds, again."

Humphrey Bell had been laying out exhibitions at the Institute for years, mostly of work of dead artists who had little say in how their work was displayed. If he had a problem with Sheranie, or the sponsorship department, he generally found a well-timed hissy fit, with perhaps a threat of resignation, would ensure he got his way. But this time was different. The architects didn't like him telling them how they should set out their work; they didn't seem to have a clue about how visitors would circulate around the gallery, or that the audience who normally attended the Institute of Art exhibitions would have a limited understanding of complex architectural drawings.

"I've just about had enough" Humphrey launched into his well-rehearsed tirade. "I've worked on a lot of exhibitions, but never one as chaotic as this. The Institute has to make up its mind. Who is designing this show – me or the architects? I was commissioned to make sure their collections of building projects worked as an exhibition, but the problem with architects is that they believe they can design everything – the layout, the graphics, the lighting – but they can't. If we carry on as we are it's going to be a disaster."

"Frederick certainly has very strong views on the way the exhibition is designed" said Tariq "and he has still to decide exactly what he's wants to put in it. He's been away for three weeks, but we have a couple of hours with him tomorrow when we can finalise the selection of projects."

"I should be at that meeting so that we can discuss the layout," insisted Humphrey.

"I don't think that will be necessary," Tariq replied, as politely as he could. "Freddie is insisting that he designs the layout of his section."

"But can't you see that is totally unacceptable?" Humphrey spluttered, 'that is *my* job! Sheranie, can you support me on this?"

"I think I should say," Tariq continued "Freddie is very insistent on this. If he doesn't have total control over the design of the room, we may well pull out from the show."

"If Freddie has total control," said Alex "then Harry will certainly insist on it too."

Sheranie was stuck. Humphrey had given good service to the Institute, but it was more important to keep her two stars happy – without them, she would have no show.

"I think we need to look at a solution where each architect is responsible for the design of their own space, but the introductory gallery would be your responsibility, Humphrey. . . ".

"I get the message, Sheranie! I was taken on to design the whole exhibition, and I'm not prepared to be handed the leftovers! I have no option but to resign!"

Humphrey pushed back his chair, gathered his papers from the green baize-topped table and strode out of the room.

Sheranie had already been making contingency plans in the event of a Humphrey walk out for some time.

"We need to find someone else to take over from Humphrey; someone who both Harry and Freddie are happy with," she announced "I propose that we ask Jason Vent to oversee the design of the introductory gallery and the graphic design of the publicity material. From what I understand, both of your firms are working happily with Jason's team on the Frampton EuroGames, so hopefully, you can all work together at the Institute."

She certainly hoped so. The organisation of this two man show so far had been a nightmare – too many egos to be soothed, too many control freaks to be contained – artists were pussycats compared to architects.

With just three months to go until the private view, Sheranie had a horrible feeling her troubles weren't over yet.

***

Sir Nigel Frith told Mayor Jarvis about his plans to take over the Media Centre for the University after the EuroGames as long as Tomo Koji's design was amended. Ed Clutton wrote to the Japanese architect specifying a range of alterations to his design. Koji responded by return, saying that he would be arriving in London in a week's time and suggested a meeting.

At the same time he emailed Rachael to say that he would like her advice on a difficult problem he was facing and he would like to meet up with her when he got to London.

Rachael's interest was pricked. She had heard that things weren't going well with Koji's project for the Games. What did he want to talk to her about? He had seemed so embarrassed after their last encounter that she had thought he would have wanted to steer clear of her altogether.

So it was with her digital recorder in hand that she arrived at the newly opened St John Hotel, just off Leicester Square. She nodded to the greenhorn hotelier Fergus Henderson in his suit made from traditional butchers' aprons puffing at a fag in the street outside. She was a great fan of Fergus's restaurant in Clerkenwell and hoped the hotel would be just as successful.

"Mr Koji is in his room. He asked that you go straight up" said the receptionist.

"Damn," thought Rachael. She'd been rather looking forward to a bit of lunch. The reviews had praised the potted pigeon and the sweetbread and she was keen to try them out.

She walked through the spare white corridors until she found Koji's room. She knocked and immediately the door opened and there stood the Japanese architect in a white kimono style dressing gown, against the backdrop of the all-white room with just the greenish tinge of the frosted glass shower partition providing a hint of colour.

"Good morning" he bowed. Rachael took two steps inside and Koji pushed the door to.

Without any pleasantries and to the journalist's astonishment, he suddenly barked in heavily accented English "Fuck me please, Rachael!" He stood without moving but allowed the gown to hang open to reveal his aroused state.

"My! my! how your English has improved!" Rachael laughed as she admired his physique. She remembered how well hung he was when she had paid lip service to it in Frampton, but she was surprised at his muscular body, there was not an ounce of fat on him. She recalled reading that he was some advanced *dan* in the martial arts. "Hitting people with sticks certainly keeps you fit!"

But Koji didn't laugh. He pulled Rachael gently towards him and their two bodies toppled onto the all white counterpane. He had been imagining this encounter for months, and Rachael's pliant responses fulfilled all his desires.

Satisfied, Koji got up from the bed and went to his bag. He pulled out a thick envelope which he gave to Rachael with a bow.

"Thank you very much. This . . .is . . . present. . . for. . . you," he said haltingly.

Rachael frowned as she took the envelope. What was it? Cash? Does he think I'm a tart? But she opened the flap and found only typed sheets of paper. She pulled out a compliment slip that lay on top. It was from Tak, Koji's assistant.

"Rachael," Tak wrote "we are very upset at the way we have been treated by the client team at Frampton. I have written down our history of the project and Koji-San's views about the situation which I have translated for you. He doesn't feel he can explain it himself in English but please use this information in any articles you might be writing about the buildings for the Games."

The next day the headline in *The Gazette* announced "Japanese designer resigns from EuroGames site".

"Tomo Koji, one of the world's leading architects, has resigned from the Frampton-on-Tees EuroGames project and attacked his former clients as 'philistines'," read the article. It went on:

"According to Mr Koji, people in Britain don't respect architects enough. 'You are not interested in ideas; money and marketing are what matter. Original thinking and debate have been overwhelmed by slick and low cost architecture. We thought very carefully about the design of the Media Centre but were forced to change it because of comments from local people who knew little about the ideas embodied in the design. We designed a building that fitted into the city but in Britain you see buildings as freestanding objects. They have no dialogue with the other buildings around them. I would rather resign than have my name associated with a building I am not satisfied with'."

"Thank you very much" said Rachael as she drove the architect to Heathrow. And she meant it. This was the second time she had made the front page thanks to Koji. A part of her regretted he was leaving, he had brought a refreshing clarity to the discussion, he had stuck by his principles and he was horny as hell.

Immediately, the EuroGames Press Office put out a statement that AAP had been appointed sole architects for the new Frith Media Centre.

***

"I'm not sure how it would work if she came back to me," said John Sims when he met Freddie for lunch at a secluded restaurant to discuss his ex-boss's relationship with April.

"Why not? You seemed to get on OK before I came along."

"Precisely. But April hates the fact that we're so badly off. When she married an architect she thought she was entering a world of smart living, and grand designs with *Elle Deco* interiors. But it hasn't worked out like that. We live in pokey flat in Islington; friends of ours who are lawyers are earning twice as much. Partners like you do well enough, but down in the engine room it's a different scene. People work for love of the job, not for the money!"

John talked about a little infill site he had found up in Highgate where he had planned to build his dream house, where he could work out some of his own architectural ideas, where every little detail could be designed to suit his taste and lifestyle. He revealed he had designed the plan to accommodate the two children he and April had planned to have. But he couldn't afford the site, let alone start construction.

"Look John, you're a good architect and you've made a great contribution to the office. I'm happy to take you back and move you up a level or two so you're earning better money, and as a gesture of goodwill – or perhaps remorse" he laughed uncomfortably, "I'll help you with the purchase of you're site. I'll give you a cheque right now for £25K."

John looked stunned; Freddie smiled encouragingly; he rather enjoyed the feeling of power he suddenly had over the couple's lives. The potential availability of the lovely April for the odd sexual encounter didn't escape him even now; it was very tempting and good value.

"But I need £50K to be able to start on site." John said, more a point of information than a bargaining ploy."

"OK, you've got it."

April accepted the deal. They would get their house, they would be better off. And Freddie wouldn't be far way.

Chapter 14

"Shall we share a water taxi into Venice?" Josh Stern had been on the same flight from London as Jason Vent.

"Yes, let's. What hotel are you staying in?"

"The Danieli"

"So am I! What fun!"

Josh and Jason, and ten thousand other architects, critics, journalists and PR people, had come to Venice for the opening of the Architecture Biennale. Every two years the International Pavilions in the Giardini, the Corderie dell'Arsenale and various *palazzi* filled with the work of architects from around the world and the *vernissage* and press day became the focus of a grand, three day, city wide party, a long weekend of discussions, debates, networking, partying, squabbles and sex.

"Could there be a more stylish way to enter a city!" exclaimed Josh. The two sat at the back of the sleek, highly varnished launch as it carved its way across the choppy lagoon, slapping hard into the wakes of passing taxis; the tanned *tassista* expertly steered his craft through the busy traffic, casually saluting his colleagues with the air of a star arriving for the Venice Film Festival rather than a mere cabbie.

"It beats the M4 any day!" Jason replied as the divine profile of *La Serenissima* drew closer, its campanile commanding the skyline as Wren's spires had once held sway over the City of London. But just as its watery bounds had protected Venice from the ancient Hun, so had they withheld the onslaught of barbarian progress: increasing heights of buildings had not absorbed the delicate tracery of its profile, neither had office towers diminished the commanding stature of the Campanile San Marco.

The water taxi drew up to the Danieli's private landing stage and Josh and Jason made their way up to the grand gothic reception space. The ducal staircase zigzagged up through the 14th century atrium, decorated ogee arches and classical columns were stacked in a riot of detail. In the low lit bar the architectural glitterati gathered to discover what they should be doing over the next few days, which events to attend, which pavilions were rumoured to be worth visiting, who was hot and who was not.

"What a great space!" Jason gasped, "it feels more Norma Desmond than Doge Dandola, but the bar is just *the* best place in town to watch the Biennale go by."

There was a strong UK contingent for the Venice Biennale that year. Rachael Dove's show for the British Pavilion, 'New Housing Solutions' and tipped by the Danieli barflies for best in show, highlighted The Infini T Tower by Amanda Stone; Jonny Spon's designs for the Frampton Pavilions formed the centrepiece of the international displays in the Corderie, the spectacular 300 metre-long redundant ropeworks; Ed Clutton had hired the Palazzo Contadore just off the Grand Canal to house an exhibition about Frampton as an architectural hotspot, with a massive model of the EuroGames's site as its centrepiece. The unknown team of Architectural Analysis Inc had won the competition to build an installation celebrating Scottish Independence on the Fondamente Zattere on Dorsodura. The huge inflatable structure made a significant impact on passing cruise ships, but ate up the whole of the region's culture budget for that year. Top of Jason and Josh's list of exhibits to visit was the new Niall Jacquet installation of furniture moulded from male body parts and manufactured by Riccardo Scappi's Marsoni furniture company.

The cost of hiring Frampton's palazzo had been sponsored by Sam Spurling and Ecoplastics. Since moving to his new factory and receiving a contract for 130,000 injection moulded recycled plastic seats, Sam had become a great fan of the EuroGames and a roving ambassador for Frampton, promoting the return of manufacturing to the city.

***

Harry and Jenny arrived early at the Giardini on the Press Day, hoping to get round the main pavilions before things got too crowded. They were looking forward to a relaxed weekend just enjoying the atmosphere of Venice. Harry only had a few official duties at the Biennale apart from appearing at a number of receptions hosted by Mayor Jarvis, and work at the office was going smoothly without him.

The tree-lined gravel pathways were already thronging with contractors putting final finishes to exhibits and caterers were setting out tables of champagne flutes in readiness for the opening receptions.

Meanwhile journalists were tracking down starchitects – that small group of designers who have become media stars and are selected for jobs for their profile as much as for their architecture – to interview. The Italian Pavilion, with its white fascist façade, formed the focus of the vista as visitors passed through the security cordon. Up the slope to right, the path led to the British Pavilion, a pompous symmetrical villa with a grand staircase up to the classical portico and central entrance.

Harry rather liked the installation of The Infini T Tower which took up the whole of the first room of the British Pavilion. A large, intricately detailed boxwood model formed the centrepiece while large-scale computer generated images of the building in its Frampton context filled the four-metre high walls. In the background recorded voices of Amanda Stone and Sid Dixon described the ideas behind the design.

"The building was conceived as a specific response to its location on the cusps of Georgian and Victorian Frampton" intoned Amanda, "and designed to provide a variety of apartments across the site as an opportunity to explore new models for contemporary housing and domestic space."

"This is very disappointing!" a voice Harry recognised only too well could be heard from the second gallery. "It's all so boring, no idea of form at all, who on earth would want to be condemned to live in this sort of stuff?"

189

"Let's go!" Harry whispered to Jenny. "The last thing I want to do is to bump into Frederick Shaw!"

"It looks like something Harry Jamb might have designed!" Freddie laughed as the *Building News* journalist jotted down the quote.

After a quick look in the German Pavilion, Harry and Jenny made their way to the Japanese Pavilion tucked in amongst the trees.

Tomo Koji's installation compared contemporary art museums (all designed by him) to Shinto temples: exquisite photographs of geometric concrete shapes set against tailored landscapes and reflective lakes were hung beside simple Shinto temples of white cypress, celebrating the harmony between deities, man and nature.

Koji was surrounded by journalists asking him questions; Yuki translated those that weren't in Japanese. A nervous cultural attaché was desperately trying to bring the conference to an end, as the Japanese Ambassador was about to arrive to officially open the show. Koji took no notice and carried on, until he recognized Harry.

"Har – ree!" he called "Good to see you!" Which was as far as he was prepared to go in English and he turned to his wife to translate.

"How are things at Frampton-on-Tees?" Yuki asked with a shy smile.

"Very good thanks – we've got planning permission and the cranes are on site. Sorry to hear about your problems."

"These people have no culture!" Yuki found it difficult to match the vitriol with which her husband spat out these words in his native language "they do not respect the art of architecture! They only want to buy the cheapest building that will do the job! They asked me to make changes which would have destroyed my design and I wouldn't do it. Your friend Josh Stern agreed to take on the project.

He should have refused! I ask the Royal Institute of British Architects to boycott the project, but they said the client can make that sort of decision if he wants to. I am an artist! The client should respect what I do. Why else do they ask me to work for them?"

At that moment the Japanese ambassador arrived. Koji turned and bowed.

"*Ohayou gozaimasu*" Harry could see from the depth of the Ambassador's bow that the Japanese diplomat held Koji in greater esteem than his British equivalent would have held Harry – if he even knew who he was.

After dipping into a couple more pavilions Harry hailed a water taxi to take them both to Locanda Cipriani at Torcello where they enjoyed a delightful, architect-free lunch in the enclosed garden, overlooked by the campanile of the Cathedral of Santa Maria Assunta. The rustic interior, the open terrace and the pergola covered in flowers and foliage was a refreshing change from the works on show in the Biennale.

"Oh Harry, you look so much better than you did." Jenny held his hand across the table as the crickets chirped among the roses, and outside the walls a noisy group of tourists recently arrived on the vaporetto made their way to the twelfth century cathedral.

"I feel great Jenny, thanks to you. We're going to need to be on top form over the next year. There's a lot to be done. I'm really happy with the way the Stadium is finally shaping up; if we get the Institute of Art Exhibition right we're going to be flying high."

That evening Astrid Sollett took over the upper room at Harry's Bar to entertain forty or so friends and contacts. Ernest Hemingway's watering hole may have become something of a tourist trap but its no nonsense 30s' interior and *risotto alla primavera* still drew in the architectural crowd. Astrid had spent a long time on the *placement*, carefully separating Harry and Freddie, and putting Koji as far away from Josh as possible; she had Sid Dixon and Amanda Stone together. There was a minor panic when Jason insisted he sat next to Josh who was by then deep in conversation with Niall Jacquet. Amanda herself sat between Ed Clutton and Mayor Jarvis.

There were plentiful supplies of the Bar's signature Bellini cocktail of white peach juice and prosecco as the guests waited to eat. It was a busy night and it took ages for the antipasto of carpaccio to arrive. No one noticed, they were deep in discussion about the works they had seen that day, making recommendations of must sees, who was good and who was bad. As the Bellini's had their effect the noise rose. There were mixed views about the British Pavilion; few disliked Koji's presentation, but felt it was rather predictable; Jonny Spon's full scale installation of one his Temporary Pavilions in the Arsenale got the thumbs up from most of the diners apart from Carlos de Souza, who felt that Jonny's consultative working methods set a disturbing precedent.

"We train for seven years to learn how to do this job; we have to work for another twenty years before we get a chance to do anything proper. How come the public can sit round a table with a fistful of crayons and tell us how to design?" Carlos knocked back another Bellini just to make his point.

As coffee was served and conversation was shifting to which party everyone was about to go to, Astrid tapped her glass.

"Dear guests, thanks for coming this evening. Before you leave I'd like to ask Rachael Dove to say a few words about "New housing Solutions". She signalled her to rise with a wave of her hand. "Rachael!"

The journalist and curator rose unsteadily to her feet. She was wearing a tight-fitting and unforgiving black jersey dress which showed off her gym-toned body to perfection. Freddie, who had been sitting opposite Rachael, was transfixed.

"We er felt. . . er. . . that. . . er" Rachael was clearly nervous; Freddie noticed her hand in which she held some scribbled notes was shaking like a leaf. Guests looked at their empty plates in embarrassment. But Rachael knew her stuff. After her first faltering words she began to get into her stride, her tightened throat relaxed, she put down her notes and looked around the room.

"We all know that the state of current British housing is in a mess; it's poorly designed, badly constructed and our space standards are a scandal. And we can't build enough of them. Because the housing industry is now controlled by the volume house builders there is little experimentation into new ways of designing and delivering the sort of homes we need. So we looked back to see what we could learn from innovative schemes developed in the post war period, which have largely been forgotten because everything from that period is tarred with the same brush of failure. And then we looked at a number of contemporary schemes that move the discussion forward – the centrepiece of course is Amanda Stone's brilliant design for a residential project in Frampton – carried out, it must be said, for an exemplary client. It confirms the maxim that behind every good building is a good client Her geometric design, elegant proportions, attention to context and spacious flats are a lesson to us all."

Rachael sat down to enthusiastic applause as Sid quickly got to his feet.

"My thanks Astrid for hosting such a splendid evening. I am a very modest man," he announced with a smile, amid hoots of laughter "but I couldn't let Rachael's comment pass without adding my congratulations to Amanda for a brilliant design. The scheme includes homes for the rich and for the less well off – all designed and built with the same care and attention. Its beautiful and. . ."

"Bollocks!"

Sid ignored the intervention as guests looked around the room for its author " . . . and sets a new standard, not just for Frampton but. . ."

"It's a fucking sell out!" Carlos, his dark oiled curls awry, glass in hand, swayed across the room ". . . there's no life! No spirit! It's all so bloody boring! I, Carlos de Souza, am the designer of the Frampton Swimming Complex" he stabbed his chest with the forefinger of his spare hand – while the other hand hung desperately to the back of Mayor Jarvis's chair as the inebriated architect attempted to remain upright. Freddie frowned. He noticed Rachael, always the journalist, was writing notes on the back of the menu.

"I designed that building. *That* is beautiful! It has real form! It is a sexy building…"

"Oh do shut up!" cried a voice and other guests joined in with boos.

Carlos staggered towards the stairs, turned to the room and raised both arms in an aggressive 'V' sign and clattered down to the bar below.

"That was exciting!" Josh giggled to Jason.

Josh had been very attentive all evening, worried that Jason might fancy Niall Jacquet. Niall's shaved head and sculpted features had been tanned to a tee in the month he had spent in his Formentera villa; the results of his regular work out was there for all to see – a muscular neck emerged from the sloping shoulders of his tight white tee-shirt, its short arms stretched by bulging biceps and its waist rippling with the profile of an impressive six pack. But luckily for Josh, Jacquet didn't fancy Jason. He had other plans and got up to leave.

As they watched his tight leather clad butt mince towards the stairs, Josh and Jason looked at each other: "Let's go back to the Danieli!"

"So *is* Carlos the designer of the Swimming Complex?" Rachael asked a pensive Freddie as they were left alone at their table.

"As you well know Rachael, architecture is a team game. Of course he has made a contribution – a very valuable one – but the designer is the firm: Frederick Shaw and Partners. It has nothing to do with individuals."

Koji, with his wife, slipped away as inconspicuously as possible from the emptying room. He felt sure that Rachael would be as diplomatic as was necessary, but he didn't want to chance it.

As the couple walked along beside the slapping water towards Piazza San Marco they could make out the figure of Carlos de Souza in heated conversation with Josh and Jason, who were trying to steer him towards his hotel.

"Geroff me!" Carlos shouted as he yanked his arm from Jason's grip, but then lost his balance and stepped backwards with a gasp into the blackness of the Bacino di San Marco. Carlos could swim but, totally disoriented, he started paddling towards a gondola full of Chinese tourists.

"Over here! Carlos! There are steps!" Jason called. The South American turned and paddled his way to the slippery stair. As he rose out of the water, he puked, narrowly missing Jason's pale suede Gucci loafers which he had bought earlier that day.

As Jason and Josh steered Carlos away from the water's edge, Koji slipped past in the dark – Josh was someone he would prefer to avoid after all the fuss over the Media Centre.

"I've had enough" Jason said "let's leave him here" as they perched the limp figure against the wall of the Doge's Palace and walked the two hundred metres back to the Danieli.

***

The next evening Frampton held a VIP special reception at the Palazzo Contadore to present an 'Update' on the buildings for the EuroGames. The Palazzo can only be reached by water taxi from the Grand Canal or by a tortuous route through the alleyways of the Dorsoduro, so the early conversations were dominated either by guests' incredulity at the cost of a two minute taxi ride, or explanations that they were half an hour late because they missed the turning by the bridge over the canal next to the street which leads to the Guggenheim. But the prattle about the problems of navigating the city of water was brought to an abrupt halt as Carlos walked into the room.

As people turned to stare Carlos smiled in response. Such recognition was his due. He was responsible for one of the great new buildings of the moment. Of course they would note his entry.

But as the normal hubbub of conversation returned it was not about Carlos's Swimming Pool Complex but his swimming in the Grand Canal.

"Did he fall or was he pushed?" they giggled.

"Who would have pushed him? Amanda Stone? Freddie Shaw?"

Tutta la Venezia knew about Carlos's escapade, as by then did most of the architectural world. Jonny Spon had witnessed the event and noted it in his blog for the *Building News* website; *The Gazette* gossip column picked up the story and ran it under the headline "Swimming pool architect makes a splash."

The giggles subsided as Mayor Jarvis walked up to the dais set up in front of the grand windows that looked out over the canal. The interior of the Palazzo was rather more basic than he had expected. His vision of a palace was one with walls of Old Masters, lots of gold leaf, huge chandeliers and maroon drapes. But Ed Clutton's budget couldn't run to drapes. The room was big enough but the lime painted walls and plain timber ceiling were a bit of a disappointment.

"Good evening Ladies and Gentlemen, let me welcome you to Frampton-on-Tees's little home from home in Venice." He looked up to encourage laughter at his wry humour. "First of all I would like to thank Sam Spurling of Ecoplastics for sponsoring this event. We are spending a lot of public money on the EuroGames, and lest anyone should be mistaken that we are squandering it on champagne and canapés, let me tell you that every penny spent this weekend is one of Sam's!"

"But the serious part of this evening is to get you to take a close look at the exhibition of the buildings we are erecting for the Games and to see how this great event will benefit our city in the long term. And on that note I would like to announce that today's meeting of the Frampton Planning Committee agreed to the changes to the Media Centre, which after the Games will be taken over by the University's Department of Digital Technology. I'd like to congratulate Josh Stern of AAP for creating the new design and all our architects for their spectacular work which will change the face and the future of our great city. The Media Centre was the last piece of the jigsaw – now it's full steam ahead – on time and on budget!"

The guests applauded heartily. The architects smiled demurely.

"Thank you for coming, and take care as you return to your hotels – we don't want you falling into the canal!" he laughed as the guests turned towards Carlos, who was clearly not amused.

The next day *The Gazette* reported that The Infiniti T Tower had been awarded the Golden Lion Award for the Best Installation in the whole of the Biennale event. Sid was over the moon; there had been a big turnout of rich Russians at the Biennale and word was that they were starting to buy 'name' architecture in the same way they were buying art.

"That's worth a few mill," he said to Veronica as the water taxi sped the couple across the lagoon to Marco Polo Airport, slapping and banging into the waves and wash of other boats. "Added value – that's what this architecture business is all about."

Part 4 – Construction

Chapter 15

"Sven Christensen, Director of the Architecture Institute, invites you to a celebration of the work and life of Sir Frank Cummins OM RIBA to be held at Gibberd Square, London WC1." The impeccable typography of the letterpress card was adorned with a black and white photo of Frank taken in the 60s by Lord Snowdon. The architect was leaning over his drawing board, sleeves rolled up, 6B pencil in hand, his aquiline features framed by flowing locks and a jaunty bow tie. A rough but recognisable sketch of his great Northern Opera House could clearly be seen on the stretched cartridge.

Harry was glad that Sven had asked him to speak at the memorial. He had liked the old man and owed him a lot professionally.

The architectural community turned out in force on the night. Everyone who was anyone was there Riccardo Scappi, Sid Dixon, Piers Gough, Sheranie Philips, Richard Rogers, Rachael Dove, Norman Foster; Bob Maxwell had flown in from Princeton and Koji from Tokyo. The Japanese architect's marathon trip meant 28 hours of travelling and just five hours on the ground in London. He had acted as the local architect of record for Frank when he was doing the extension to the Tori Foundation's gallery in Tokyo. The impact that working with the great man had had on the young architect and his approach to design – indeed his whole career – was such that he felt obliged to pay his respects.

Freddie had sent his apologies; he was on a site visit in Guangzhou.

Such events are as much about catching up with people you hadn't seen for years, as they are to honour the dead, Harry mused as he looked out over the crowded lecture theatre. The sea of grey heads interspersed with those of enthusiastic students keen to experience the fading pulse of their antecedents and three generations of practitioners who had cut their teeth in Cummins' studio. He started his speech.

"Frank once told me that an architect has to be both a charmer and a shit," an embarrassed titter rippled across the room, old heads jerked up and frowned. Damn, was that too risqué for an occasion like this? Harry worried as he continued "I always found Frank to be the former. He was a wonderful mentor to me as a student and young architect. I learnt much about design, and about the ways of the world. Indeed, I run my practice today along very similar lines to the way Frank ran his – except I pay my staff more!" This little joke went down better among those who had toiled for minimal financial reward in the Cummins office.

"As an architect trained in the Beaux Arts tradition who espoused the Modernist cause, Frank could be described as the last of his kind. He could draw like an angel, illustrating complex ideas with a few deft lines. . . erm . . ." Harry hesitated as he sensed a commotion in the front row. Frank's widow Moira was scrabbling in her handbag and finally withdrew a handkerchief into which she buried her head, sobbing, her 40-something son and daughter on either side were looking across the rows in some astonishment towards a late arrival, squeezing himself into a seat next to Dorothy, Frank's faithful and long serving secretary.

The man was in his late thirties, tall with long, flowing hair and a familiar face. Dorothy, as prim and neat as Harry remembered, her white hair pulled back in a tight bun, smiled fondly as the man sat down and the Cummins siblings stared open mouthed across the room.

"I am pleased to say" Harry continued "that Moira has generously agreed to present Frank's stunning collection of drawings to the British Architectural Library." It had been a close run thing Harry had learnt. The children had dumped much of the archive in a skip as they cleared out the great architect's effects. Not through any ignorance of their value, but for revenge. Revenge against architecture. Revenge against the world to which Frank Cummins had devoted his life; the world that sent them away to school, that absorbed his every waking hour and ensured their father remained a distant and rather frightening figure. How good they felt as they tipped cardboard tubes full of old tracing drawings, ancient copies of *The Architectural Review* and Le Corbusier's *Oeuvres Completes* into the skip.

An architect neighbour alerted the BAL's Librarian and within the hour an astonished curator, his heart pounding like a rollover lottery winner, was loading the treasure trove – for which the Getty or the Canadian Center for Architecture would have paid millions – into the back of a borrowed van.

Harry sat down and listened to the other speakers. Sven was fluent and passionate, choking several times as he recalled his long friendship with Cummins. Others discussed his architecture, his good deeds, his love of wine, holidays in France and Italy, and amusing incidents.

Harry heard little of it as he tried to work out what was going on in front row. The Cummins family seemed very restive, whispering amongst themselves and eying Dorothy who sat quite upright, listening attentively to all the speakers.

"Everyone is welcome upstairs for drinks." Thor announced as the speeches finally ended. "The wine is from Frank's extensive and excellent cellar so I am sure you will all enjoy yourselves in a manner of which he would have approved!"

As the guests got to their feet – not an easy task for some – Harry made a bee line for the faithful secretary.

"Hello Dorothy! How nice to see you! It must be 25 years!" He kissed her warmly on both cheeks.

"Yes, but I have watched your career with great interest. You have done so well!"

Harry looked at the tall man who was hovering.

"This is Francis," Dorothy said looking directly at Harry ". . . my son."

Harry could not contain his surprise. He started to speak, but Dorothy anticipated his question.

"No, I'm not married, and never have been. Frank was his father. This is the first occasion that we have come out of the closet, so to speak."

"So that was the familiar look!" thought Harry.

"No one ever knew," Dorothy continued "at least not until the funeral. The family were even more astonished than you are. So when Frank left a big part of his estate to Francis you can imagine Moira and the children were pretty upset. As you noticed they weren't too happy that Francis came today, but this is an architectural event and we were part of his architectural life. To his family it was just his job, to me it was everything."

Other past members of the Cummins' office recognised Dorothy and she and Francis were swept up into the crowd as they tucked into the remnants of Frank's cellar. Harry label-checked the bottle as the waiter – an Institute student earning a bit of pocket money – poured him a drink. Chambolle Musigny '93. "Very nice" he murmured half to the young student and half to the spirit of his mentor. He raised his glass "Cheers! To Frank! To Architecture!" As he did so he watched Moira Cummins and family slipping unnoticed from the room.

***

"It's the most difficult job I've ever built." Joe Porley pointed up to the converging cantilevers of steel that completed the huge sphere that formed the roof of the Swimming Complex.

"Those steel beams are massive – they're 30 metres long and weigh 70 tons apiece" he explained to Mayor Jarvis as they took a tour of the Games's site, "and until they join at the top we've got to make sure they don't all fall down. It's not a new problem, Wren had it at St Paul's Cathedral and Brunelleschi in Florence." Jarvis looked around – the sky was filled with a tracery of cranes, on the ground, trucks, bulldozers, scrapers, road cleaners, delivery lorries criss-crossed the site – the roaring engines and flashing warning lights adding to the air of excitement. Ed Clutton's masterplan snaked out across the old steelworks and Jarvis could finally relate the physical layout to the multitude of drawings and plans he had been studying for the past three years.

He could also make out the forms of the buildings as they rose from the ground: Harry Jamb's jewel box Stadium, the simple form of Josh Stern's amended Media Centre design and Frederick Shaw's dramatic Swimming Complex dome that was taxing Joe Porley's construction team.

The Mayor felt a real sense of pride. He was a patron of architecture. It was so much more than just being the 'client'; he had set out to get some of the best architects in the country and around the world to design the best modern buildings that would bring real change and a new life to Frampton. Florence had the Medicis. Modern Frampton had Richard Jarvis. He would leave a legacy to the city as powerful as that of his Victorian antecedents.

Joe stopped and turned towards Jarvis. He looked uncharacteristically worried. "It's going to be really hard to stay within budget on this one."

The Mayor's was startled out of his reverie.

"What on earth. . .? You said you'd got the budget sorted!" Jarvis said sharply.

"I had," Joe cut in "but the recent terrorist bombings have meant the EU Organising Committee has demanded additional security measures and because of its complexity this building is much more difficult to adapt than the others. On top of that they've asked for an increase in the specification for the VIP areas. They're worried their sponsors won't like the designs that we have at the moment."

"And there's nothing you can do?"

"We can start cutting some of the quality from the public areas, we could omit the internal ceiling from all the circulation space – it wouldn't look very nice, but it would work."

Throughout the whole process of getting the games to Frampton the Mayor's team had juggled three factors – time, cost and quality. The timing was fixed – if the buildings weren't ready on the allotted dates there would be no games – at least not in Frampton. As the date got closer so the room for manoeuvre reduced.

Cost was a political issue as much as a construction one. What was too much? How much would the public accept? How many hospitals or schools or houses could you build for the money? Cost was the topic that so exercised the media and thus was always in the forefront of the politicians' minds. But as he saw these great temples of sport rising around him, Jarvis knew his priority must be to maintain the quality. In a few years' time the press and the people would have forgotten the debate about costs, while these magnificent structures would still be in use and would be the symbols of the city in the twenty first century.

"No, Joe, don't cut the quality. I'll find the money," the Mayor said firmly. He raised himself to his full height and marched across the mud-strewn site. He felt very proud of himself.

***

Alex La Touche, architectural photographer, made his way up to the top of Abraham Darby Tower on the Conway Estate. The paved area and the fluted concrete structure that housed the lift motors were a nod in the direction of the rooftop playgrounds of Le Corbusier's *unités d'habitation,* the model for so much post war council housing. The French architect's vision of healthy Marseilles children enjoying fresh air and sunshine twenty floors up had not transferred well to post industrial Britain. Health and Safety legislation had long banned any legal use of the space which had become the domain of truant teenagers, glue sniffers and drunks. The rough concrete walls, the boardmarks of the timber shuttering lovingly specified by a member of the Frampton Architects Department (closed down by Maggie Thatcher in the 1980s), were now covered in graffiti.

The photographer set down his tripod amongst the discarded plastic bags and needles and looked down on the Games site. The cloud was patchy and he prepared for long waits for sun between shots. From twenty three floors up he could see each of the main buildings – the powerful shapes of the Swimming Complex filled the foreground; from La Touche's bird's eye view the oval plan of the stadium could be understood against its severe, almost classical façade, while the cuboid volumes of the Media Centre created a solid backdrop to the composition. He took a number of wide-angle shots that showed the site in its Frampton context – they were informative but unexciting. He changed to a longer lens and adjusted the focus. The foreshortening of the image accentuated the geometric forms of the buildings. As he watched the monitor screen on the back of the Nikon the clouds moved away and the sun threw the three structures into sharp chiaroscuro and, to La Touche's delight, highlighted the Palladian façade of Frampton Hall at the end of the valley, which, through the flattening effects of the telephoto lens, seemed to be looking over the shoulder of the new architecture.

"Gotcha!" he shouted to the view as he kept his finger on the button on continuous shooting mode. The camera whirred away as the sun moved across the screen.

La Touche emailed the photo to picture editors on papers, magazines and website around the world under the heading "Ancient and Modern". The striking juxtaposition of the Duke of Frampton's country seat, its honey limestone front spotlit by the afternoon sun, the powerful forms of the sports stadia and the sea of cranes dropping the last pieces of structure into place, appeared on the front pages of the *Asahi Shimbun, Straits Times, Washington Post, Frankfurter Zeitung* and *Le Monde* as well as a host of architectural magazines and sites.

The *Frampton Times* ran the photograph as a poster across the centre spread. The paper's leader was fulsome in its praise.

"As the buildings for the EuroGames finally take shape we can start to see how this great event will change Frampton – not just in the way the world sees us, but in the way we see ourselves. After years of decline, the loss of our major industries and debilitating unemployment, Frampton can once again hold its head high."

The majority of letters to the editor that followed were also complimentary.

A typical example was: "Whilst I am not personally a fan of modern architecture I have to write to you to say that the designs for the Games buildings are a cut above the usual rubbish that we get in Frampton. I particularly like the bold design for the Swimming Complex which to me represents what these games are all about – the building sits like a pearl on its shell, revealing to the world what a 'pearl' of a city Frampton-on-Tees is." The letter was headlined 'The Pearl of Frampton'.

In *The Gazette* Rachael Dove reviewed progress on the site. "The bold geometric forms of the Frampton buildings are reminiscent of the work of the 18th century French architect Étienne-Louis Boullée; distorted and stretched perhaps by the possibilities of modern day computer aided design and structural calculation but monumental and powerful nevertheless. The most striking reference is that of the Swimming Complex – locally nicknamed 'The Pearl' – to Boullée's 'Cenotaph to Newton', a design that Frederick Shaw would know well."

"All iconic buildings need a nickname," Ed Clutton told the Mayor. "You should use 'The Pearl' in your speeches in the future."

"What about the Stadium, don't we need a nickname for that too? We could call it 'The Oyster!' "

"No, the 'Hester Stadium' is perfect. Even more so now Martin is paralysed. Did you see him on the news the other day? It's amazing what he's able to do with that wheelchair. You'll be able to see for yourself next week – he's coming to the topping out ceremony. It's all going to be a bit embarrassing with Harry Jamb there as well."

***

Frederick Shaw had made up his mind. Carlos de Souza, his senior designer, had to go. He was acting very strangely in the office with frequent emotional outbursts, and was definitely getting too big for his boots.

Ever since Carlos's outburst in Venice, Freddie had noticed how the South American was increasingly claiming authorship for a number of buildings designed in the Shaw office; the Swimming Complex – or 'The Pearl' as everyone was now calling it – in particular. It was never to his face, but reported conversations, comments in the architectural press and snippets of gossip confirmed to Freddie that Carlos was out to steal his thunder.

Architecture was a team game he was keen to tell clients, it took a wide range of skills to design a major building, but Freddie led his team from the front. He was the face of the practice, he formed its philosophy and he monitored the design of every project. Nothing left the office without his sign off. It was often a frustrating process for the design team. Freddie would be away for weeks and then turn up in the studio and change everything.

The most frustrating bit was that he was normally right. Team leaders would be called into the office at weekends when Freddie would painstakingly go through the drawings on a scheme, marking them with his distinctive green Pentel. He would sketch the changes that he expected to be done on the side of the drawing – he never used a computer to design, he didn't know how to anymore, the technology had become too sophisticated. Anyway, he didn't need to, he had an office full of people who could do it for him, who could turn *his* vision into the perspectives, plans, sections, calculations and schedules that would allow others to turn them into reality.

All the drawings for The Pearl were complete and the team who had worked on it were twiddling their thumbs; there were a few queries from Joe Porley, but most of their work was done. They needed another project.

"There's not a lot of work in the UK at the moment" Tariq said "and the current downturn is likely to last a few years. We've been lucky to have the Games to keep us going. We've got to concentrate more on our overseas offices – Abu Dhabi and Shanghai in particular."

"We could transfer The Pearl team to Shanghai to work on the Ho towers project. Wallace Ho tells me we'll get the go ahead on that soon. But I'm not sending Carlos – I want you to get rid of him."

"Blimey. That's going to be tricky. On what grounds?"

"I don't care what grounds. Just sort it out. I'm in China next week with Wallace. Do it then."

***

"You cannot be serious!" Carlos responded in disbelief when Tariq told him the news.

"With our falling workload we've got to make cuts and we've got more senior designers than we can find work for."

"It's nothing to do with that and you know it Tariq! Freddie feels threatened. They are my designs that are making the name for the practice. I designed The Pearl. Before I joined the practice all the work was boring, boring, boring! After I came it all changed!"

Carlos knew that Freddie had been freaking out over his outburst in Venice and his claims of authorship, but he had never dreamed he would be fired.

"He needs me! Without me, Freddie wouldn't know how to do that sort of stuff."

Tariq too knew how important Carlos had been to the development of the design philosophy of the firm, but he felt that the ideas were well embedded amongst the design teams by now, the more sensuous architecture that he had brought to Frederick Shaw and Partners was now part of the firm's DNA.

"I'll sue you, Tariq. I can prove that The Pearl design is mine! I showed Freddie my final year thesis at my interview. The Frampton building is based on my student project and I'll prove it!"

"I'm sure we can agree on a reasonable settlement, Carlos, and my advice would be to take it. You won't get anywhere on the copyright issue. This sort of thing happens all the time." He handed Carlos his P45.

"I'm going to speak to a lawyer. You haven't heard the last of this! Freddie is such an ungrateful arrogant bastard. I'm going to get him!" he shouted and stormed out of the office.

***

One Saturday morning Harry was out shopping in Borough Market when he caught sight of Amelia through the crowds. The early morning sun filtered through the green painted filigree Victorian iron roof; Farmer Sharp's stall was piled high with joints of Herdwick mutton.

"Amelia!" Harry called, and she looked round. She was undoubtably pleased to see her father, but she looked worried.

"Daddy! What are you doing here?" She kissed him on the cheek. Where were the hugs he expected?

"The same as you probably," he answered.

The tall youth standing beside Amelia looked at the ground as though eye contact would draw attention to his presence.

"You remember Ben Shaw, Daddy. I've been meaning to tell you for ages, but I just couldn't do it. I didn't know what you'd say" she blurted. "We're living together and we want to get married." Ever since they started seeing each other after she had bumped into Ben at the Siena Palio, the couple had worried about their parents' reaction to their relationship. While Amelia thought Harry could come to terms with it, Ben knew that his mother would not.

"Let's go and have a bit of breakfast at Roast," Harry volunteered and led the way to the elegant wrought iron restaurant building which had once sat next to the Royal Opera House in Covent Garden, but after that building had been refurbished, unwanted bits of the structure had been moved to Borough and now sat there as though it had always been thus.

He ordered coffee and toasted cottage loaf all round – no one had the appetite for a 'Full Borough Breakfast'. Harry needed a bit of time to think.

Since their student days, his and Freddie's life had been so intertwined that there seemed a bizarre inevitability about Amelia's and Ben's relationship. Their successes and their failures spiralled through their professional lives – when they pitched for jobs the success of one was failure to the other – that there was something almost fraternal about their fighting. Deep down Harry hoped that one day the barriers that divided them would dissolve – but he still seethed when he remembered Freddie's rejection of his proffered hand in the square in Siena.

"I went to stay with Mummy in Marrakech the other day."

"How is she?"

"Pretty depressed and miserable. She can't face coming back to London. She's thinking of moving to Tuscany; Grandpa's going to buy her a house in Lucca. Why don't you go and see her? She feels so guilty."

"And so she should."

He had not gotten over Eleanor's affair with Hester and felt little sympathy over her shocking departure. He had no desire to alleviate her feelings of guilt. He changed the subject.

"Anyway, congratulations! I don't have a problem with you two getting together. But I think you will find your father and mother will be more difficult to convince, Ben."

209

"I know. But he's abroad a lot at the moment. The firm's starting work on a big project in Shanghai."

"Well he should be working on our 'two-man' Institute of Art Exhibition, it's only six months away and we haven't decided on what we're putting in it yet. It doesn't help that we don't speak to each other. It's a crazy situation. Somehow we're going to have to sort it out!"

***

"I would not advise suing Frederick Shaw and Partners over the copyright of the Swimming Complex, Mr de Souza" said John Bridges of Binghams, the intellectual property lawyers. "It's always hard to prove, and anyway you have been working as part of the team designing the 'purloined' building. It could cost a lot of money – look at the case of Pearce vs Koolhaas. That totted up costs of over three quarters of a million pounds. It was also a case where a student project was allegedly copied – in this case the design of a completed building in Holland. He was unsuccessful. Yale architecture student Thomas Shine didn't have much success when he tried to sue Skidmore Owings and Merrill over a design for the Freedom Tower in New York. He claimed that the architect David Childs had seen his design during a student jury at the school."

"But they are building a design that was done by me!" Carlos was becoming very agitated. "I don't get any recognition. All I got was a salary, and a small one at that!"

"I'm sorry Mr de Souza, but as an employee of Frederick Shaw and Partners your contract did not include any other payments. In my view the firm has already been very generous. If I were you I would drop it."

The haunted figure that sat in front of the lawyer was a shadow of the designer who had so confidently fought his way through the presentations, the design and construction of The Pearl. His once tanned skin was now pale, his hair lank and unwashed and clothes crumpled and dirty; his red-lined eyes only came alive when he discussed the building that had been the focus of his life for the past five years.

"You don't understand what that building means to me. Every column, every beam, every bolt is etched in my brain. I worked seven days a week to make sure it was perfect. I fought the philistine planners and project managers to protect its quality. And now it has all been taken away from me."

"I would suggest it's best to put this behind you. The settlement you received from Shaw's is very generous."

John Bridges ushered the architect from his office and watched as he walked out into the busy street. He frowned. "I hope he doesn't do anything stupid," he said to the receptionist "that's a guy who looks like he's close to breaking point."

Chapter 16

 As the buildings neared completion, Ed Clutton organised regular tours of the Games site for sponsors, VIPs, press and the local community. It was never easy; security on the site became tighter and tighter and it took time to get groups past the gate. There was always someone who hadn't read their invitations and failed to turn up with photographic I.D. The site was still busy even as Jonny Spon's later scheduled Temporary Pavilions –ticket booths, ice cream kiosks and temporary hospitality tents – were being installed.

The EuroGames Commission, led by the EU Minister of Sport, visited Frampton to check on progress. The smiling Minister was photographed in the centre of the Stadium shaking hands with Mayor Jarvis, the primary colours of the Ecoplastic seats providing an eye-catching background.

"Zis will be the best EU Games ever." The Minister's progress up the political ladder depended on it.

The Mayor and the Minister were gratified at the response the Games complex was receiving from visitors and press. The early scares about costs and time had proved unfounded, so now the debate turned on how good the buildings really were. How did they compare to Munich, Paris, and Milan? Journalists drafted in by their editors to dig up dirt were frustrated and they inevitably ended up at Frampton Hall where the Duke was always good for a negative quote.

Photographs of the grumpy aristocrat leaning on his balcony wall looking out towards the city whose name he bore appeared in newspapers around the world. In the background the recognisable forms of the three showcase sporting buildings created a composition which was having just the sort of impact on international awareness that Jarvis had dreamed of.

"You've got to see Frampton not as a place but a brand!" Jason Vent told him.. Today, when people think 'Frampton-on-Tees' we want them to think of winning, of success, or a modern city with great buildings and great places . . . not a place associated with heavy industry, belching out smoke and leaving a layer grime."

So, for bored journalists the stories started to revolve round the conflicts and competition between the architects. Both Harry and Freddie were starting to make regular, but separate, appearances on TV and radio chat shows. They would be called up for a comment by the BBC's *Today* programme if there were an architectural or environmental slot to fill. Preparations for the Institute of Art Exhibition were well under way and the show was expected to be one of the highiights of the cultural calendar. Both the Stadium and The Pearl were on the shortlist for that year's prestigious Frazer Prize. They became fair game.

The Gazette managed to track down Eleanor in Tuscany and ran a double page interview about her, Harry and Hester. Other papers ran stories from former members of staff from the practices and highlighted the tension between the two men.

The irony of Harry and the Hester Stadium was not lost on commentators. "Harry Jamb's testament to the man who stole his wife" is how Bert Field described the building in *The New York Times*. But the real bombshell came when *The Gazette* ran an interview with Carlos de Souza. The editor had asked Rachael Dove to write the piece, but she refused. "The guy's a paranoid nut case," she told the editor. So the story was given to the news desk to piece together.

Nut case or not, Carlos made the headlines. Next to "Architect stole my designs" were photos of Carlos holding up drawings of his student scheme which, in broad outline had recognisable similarities to The Pearl. Freddie was furious but he was also shocked by the photos of his former associate. His face was thin and emaciated, his once wavy oiled hair was now long and lank, the winning smile now twisted into a despairing grimace. Carlos was clearly going through some sort of mental breakdown.

"Bookies offer joint odds on Jamb and Shaw to win Frazer Prize" ran the headline in the *Building News*. "Bookmakers have named Frederick Shaw and Partners' 'Pearl' Swimming Complex and Jamb Associates' Hester Stadium as 7/2 favourites to win this year's Frazer Prize. The announcement of the winner of British architecture's top prize will be made by artist Sophie Senior at a gala dinner to be held in the Gothic splendour of Giles Gilbert Scott's Frampton City Hall."

Elsewhere the paper's gossip column added to the tensions. "The live TV cameras will be focused on the faces of Harry Jamb and Freddie Shaw when the Frazer Prize announcement is made in Frampton. The former partners, whose acrimonious 'divorce' has meant the two have not spoken for over a decade, will surely be attempting to disguise their divisions as their lives are inexorably drawn together once again. Not only is their joint Exhibition 'Divergent Paths' to take place next year at the Institute of Art, but the two will be in the forefront of the promotion of the Frampton Games in June. In the biggest architectural needle match since Street and Gilbert Scott battled it out over the Royal Courts of Justice, Frazer Prize organisers are praying that there are no punch ups between the two camps when the results are announced."

***

"I'm sick of all these computer visualisations of my buildings." Sid Dixon complained to Jason Vent as they discussed the sales promotion of The Infini T Tower. "They end up making everything look the same. I want something different; something nobody has done before; something classier. But nothing cheesy."

"I need a better brief than that," Jason responded, "why don't you show me the sort of thing you have in mind?" Jason flicked through a pile of books sitting on the developer's desk. Sid kept a selection of architectural monographs in full view to impress visitors. It reinforced his design credentials. Jason picked up a new book that had been sent to Sid that morning: *Historic Frampton-on-Tees – A Guide to the Host City of the EuroGames* by John Veduty. The book was a spectacular collection of full plate photos of Frampton's best buildings. Shot in bright sunlight, the soft stones and the red terracotta stood out against clear blue skies. Intricate pencil sketches of details of the buildings – classical capital, gothic ogee arches and carved pediments – were interspersed with the four colour images.

"There! That's the sort of thing!" Sid grabbed the Veduty book and pointed to a drawing. "Get the artist to meet up with Amanda and see what they can come up with."

Jason looked to the front of the book for the credits.

"Hey! They're by Petronella Conway! The Duke of Frampton's daughter!"

"Even better. Get her to go and see Amanda to sort out the best views to use."

***

The Grand Hall in the Civic Centre was a sea of circular tables; above the dinner settings, huge Victorian chandeliers sparkled as the Channel 4 TV crew adjusted their powerful lamps. Along the maroon damask walls former Mayors of Frampton looked down as Rachael Dove – who was due to introduce the Frazer Prize winner – rehearsed her entrance onto the stage. She was dwarfed by the giant screen behind her, suspended from the dark oak hammer beam roof onto which were projected images of the shortlisted buildings. There were eight selected projects, but it was generally felt that none of the others stood a chance. It was a two horse race between Harry Jamb and Frederick Shaw.

The guests gathered in the reception area where waistcoated waiters sporting colourful badges inscribed 'EU Games – Frampton' plied them with champagne. Mayor Jarvis worked the room, moving from group to group as though it was his party. Partners and staff of hopeful practices, engineers, cost consultants, clients and journalists discussed who they thought the winners would be. Freddie's supporters suggested that the jury was biased in favour of Harry; there were rumours that the judges couldn't make up their minds between Jamb and Shaw and therefore were going to select a less controversial building. They looked around the room; where was Frederick Shaw?

"He probably won't turn up if thinks he hasn't won" said Sir Richard Frank to Sid Dixon as the toastmaster announced that dinner was served.

Freddie and Harry had both booked two tables for members of the teams involved with their buildings. The table planners had placed the two parties on either side of the hall. In between was the Frampton table with Mayor Jarvis and Ed Clutton who had invited Joe Porley and Sir Nigel Frith as their guests. Sid Dixon had taken a table too. His wife Veronica was with her new toyboy, the 24 year old artist Warwick Kent; Amanda Stone was sitting next to Petronella Conway – the two had become inseparable since the Duke's daughter had started working on a series of drawings of The Infini T Tower – while Sid entertained Emily Rutland, the residential property correspondent of *The Gazette*.

"Petronella's done these great drawing of The Infini T Tower. I'll give you an exclusive on them. . ." Sid's voice was drowned out as the thumping beat of the intro music announced the start of the awards ceremony. The lights went down and a spot picked out Rachael Dove who teetered onto the stage. Sid marvelled at her sleek figure. In the glare, the clinging black jersey dress was unforgiving, but he could find no fault. His mind wandered back to the night in The Carlton at Cannes. Perhaps it was time for a return match. Freddie was having similar thoughts, as was his guest of honour, Edmund Ho.

"Mayor, ladies and gentlemen, I'm Rachael Dove and it gives me great pleasure to host the announcement of the country's most important architectural award – the Frazer Prize – sponsored by Draw Cad Computing Systems, Marsoni Furniture and Ecoplastics Ltd."

There were wild cheers at one table at the mention of Ecoplastics. Sam Spurling had splashed out on one for his sales staff in recognition of a record trading year, and the team were determined to enjoy the party.

"We have come to Frampton-on-Tees to celebrate this premier architectural prize because the buildings for these EuroGames are some of the most significant erections. . . " Rachael paused as the Ecoplastics team hooted at her choice of words "of the decade. And we will see shortly whether one of the two major buildings designed for the Games will win the Frazer Prize this year. I would now like to invite Sophie Senior to the stage to announce the winner.

The celebrity artist walked unsteadily towards the steps of the stage as the thumping royalty-free muzak blasted out again.

Sophie Senior, the radical video artist and winner of that year's Turner Prize, had been invited onto the Frazer Jury to provide the layperson's view, although her ideas about architecture were hardly those of the man in the street. Neither were they those of the other members of the jury and Senior had refused to accept the majority vote. She was not in a good mood. She stumbled alarmingly as she made her way onto the stage.

Senior walked to the microphone and Rachael handed her a large black envelope.

"The winner. . . of the Frazer Prize is . . ." she struggled with the envelope ". . . oh bugger it's upside down!. . . got it!" she pulled out a card, turned it the right way up and read "The Hester Stadium by Henry Jamb Associates!!"

Harry's team leapt to their feet as one, hugging each other, shaking hands, doing high fives. Harry signalled to the group to join him as he walked between the crowded tables towards the stage. As he passed the Frampton party, Mayor Jarvis leapt up and enthusiastically shook Harry's hand.

On the other side of the room the Shaw group sat in stunned silence. The other diners seemed more interested in the reaction of the loser than the winner. Where was Freddie? He hadn't sat down to dinner. Had he been tipped off that he wasn't going to win? Or was he waiting in the wings just in case?

A beaming Harry stood with Jenny in front of the microphones, surrounded by his Hester Stadium design team.

"I'd just like to thank all those involved in the design of this building for their brilliant work, and to the city of Frampton-on-Tees for the opportunity to produce a building of this quality." He looked over to the Shaw table, "and I'd like to congratulate the other shortlisted teams. Selecting one out of such a group is a hard task – they are all winners!" And he raised the Frazer Prize plaque – which would be fixed on the front of the completed building – above his head. Harry soaked up the applause and the cheers as Jenny held onto him and kissed him hard on the cheek.

After the Frazer Prize announcement Freddie kept a low profile. Sheranie Philips was chasing him for the final layouts of his part of the Gallery in the Institute of Art Exhibition.

"We've only got three weeks to go and I can't get hold of him!" she complained to Exhibitions Committee Chairman Sir Richard Frank at the monthly meeting.

"But you've all been working on this for months – the plans should have been fixed weeks ago! What's going on?"

"Carlos de Souza had been our main point of contact, but he's no longer there. Tariq Ali has just told me that Freddie wants to make changes and will do them when he returns form China. He says not to worry, Freddie often does this and they'll make sure it's OK on the day."

"He's sailing far too close to the wind for my liking," grumbled Sir Richard, but there was little he or Sheranie could do but await Freddie's return.

Freddie redesigned the layout of his section of the Exhibition with two weeks to spare and the contractors worked through the weekends to install the giant models and huge blow up images. Having virtually ignored Sheranie for the past six months, Freddie became totally involved in the preparations and to the curator's dismay continued to change the display.

"You lost out to Harry Jamb over the Frazer Prize but you'd better make sure you don't come second best in the Institute of Art show." Harriet had urged.

Freddie had been keeping an eye on the progress of the installations in Harry's gallery and decided that he needed to increase the size of his model of The Pearl.

"I need something that seems to fill the space," he instructed the worried model maker who would normally need several months to make a model of that scale. "I don't want a lot of detail – something that highlights the geometric form."

***

The night before the press view of the show Harry and Sheranie gave a final inspection of his room.

"It's looking great, Sheranie!" he approved, "I'll see you in the morning" as he pulled the grand gallery doors shut and made his way home.

Meanwhile, in the introductory area Jason Vent was overseeing some last minute touches to the graphics. A contractor was rubbing down huge cut out lettering onto the gallery walls – on one side it said 'Harry Jamb Associates', on the other 'Frederick Shaw and Partners'.

It was midnight and Jason was keen to get home and get a bit of sleep before the Press Conference at 11.00 the next morning. All he was waiting for was the large-scale model that Freddie had decided to have built at the last minute. The model makers had rung to say the lorry was on its way. The contractors were sitting around on the floor or outside smoking as they waited for the last piece of the jigsaw to arrive.

"They'll have to come down!" Jason turned around to see Freddie pointing to the names of the firms which he had spent the whole evening carefully positioning. "Harry Jamb's name is almost twice the size of mine!"

"But they're the same width" Jason responded "you've got more characters in your name so the height comes out smaller. It's designed to fit with the text underneath. I can't change it."

"Why don't you put it here?!" Freddie said crossly, pointing to a piece of wall that didn't seem to have anything on it at all. Jason, tired after a long day and frustrated at this last minute interference, had had enough.

"I'm not going to change it. The design of this section is my responsibility and it stays as it is!"

Jason's intricate design had attempted to merge the contrasting styles of the two architects with a series of giant diagonal shapes crashing into each other. He had placed models at disturbing angles and suspended projection panels from the gallery's vaulted roof. He had thought carefully about the location and impact of every piece of the composition. The problem with these bloody architects, he thought, is that they think they can design everything. Why don't they stick to buildings?

"If you don't change it I will instruct the driver to take The Pearl model away right now," came Freddie's retort. "I don't think the Institute would be very pleased to have a big gap in the show on the Press Day, do you?"

Jason was taken aback. Was this a massive bluff? Or was Freddie capable of being this bloody-minded having lost out to Harry Jamb for the Fraser Prize? Jason chose discretion rather than valour.

"I'm going to call Sheranie" and he punched his mobile. looking nervously at the clock.

"It's two in the morning!" protested the bleary eyed curator as she arrived back at the Institute to sort out her squabbling exhibitors. "I can't believe this is happening!"

Jason and Freddie argued their case, each remaining as intransigent as the other. Sheranie weighed up the odds. To offend Jason would be bad but not catastrophic. He'd cause a flurry and ring the gossip

220

columns but she'd still have a show. But a show with a big hole in the middle was a different matter. It couldn't happen. Anyway, she had had enough of the ongoing bickering between the two architects, the indecision and the clash of egos.

"Take them both down," she said curtly, directing her comments at the two contractors who had been watching the arguments with the patient boredom of those who are used to the clashes and changes of mind endemic to their creative clients. "There's no time to have new graphics done before tomorrow morning," she added quickly to head off Jason's nascent protests.

As the two operatives started to pull down the work they had spent half the day carefully positioning, Sheranie turned on her heels and walked out of the gallery without a word to Freddie or Jason. She didn't want to give them an excuse to continue the debate and she was confident that there was no way that Freddie, having stamped his foot and won a pyrrhic victory, would now carry out his threat and exclude the centrepiece of his display.

***

There must be a couple of hundred journalists here, thought Harry, as he looked out over the room and waited for Sir Richard Frank to open the Press Conference. A melée of TV cameramen and photographers jostled each other at the side of the room while gnarled hacks looking for a gossip story, stubbled feature writers from *Blueprint* and *Icon*, incredibly stylish girls from *Vogue* and *Elle Deco*, seen-it-all critics from the nationals and a delegation of foreign correspondents sat with their pads and press packs on their knees, pens at the ready. In the front row sat the team from Loftus Global PR who were there to ensure maximum coverage for Frederick Shaw and Partners. Above the muted conversation, the banging of the contractors, still adding the finishing touches to Freddie's model, advertised the just-in-time strategies that had prevailed on the whole project.

Harry was sitting at one end of a long, green baize-covered table raised on a dais. At the other end sat Freddie Shaw. Sheranie Philips and Sir Richard Frank separated the two.

Sir Richard cleared his throat and pulled the microphone towards him. "Good morning ladies and gentlemen and welcome to this important exhibition which displays the work of two of the country's leading architects. We are sure you will be excited to see their projects in a comparative display which focuses on designs for the Frampton Games. The undoubted international interest in the event and the images portrayed by their architecture will ensure the significance of this show both in terms of placing the Frampton Masterplan in a specific modernist context but also in progressing the tectonic debate." Frank continued on in this vein for some time until, as the writers stopped taking notes, Sheranie took the opportunity of a brief pause to butt in:

"I think we should move on to questions, Sir Richard – I'm sure everyone is dying to get in and see the show."

The man from *The Daily Mail's* hand shot up.

"There have been widely circulated rumours of difficult relations between the two architects," he directed the question to Sheranie, " that they haven't spoken to each other during the preparation of the exhibition. Is that true?"

"Inevitably the media are interested in personalities," Sheranie gave her carefully planned reply to the predictable question "but we have worked very successfully with the professional teams from both of the offices. The installation has been brilliantly coordinated by Jason Vent who has acted as go between so that there have been no greater difficulties on this project than one would expect with a major exhibition of this scale. I don't know if either of the architects has anything to add," she looked towards Harry and then to Freddie – both architects gave a brief shake of the head.

"Harry, has Martin Hester visited the Stadium that he has become so closely associated with yet? What does he think of it?"

Harry frowned. The 'H' word was becoming increasingly difficult to avoid. He had instructed all his drawings, photo captions and press releases to be labelled 'The Frampton Stadium', to avoid using the name of the man who had made a cuckold out of him, but as the building entered the public consciousness he realised he was fighting an unwinnable war.

"Yes, of course he has," Harry tried to maintain an upbeat tone to his voice "and he has said that the disabled access is the best he has come across in any building of this scale."

"And has your wife seen the building?" the reporter persisted with a smirk.

"I think we should move on to another question," Sheranie said sternly "Yes?" and she pointed to one of the many waving hands.

"William Hyatt from *The Telegraph*." A young man in a tweed suit and waistcoat announced languidly "The Duke of Frampton has described the buildings as 'abominable' and out of context in the city. How do you respond to that?"

"The Duke knows little about architecture," Freddie immediately launched into an attack. He had become fed up with the Duke's sniping but also knew that a robust response would make the headlines. "He's always talking about a battle of the styles, but architecture evolves, it responds to changes in society – changes towards equality and freedom that I guess the Duke finds that hard to accept. A reproduction of Rome's Coliseum in Frampton might keep the Duke happy but would make a laughing stock of modern Britain."

After half an hour of questions Sheranie announced it was time to tour the show. As the uniformed security guards pushed open the grand doors to the galleries, the model makers, who had been putting finishing touches to Freddie's giant model, squeezed their way out through the throng of eager critics.

"Wow!" said the girl from *Wallpaper*. She had expected a sedate arrangement of models and drawings but Jason Vent's crashing diagonals and bright colours gave the display a vitality and excitement that had an immediate impact on the visitors. "Jason, the idea of setting the models against that big blank wall in the entrance is brilliant!"

"Thank you darling," Jason replied, still smarting from the previous night's argument with Freddie but unwilling to deny the serendipitous nature of the composition.

Sheranie had arranged a special tour for the most important writers and critics – the half dozen who helped form the opinion of the rest whose comments would help make the 'Divergent Paths' show a success for the Institute and make or break reputations.

"We've got just half an hour for the tour so it's essential we keep to time, after this we've got TV interviews and the photocalls, so there's no flexibility in the schedule," she instructed Freddie's PR team.

John Earnest from the *Financial Times*, Fred Blom from the *New York Times*, Terry Slight from *The Independent*, Tim Tinker from *The Times*, Ellen Pelly from *The Guardian* and Rachael Dove from *The Gazette* gathered round Freddie as he explained the ideas behind his display. In his signature black suit and white collarless shirt the architect made a striking figure, picked out by the powerful Erco display lighting as he stood in front of the giant model of The Pearl, the curve of the spherical structure creating a huge halo to his fine chiseled features. The dark jacket highlighted his slim frame against the pale abstract backdrop.

"I have placed this great model on the axis of the gallery against the end wall so that the visitor sees it as they first enter the gallery and are drawn towards it as they make their way through the other exhibits."

He led the group on through the space, shepherded by the team from Loftus Global PR, stopping at each of his exhibits to describe in detail why he had selected it and what its significance was. After thirteen minutes of talking he was hardly halfway up the gallery.

"A couple more minutes, Freddie, and then we must move on," Sheranie said quietly. Freddie gave no response.

After 15 minutes Sheranie's interventions became louder and more urgent; "The group really must go to meet Harry Jamb now.".

"Nearly finished" Freddie replied but continued at his own pace.

"We must now move to the other gallery," an exasperated Sheranie announced to the group as her watch told her that Harry would have to squeeze his tour into ten minutes.

Freddie began walking slowly to the exit of his gallery, talking to the writers as they went. As the hacks were about to leave, the team from Loftus handed out Freddie Shaw and Partners' own Press Release and a copy of the firm's book of their collected works *Form and Place* with a glowing introduction by *The Times's* Tim Tinker.

Sheranie looked at her watch again.and led the party across the link between the galleries to where an agitated Harry was standing, with Jenny in the background. "I'm sorry Harry, you've only got five minutes."

"That's impossible! I can't do it that fast. Bloody Freddie – he did that on purpose!" he exclaimed quietly and unnoticed by the gaggle of critics.

"I'm sorry we have so little time," Harry gathered his wits quickly to address the select journalists, "but I'm sure you can gather what information you need from the work on display – which I believe speaks for itself. We believe in beautiful buildings that deliver a spiritual engagement within and a visceral response without. . . as opposed to other architects," he added pointedly looking briefly towards Freddie's big white model "who feel the need to show off or use cheap tricks to attract attention. Thank you and enjoy the show." He smiled as enthusiastically as he could. The BBC researcher pulled him across to the camera set up in front of the Hester Stadium model.

The interview went off without incident and Harry went over to Sheranie.

"So now what?"

"*The Times's* photographer needs to shoot you both," said Sheranie, " he's over in the other gallery."

The bearded figure in jeans and safari jacket with lots of pockets was standing talking to Freddie. Sheranie and Harry walked up to the group and Sheranie introduced the photographer to Harry. Over the morning Harry and Freddie had still not exchanged one word. They had somehow managed to stand together without visibly recognizing the presence of the other. Onlookers unaware of the gulf that still separated the two would have noticed little amiss.

"I'd like you to stand over here," instructed the bearded snapper "nice and close together so that I've got the big model in the back ground, it creates a brilliant frame."

Freddie felt vindicated in his decision to add in the big white model of The Pearl. He could see from the way that all the photographers were snapping away that his composition was the one that would make it into the papers. He knew that picture editors would love the powerful graphic shape created by its abstract form and chiaroscuro lighting.

"I'm not bloody doing that," Harry protested: "Why on earth would I want to be photographed 'framed' by a Freddie Shaw building! You must be joking!"

"Well mate, either you want your picture in *The Times* or not.," quipped the irritated photographer, more used to directing grateful minor celebs than being told what to shoot by a couple of self-important tossers.

"Well, not like this actually." replied Harry as he strode off to the relative familiarity of his own space.

The stunned photographer turned to Sheranie: "My instructions are to shoot them both together, Sher. Sorry but if one's not playing ball I'm buggering off."

The team from Loftus PR high fived as they looked through the press cuttings from the 'Divergent Paths' private view. Most of the papers had used a picture of Freddie with the profile of The Pearl in the background. All the serious reviews were full of quotes from Freddie. Harry's 'The architecture speaks for itself' was hardly noticed.

Chapter 17

As the EuroGames drew near, the excitement in Frampton was palpable. Public spaces were spruced up, hotels completed their refurbishments – generously funded by grants from the European Union, banners decorated with Jason's colourful logo were fixed to lamp posts throughout the city, shops gave their window display a sporting theme, the Black Cat club re-equipped its dungeon and the Bishop of Frampton-on-Tees warned against the dangers of increased prostitution. Against this flurry of human activity, the giant forms of the Hester Stadium and The Pearl competed with the cathedral for domination of the city skyline.

For months the schoolchildren of Frampton and surrounding areas had been practising for their appearance at the Opening Ceremony. Jason's brief for the spectacular was to create a televisual event – expected to be watched by 1 billion viewers – that reflected the "rich heritage of Frampton-on-Tees as well as its vibrant future".

John Veduty helped Jason's team with the research into the city's history.

"St Benedict came here in the seventh century and thought about building a monastery here before he settled on Jarrow," Veduty had reported "but you won't be able to use him. He doesn't fit in with the council's diversity policies! The Vikings ravaged the area in the 850s but the Danes won't like it if you include that, and the Framptonians were a pain the neck for William the Conqueror until the massacre of 1069 and that's certainly not a feelgood story! But I did find out about a skirmish between Cromwell's troops and the Royalists in 1643 that happened close to the site of the Games. The result was inconclusive, so no one can complain if you put that in. Roundhead's versus Cavaliers – it's a classic confrontation – ascetics versus romantics, minimalists vs. post modernists, Stadium versus The Pearl, Harry Jamb versus Frederick Shaw."

A month before the Games were due to open, and before the security lock-down began, Jason organised a dress rehearsal for the Opening Ceremony and invited the teams that had been involved with the buildings to watch.

Harry and Jenny sat up in the very top of the Stadium to watch the Frampton school kids with helmets and pikestaffs race across the stadium floor. Massed ceilidh drummers pounded out a beat based on the pulses of athletes. Every clog dancer in the region had been recruited to respond – their amplified clacking filling the empty amphitheatre, a local pop star who Harry didn't recognise sang a song about winning. The long lines of flag wavers, their bright colours fluttering across the ground before being flung high into the air, brought back memories of Siena some four years earlier. Harry tightened his grip on Jenny's hand. The days of long family lunches in the Tuscan sunshine were over and seemed a lifetime away. Much had changed. Harry was now in the architectural big league, Amelia and Tom seemed to be happy, living together with their new baby, and he was comfortable in his relationship with Jenny. But Eleanor's infidelity still hurt and he felt a pang every time he heard someone mention the name of his building.

"Welcome to the magnificent Hester Stadium!" Jason stood in the centre of the circular space, a tiny figure picked out by a tracking spotlights, while his lean features filled the huge screens at either end of the Stadium. "That was fantastic! We can't do it now, but the next part of the ceremony will be a huge firework display." Jason had based his concept on the flying molten metal that exploded from the city's Bessemer converters when Frampton-on-Tees was the centre of the steelworks industry. "Then a local athlete, who is being selected through a public ballot will carry the EU baton into the Stadium. We won't know who that athlete is until he appears on the night – it's being kept a secret!"

The spotlights went out and the 500 piece Massed Brass Mill Band struck up with Wilcocks's *The Champions*. As the chiming sound of the cornets and euphoniums filled the stadium, the Roundheads and Cavaliers threw off their costumes to reveal skin-tight leotards each one covered with a thousand sparkling LEDs. The school children joined hands to create a kilometre-long conga.

"The children are the future of the city," Jason explained to Roger Chase the editor of the *Frampton Times* "their digitally controlled costumes signify the new technologies that Frampton seeks to attract, and they dance in unison in contrast to the battles and conflicts of the heavy industrial past. The whole event will be relayed to giant screens in The Pearl which will be reserved for local people, so that everyone will be able to be a part of the event."

Freddie left the rehearsal early on and walked across the empty site towards The Pearl. The mud, the swinging cranes, the flashing lights of the dumper trucks, the clatter of jackhammers and flash of the welders had gone. He walked into the huge circular entrances, their concrete surfaces textured to give a rippling, water-like effect.

"Good evening Mr Shaw." The security guard had been working on the Games since construction first started and recognised Freddie from his previous site visits. "That Mr de Souza has left you this package, he said you would be coming here to take a look this evening. He didn't look well at all. He's changed a lot. At first I thought he was a down-and-out. But he said you'd be needing these."

"Thanks." Freddie took the package with a frown. What could Carlos be up to? The only things he was expecting from Carlos were lawyers' letters. The lumpy package he held in his hands certainly held more than that.

He walked up into The Pearl's great domed space and sat down in one of the poolside seats. The complex of curved beams, hung with Jason's now familiar flags, created a spectacular backdrop to the brightly coloured seats, the iconic form of the 15 metre high diving tower and the mirror-smooth pool. It was the first time he had been to the building since it had been finished. The space was so familiar, he had seen it in his mind's eye in sketches, in plans and sections, in models and photo-realistic computer generated images but there was no substitute for the real thing. It was rather good, he thought to himself. The 50,000-seat space was big, but it felt quite intimate. Filled with people it would generate the sort of atmosphere that feeds the buzz and excitement of competitive sport.

Images of the LED leotarded kids from the rehearsal swirled across the giant screens suspended above the pool as Freddie studied the padded envelope on his lap, his name written with bold marker pen in Carlos's unmistakably florid script. He pulled back the little red tag and peered into the opening. . ..

Freddie went cold and felt sick to the pit of his stomach. Inside the package were two large bolts, and a note: "I have removed these two bolts from a key part of the structure of the dome that was designed by me. Without them the banks of seating when they are full of people will collapse. Since you claim it is your building you will know where they came from." Carlos knew very well that Freddie had had virtually no contact with the detailed design or the construction of the building and wouldn't have a clue where the bolts come from. "I will tell you where I took them from if you publicly announce that The Pearl was designed by me, Carlos de Souza."

Freddie's head reeled. The thought of his building collapsing cut to the very core of his life's work. Every design, every decision is predicated on stability and safety. Collapse would also bring professional ruin, yet Freddie was determined not to accede to Carlos's demands.

Carlos was right to think that Freddie hadn't a clue where the bolts might be from and he didn't know how he was going to find out. The two site architects who had worked on the project were letting their flats at vast rents to visitors to the Games and had gone trekking in the Himalayas. If he contacted Joe Porley the secret would surely get out, and Freddie couldn't afford for that to happen.

"Good night Mr Shaw!" Freddie didn't even acknowledge the cheery security guard as he left the building. He was scared out of his wits. The highest profile project of his career, his launch pad to the rarefied community of global starchitects would come crumbling down – literally – unless he acted fast. The site was going into security lock down the next day and he wouldn't be able to get back onto the site however familiar he was with the security guards. The next time he could get into the building would be in the company of the crowds who could cause its collapse.

Freddie walked out into the dark night. The main lighting had been turned off and only the dim safety lights illuminated the wide boulevard that connected The Pearl to the Hester Stadium. The black shapes of the buildings were silhouetted against the cloudy sky. It was drizzling lightly. Freddie needed to look at the working drawings. He pulled his black jacket around him and quickened his pace as he walked towards the construction office which had moved from temporary site huts into a basement office beneath the Stadium.

***

"Thanks everyone – that was brilliant! See you back here in three weeks at the Official Opening Ceremony of the Frampton Games!" Jason put his hands above his head and applauded his performers.

Harry and Jenny made their way down the steps to the exit.

"I'm going to stay here for a bit," Harry said "I want to look round on my own. You take the car back to the hotel, I'll walk over when I'm finished." He handed her the car keys as she kissed him lightly on the cheek.

"See you later." she smiled. Harry was back to his old self: the Harry she remembered from the days she first knew him. Success suited him and a new, slicker wardrobe of tailored suits and handmade shirts she had selected seemed to add to his confidence and stature. Their relationship was all that she could have hoped for. Although she felt that some of Harry's architect friends rather looked down on her – "Did you know Harry's got off with his *secretary?*" she could hear them saying – now that his life was a hectic round of world trips, receptions, interviews, and presentations as well as running the practice, he needed a well organised wife. Their sex life was exciting, and with that in mind, Jenny had booked the best suite in the Frampton Arms. "This should be a great night" she thought as she turned the car out of the Stadium car park.

Vomitorium. Surely someone could have come up with a better word by now, thought Harry as he walked through the huge exit that in a few weeks time would suck in and disgorge thousands of spectators a day just as the *vomitoria* of the Coliseum in Rome had done two thousand years ago. Not much had changed in the basic layout of stadia in the intervening millennia. Except we don't kill people now, he mused – no dead gladiators in the arena and no dead spectators in the stands. The horrific events of Heysel and Hillsborough had tightened up the regulations so such buildings were safer than they'd ever been and computer simulated movement of crowds helped designers develop layouts that made sure everyone could get out in the event of a mishap. The final building was a pretty good reflection of Harry's first sketches; but the struggle of holding onto that concept through all the detailed design, the Health and Safety Regulations, the cost cutting and the political interference had been the most stressful experience of his professional life.

As he walked out onto the grand boulevard that linked the Stadium to The Pearl, Harry felt a load fall from his shoulders – for nearly five years, every day and every night, he had thought about that building, imagined it in his head, struggled to turn it into three dimensions, planned strategies to defend his design, but now he could put that behind him. He knew it was one of his best buildings and would help to boost his reputation around the world. He felt content.

He looked up to see an unmistakeable figure walking towards him. Freddie! Harry's mood instantly changed.

"Shit! The one person I really don't want to see right now" Harry thought.

If they had wanted to avoid each other it was impossible. They were two lone figures standing like chess pieces in check on the gridded paving of the park. Freddie had stopped; he was clutching a large envelope. Harry flashbacked to the time he had offered his hand to Freddie in Siena and remembered Harriet's warning glance. She had poisoned the relationship; she had hated Eleanor and encouraged Freddie to maintain their feud. But now she wasn't here, thought Harry, perhaps this time things might be different.

Freddie was halfway between the two Games buildings when he saw Harry coming out of the Stadium. He stopped. His first reaction was to walk away just as he had done for the past decade whenever his former partner hoved into view, but there was nowhere to hide. Looking down at the bag of bolts, the enormity of his predicament suddenly hit him: bow to Carlos's demands and he would be revealed as a fraud; tell Joe Porley and he would have to institute a full scale health check on the building, potentially impacting on the schedule of the Games. It was bound to get out; do nothing and, if Carlos was right, the outcome was unimaginable. Buildings don't collapse these days. It would be the end of his career. The Frampton Games would go down in history for all the wrong reasons, the aspirations of the city dashed in the tangled steel of Frederick Shaw's crumpled bleachers.

Freddie walked urgently towards the figure framed by his masterpiece.

Harry stopped in his tracks as his erstwhile partner came closer. Was it some sort of trick? A press stunt perhaps. He looked quickly around to see if there was anyone else there. The site was deserted. A chill North Sea breeze pierced his new Paul Smith jacket.

"Hullo Harry" Freddie managed a wan smile: "Can we talk? I've got a bit of a problem," and he handed him Carlos's note. Harry read it under the drizzled glare of the boulevard lights.

Freddie's discomfort was clear and his arrogance gone. Harry was his only hope – he had always been the one who understood and enjoyed the detail of his buildings. More importantly, Harry was the only one who could operate the computerised Building Information Modelling software that had been used to design The Pearl. The complex programme included all the design and technical information needed to erect the building, but Freddie had never found the time to learn how to use it, or the inclination.

Harry enjoyed using the computer and found it a really useful tool for designing – he could see his ideas in three dimensions, view them from every angle, check the way light affected them and see how the different bits of the structure all fitted together.

"I'm up shit creek Harry," said Freddie disconsolately holding up the now soggy bag of bolts. "If I can't get them back in place tonight I'm going to have to call Joe Porley, and that would be a disaster. . ."

"Why on earth should I help you Freddie? Ever since we split up you've acted like a real shit. Why don't you sort it out yourself? you've got a big enough office!"

"I'm not asking you to do it just for me! This could have a really serious impact on the Games. On your building, on Frampton, on everyone else who has worked to deliver these Games! Please, Harry, help me!" he pleaded. He hung his head in that guilty schoolboy look that Harry remembered from long ago.

"OK. Let's go to the site office." Harry took command of the situation. He was only too aware of the wider implications of any delays in the programme. "We've still got a desk and computer there. We should be able to get the drawings up and I'll have a look."

Neither architect spoke as they strode through the empty, echoing corridors, the smell of fresh paint and new carpets made Harry feel slightly nauseous. This was the basic end of the building – plain screed floors, white painted blockwork walls with open trays hanging from the ceiling carrying a myriad of wires and ducts.

Harry noted with pleasure that even in the deepest basement (which few people would visit) the block layers had done a neat job with clean and tidy pointing. His heart was pounding. He had tried to bury the hatchet with Freddie a number of times but had been painfully rejected; once Freddie didn't need him any more would he return to his same old ways? For the moment there wasn't time to speculate.

Harry placed his security pass on the lock pad and pushed open the door to the empty site office. The lights automatically flickered into life. Huge print outs of computer-generated images of The Pearl and the Stadium decorated the walls. Photos of site progress were pinned up around the various workstations; these showed the changes that had taken place as the old steelworks buildings were demolished, the ground was flattened, the foundations were dug and the structures started to emerge. There were numerous shots of Mayor Jarvis in hi-viz vest and hardhat showing round a varied cast of VIPs – a few royals, Ministers, sports personalities, TV soap stars and local community leaders. The tall tanned figure of Martin Hester appeared in many of the early images, standing behind the Mayor and providing a powerful link to the purpose of the whole endeavour – the quest for sporting excellence. In the last photo in which he appeared, Hester could be seen smiling and pointing to the huge steel beams being craned into place on the Stadium roof. After that the Mayor can be seen entertaining his guests on his own, Hester conspicuous by his absence.

"Serves you right," Harry would often say under his breath as he passed the pictures, but that night he was focused on sorting out Freddie's problems – and with that, he hoped, his longstanding feud with his former partner.

He logged on to The Pearl construction files and started flicking through the drawings, zooming in to details as the three dimensional digital model swung round the screen. He checked against the specification of the bolts and narrowed down the possible locations. He studied the engineers' notes and tried to get into Carlos's mind – where would he think the removal of a few bolts would have the maximum effect? And since he had clearly removed them that day, where could he have had relatively easy access to the structure?

"This modelling system is amazing!" Harry enthused as he spun wire diagrams of the structure around on the screen "I can see everything the contractor has done, which links right back to Carlos's original drawings. "Look here" he pointed to the junction of the diagonal steel beams that supported the banks of seats and columns that ringed the pool. "This is different to the rest of the structure. It's not the sort of thing Carlos would have done. Looks like Joe Porley's had a hand in this."

Freddie remembered the time that Tariq had agreed to changes with Joe when they were getting behind schedule.

"That's it! Carlos always hated that detail," said Freddie.

Harry zoomed in on the steelwork drawing. A set of eight bolts supported the cantilevered seating; take away four of those, add several hundred excited spectators jumping up and down and there'd be trouble. A Mexican wave could literally bring the house down.

'Well, there's around three hundred places where he could have taken the bolts from. They're each encased in fire proofing panels; hopefully we'll be able to see if they've been tampered with. We'd better get going."

Freddie and Harry walked briskly from the Stadium as fast as they could without raising the suspicions of the security teams that patrolled the otherwise empty park. They signed into The Pearl and made their way up to the spot that Harry had pinpointed on the computer. A man-sized service duct ran around the base of the beams. Harry ignored the 'Keep Out' sign and squeezed into the pitch-dark space. He switched on a torch he had picked up in the office and pointed its beam towards the steel work immediately above their heads.

"There's the joint. It'll be one those for sure." The space was tight and several times their helmets cracked noisily on the beam casing above. "Shhhhh! The place is crawling with security," Harry urged.

Each bank of seating was separated by the entrance to the stands where the duct came to an abrupt halt. The two architects scuttled across the space looking round desperately to see if they had been spotted by one of the guards. This is ridiculous, thought Harry as he pushed his way into the duct for the fourth time. Two grown men, top professionals, the architects responsible for these very buildings, acting like schoolboys. Harry's adrenalin was pumping.

With Freddie by his side it felt like those early days of the practice, when it all seemed to be fun and excitement, before business became a burden.

As the two emerged from the fifth duct, Harry started as the guttural South African accent of the security guard echoed across the cavernous space.

"Evening, Mr Shaw. Is everything all right?" the man called up from the edge of the pool.

Freddie slowed and put on his most charming manner.

"No problem at all. Just having a last look around before all the fun starts."

"Thank you Sir, good night." and the guard continued on his round.

Under the sixth bay the torch spotlighted a section of fire insulation board was hanging loose; a large spanner lay abandoned on the floor. Harry pulled back the panel and there were the empty drilled holes that were home to the errant bolts.

"Hand them to me!" Harry urged, as he reached up into the space and, one at a time, pushed the four steel pins into their holes. "They're back in! The structure hasn't moved – God we're lucky, it only needed the slightest shift and they'd never have fitted."

Harry tightened the nuts for each of the bolts, hid the spanner in the casing and pushed the dislodged fire panels back into place.

"Let's get out of here! I need a drink!"

The two architects didn't want to arouse any suspicion, so they decided to walk quietly walk back to the Frampton Arms Hotel.

No sooner had they turned the corner into the Conway Estate than they looked at each other and burst into fits of uncontrollable giggles. The release of tension and fear and the adrenalin-rush of the last few hours collapsed into warmhearted camaraderie that recalled the early days of their collaborations, the all night working, pushing the boundaries of their work and pitching to clients who had never seen anything like it.

"Thanks Harry. I owe you one." Freddie said as they walked past the tall concrete towers, their gloomy silhouettes punctured by the illuminated windows of a handful of insomniacs. The earlier rain had stopped and the pinpoints of light were reflected in the wet road. He suddenly stopped and turned to Harry. "I've been a complete prick. . . maybe this was meant to happen . . . why don't we see if we can start over again," and he put out his hand.

Harry need no further encouragement: he took his ex-partner's hand in his and shook it strongly. He could hardly speak but managed to blurt out:

"Now I really need that drink!"

The two walked in silence as they made their way into the city centre. Words weren't necessary to communicate the relief that each of them felt and any explanations might damage their fragile cease-fire.

Freddie had always been a great believer in the maxim "Never apologise, never explain" and it seemed best not to change his ways now.

He had always felt a bit foolish that he had let Harriet force him to continue the feud for so long. Her dislike of Eleanor, which hadn't been an issue since she went off with Hester, was just one of the problems she had with Harry. She had blamed Harry for the break up of the practice and feared the professional competition he represented on his own.

As they got closer to the hotel they passed groups of binge drinking girls in their micro skirts and skimpy tops emerging from the clubs, squealing and squabbling as they teetered unsteadily down the street. Both architects couldn't help staring. A muscular bouncer with died blond hair stood outside the Black Cat Club and looked enquiringly at the two men as they passed.

"Frampton-on-Tees's most luxurious apartments!" The brightly lit sales hoarding for The Infini T Tower announced. "A development by Sid Dixon designed by leading architect Amanda Stone." A sticker mounted across the corner of the hoarding and printed in bold red lettering proclaimed proudly "75 per cent sold." The contractors were still at work under floodlights as they raced to finish the landscaping for the grand opening later in the day. Paving stones were being laid, plants transferred from pot to soil while a small army of cleaners swept and buffed the polished marble in the double height reception space. Sid had done well. The building had finished before the Games and demand for the flats was high.

"Not a bad building that" Freddie remarked as they stopped to study the architecture. "Amanda's done well. Are you going to the opening tomorrow?"

"Absolutely I am. Sid always puts on a good party."

The Frampton Arms was all locked up and Freddie rang for the night porter who opened the door bleary eyed.

"Doesn't look like you'll get that drink after all, Harry! But thanks for all your help and get a good day's sleep!" he shook Harry again by the hand and the two embraced awkwardly before making their ways to their respective rooms.

"Where've you been? I've been waiting for you." Jenny murmured sleepily as Harry tiptoed into their room.

"You'll never guess!" said Harry as he excitedly tore off his clothes. The excitement of the night and the overpowering sense of relief that his feud with Freddie was over had aroused him. As they made love, Harry told Jennie the story of the bolts and of the reconciliation.

"It's over Harriet," said Freddie firmly the next morning after he had described the events of the night before over breakfast in their hotel room. "It's over. I hope you will accept that it is and treat Harry accordingly in the future. I know you never liked Eleanor, but she's not around any more so that's not a problem. And he's got me out of a big hole without a murmur of discontent. I owe him big time."

"But he's still the biggest threat to your practice. He's the one you're going to be up against in the future in all the competitions, all the pitches. It's you or him, and I'm supporting you."

"I'm really grateful for your support, but you've got to accept that things have changed . . . fundamentally. It's a huge relief to me that it's over and it's important to me that you can see that. I think all the stories about our feud have been very damaging, it's made us seem petty and childish. It's much better for the business that we're seen to be acting like adults."

"If that's what you want Freddie. . . I'm perfectly capable of being very nice to him when I see him; but never forget, he's your competition."

***

Huge flames shot into the sky in a dramatic dance as computer-controlled flare machines ranged along the rooftop of The Infini T Tower responded to the music of the Frampton-on-Tees Philharmonic playing in the recently landscaped courtyard below. Sid, resplendent in white tuxedo, greeted the guests as they walked up the paved pathway to the building's entrance. He could hardly believe his eyes as he saw Frederick Shaw and Harry Jamb, followed by Harriet and Jenny, walking towards him, deep in conversation.

"Freddie! Harry! How nice to see you! And together! Welcome to The Infini T Tower. Not a bad building eh?"

Freddie hesitated to comment; he still felt rather miffed that Sid had given the job to Amanda in the first place.

"It's really good" Harry jumped in, "we both agree, we were discussing it last night. Amanda's got a great feel for this sort of building. It sits really well in the site without being too condescending to its surroundings. Congratulations."

"Why don't you tell her yourself?" and Sid steered the two of them towards a group, including Jason Vent and Josh Stern, clustered round the designer of The Infini T Tower. On the edge of the group Harry saw Amanda's chief designer Emily Boudin who looked close to tears.

The cluster opened up as Sid approached. Harry thought he recognised the tall figure next to Amanda.

"Hi Harry!" Amanda said and stopped as she saw he was with Freddie. "What's going on? I thought you guys didn't speak any more?"

"We've kissed and made up," Harry laughed. "We decided it couldn't go on for ever."

"Talking of kissing and making up, do you know Petronella Conway my new partner?"

Harry remembered where he had come across the willowy pre-Raphaelite before and recalled the scene four years ago in the Civic Hall when Petronella had flounced out alongside her father.

"Is that partner as in life or business?"

"Definitely life" answered Amanda "and a bit of business too. Pet's been working on all these brilliant drawings of The Infini T Tower," and she pointed to a series of framed illustrations that hung against the polished marble walls. No wonder Emily was upset, Harry thought.

"And what does Daddy say about that?" asked Freddie with a smile "Amanda's architecture is hardly his 'cup of tea'."

"He's finding that bit hard to take. He thinks it will reduce the impact of his anti-modern message."

"It probably will," said Amanda "but to give the old boy his due he hasn't any problems that we're a couple of girls. He's really quite liberal like that."

"It's not that he's liberal" Petronella gushed as the champagne took effect. "He just knows he can't criticise others. His own affairs have disqualified him from that! It's a class thing. I think he still almost believes in the *droit de seigneur*. He screwed all our nannies for sure, and my school friends from St Mary's used to call him 'the groper' after they stayed at the Hall. His favourite line was 'can I show you the roof?' where he'd goose them as they admired the views. It's like a disease and it's something my mother never got used to."

"But that doesn't necessarily make him more tolerant to gay behaviour," Jason interjected, fascinated by the turn in the conversation and the alacrity with which Petronella pursued the topic. A certain innocence combined with Sid Dixon's generous supply of booze was providing him with some wonderful gossip.

"Well he mixed with a pretty gay crowd when he was at Cambridge. I can't think they never did *it*!" and Petronella collapsed into hoots of laughter.

Meanwhile Sid Dixon had walked over to a specially-constructed dais and welcomed his many guests.

"My Lords, Ladies and Gentlemen," Sid began "welcome to The Infini T Tower – Frampton's finest new development. I exclude of course any comparison with the buildings for the Games – I wouldn't want to upset Mayor Jarvis." The Mayor laughed at Sid's attempt at humour and a titter spread round the room. "But to be serious for a moment. . . I want to say that this development reflects my faith in the future of Frampton-on-Tees as a city in which to do business. I've invested a lot of money here at The Infini T Tower," (he omitted to mention that none of it was his own but belonged mostly to a middle Eastern Sheikh who had put up all of the capital) "because we are seeing a major change in the demand for city living, when people want to come back into city centres. They like the convenience, the cosmopolitan atmosphere and they need high quality accommodation designed to suit their way of life. I congratulate Amanda Stone on the wonderful design and all those who have had the foresight to buy an apartment. Buy now while stocks last!"

A few days later Mayor Jarvis received a thick cream envelope marked 'Confidential'; on the reverse flap was the unmistakable coat of arms of The Duke of Frampton.

"What can the old blighter want now?" Jarvis said to Ed Clutton who was in his office to go through some of the last minute details of the Opening Ceremony. "I thought we'd heard the last of him."

He opened out the monogrammed sheet. The letter was short and in ink in the Duke's bold copperplate handwriting:

> Dear Jarvis
>
> I realise that my threat to withdraw funding from the new Library has been singularly ineffective and I wish to reverse my decision. In the light of much of the execrable designs recently erected in the City, I believe there should be at least one example of an approach to new architecture in Frampton that can set an example for the future. I am therefore happy to continue supporting the project as long as the architect remains Inigo James and it is carried out in the Classical style.
>
> I remain etc
>
> James Conway.
> HG The Duke of Frampton

"Execrable designs my foot!" Jarvis was very pleased the way all the buildings had turned out. They had happened because of him; without his foresight Frampton would have continued its steady economic decline. Now the city was poised at the start of a new economic era thanks to the Games – and to The Mayor.

"I think he is referring in particular to The Infini T Tower which he well knows is designed by Amanda Stone. I'm not sure if you know this or not, but his daughter Petronella has moved in with Amanda as her partner. The Duke's pretty upset. He couldn't care less that his daughter's a lesbian, but he's incandescent with rage that she's gone off with a Modernist architect."

"Good news about the Library though. Don't tell any of your architect chums, but quite frankly I don't care what style it's in as long as it works and it provides much needed facilities for the people of Frampton."

***

Sid Dixon had loaned Jason one of the studio apartments in The Infini T Tower in the run up to the Games. Not only had Jason played a key part in successfully marketing the development but also Sid knew that the designer was well connected and just through his own network would boost the image of the place and attract a fashionable crowd.

At the end of each busy day, checking on all the team rehearsals, visiting the prop and costume makers, checking sound levels on the PA system, and talking to the local school kids, Jason would take a meal on his own in Alessandro's Restaurant which had just opened on the ground floor of The Infini T Tower. The TV chef Alessandro Timosci had recently sold out to the catering conglomerate Northpoint and was rolling out the brand across the country.

"Ciao, Alessandro," Jason called as he entered the tan and maroon interior – 'contemporary Venetian' was how the press releases described it. Timosci was spending a lot of time in Frampton training up the kitchen team and doing numerous photo calls for the glossies. Each night Alessandro would pick a special wine for Jason to sample with his meal.

"Try zees one – eet ees very nice Montepulciano of two zousand and one. Zees was the very best year for Tuscan wine. Very mellow wiz good flavours."

Alessandro was right. It was a very fine wine and went down a treat with Jason's *stinco di vitello*.

As Jason was about to finish off his espresso and head for bed, Alessandro emerged from the kitchen once more and sat down next to Jason. He called to one of the waiters.

"Grappa! Alfredo and two glasses."

Alfredo duly complied and poured out two shots full to the brim.

"Bottoms up!" exclaimed the Italian chef and tossed back the fiery clear liquid. Jason had little option but to follow suit. He did the same a second time, but when Alessandro called "Bottoms up! for the third time Jason knew he had to decline or he'd never be able to walk out of the restaurant unaided.

"I really must go! I think I'll take a walk before calling it a day." He desperately needed some fresh air as the grappa made his head reel.

Jason weaved unsteadily through the newly planted shrubs and semi mature trees of The Infini T Tower into the more familiar streets and alleys of old Frampton. He knew where he was going; these were familiar routes. He usually went to the Black Cat with a friend, but this night, emboldened and befuddled by Alessandro's hospitality, he thought he'd see if he could pick up a local lad.

Greg, the blond bouncer was at the door and greeted him as he entered.

"Evening Mr Vent. Been making a bit of a night of it I see!" Jason clattered down the stairs to the bar and perched himself precariously on one of the stools.

"*Grappa, per favore*, Gary" he demanded before turning and staring shamelessly at the man next to him. "Aren't you a big boy" he exclaimed as he squeezed the biceps of the rather shy six foot four building worker who was out on the town spending the bonus he received for finishing The Infini T Tower on schedule.

The builder was not a great conversationalist and Jason soon got bored of the small talk, so he suggested they move into the back room.

The builder was indeed big, and he was rough. Jason loved it and begged for more until they were both exhausted and collapsed into the comfy chairs that formed a sort of reception to the labyrinths of cubicles and dungeons. They watched as new visitors entered and figures in various harnesses, straps and masks moved between the different rooms.

Jason noticed a tall, upright elderly figure, with a full head mask and a latex suit that covered the thin and stooping figure. Jason watched as the man turned to go into the Turkish bath area. Jason recognised the limp.

Sir Nigel Frith! Josh had never mentioned it. Perhaps that explains the steady workstream AAP has been getting from the University all these years, thought Jason!

***

Posters were pinned up around Frampton: "Palladianism and the Modern City – A lecture by Inigo James RIBA".

The Frampton-on-Tees Civic Society had invited the architect of the new City Library to address a public meeting to describe his designs for the building. The Duke was keen to make sure that the proposals, based on neo classical lines obtained the maximum local support prior to the planning application. He didn't expect any trouble, but knew it was better to be safe than sorry.

The Duke had invited James to stay at the Hall. When the date was set six month's earlier the old man still harboured hopes that Petronella would get hitched up with the architect, but that now was a non-starter.

Inigo James was something of a caricature of a country figure – he invariably wore a heavy Harris Tweed suit with waistcoat and waxed country shoes from Crocket and Jones. His plummy county accent disguised a more lowly background, but he had from a young age harboured a hankering to inhabit the drawing rooms of England's great houses.

His real name was John, but he had started using Inigo when he was doing A-level Art and visited the Queen's House at Greenwich. He spent many weekends when a student touring the countryside and knocking on doors of Palladian villas requesting a tour. Sometimes he was sent away but more often than not the owners let him in and proudly guided him around their heritage.

The Duchess served tea at the Hall before the Duke drove James down to the Civic Centre. James clutched a rusty carousel of photographic slides, he did not like computers and refused to use them. The delights of Power Point were lost on him. The technical team at the Civic Centre had had to rummage in the cellars to find a rather dusty slide projector that James could use.

When they arrived at the 200-seat lecture theatre there was a smattering of Civic Society members already seated. They seemed to James to have an average age of 75, at least.

William Hyatt of *The Daily Telegraph* was the only journalist who had responded to the Society's invitation to attend. As the technician struggled to get the carousel to work without jamming, a handful more punters turned up but still the room felt sparse.

James found it hard to get into his speech, there were more gaps than people and half those seemed to be nodding off. He was relieved when he could ask for the lights to be dimmed and he got into his slides.

"Are there any questions?" he said plaintively as the lights came up to polite applause. Already those keen to get home for supper were slipping out and none of the remaining had anything to ask.

"I don't know why I bloody bother!" the Duke complained as the Rolls climbed the drive to the Hall. "Where was everyone?"

"Maybe we haven't got a lot of support, but then no one's going to complain either," said Inigo James, "I always like to look on the bright side."

***

Riccardo Scappi's Chelsea garden was resplendent. The gardener had been working all week to tidy up the herbaceous borders, mow the lawn and clip the edges to billiard table perfection. The large, white-painted Regency house had an impressively large garden compared to most in Central London. The ground floor was at street level, but the garden dropped down a floor – so a wrought iron balcony with a curved stairway, thick with wisteria, led down to the lawn.

Riccardo was holding a party of the design world's glitterati to celebrate the completion of the latest range of Marsoni furniture, designed by Harry, prior to the big press launch the next day. The collection of reception chairs and tables, to be marketed under the "Jamb Today" brand, had been created specifically for the VIP suite in the Stadium. Harry was co hosting the party and had invited Freddie – their first appearance in public since their reconciliation.

Harry and Jenny arrived early to make sure everything was in place. Riccardo greeted them both warmly but noticed that Jenny seemed very nervous. This was the first time she had met Eleanor's father since she got together with Harry and she was terrified to come face to face with the Italian.

They looked out over the garden as black suited staff arranged glasses and tables, banks of bottles of sparkling Tuscan wine and huge wheels of parmesan cheese, their contents broken into finger bite size pieces.

"Jenny, I can understand this is a difficult for you here, but you must realise that although I love my daughter very much, she did a bad thing to Harry." Riccardo said to her. "I don't blame Harry for what happened one bit, and I still love him as a son. So please feel very welcome in my house."

Eleanor had settled into life in the Italian countryside and barely mentioned her former life. The old man liked to see her responding comfortably to her Tuscan roots but he was beginning to worry about what was going to happen to the business into the future. He had always hoped that Eleanor would take it on but that seemed unlikely now.

He was harbouring hopes that his granddaughter Amelia might start to take an interest; she had a bit of a business brain. She had given up painting and started an art gallery in Deptford which seemed to be doing rather well. Riccardo had been very impressed when he met her boyfriend Tom who was doing an MBA at the London Business School. The last few years had been tough for them, but maybe things were looking up.

The doorbell rung as Riccardo kissed Jenny on both cheeks and hugged her to his bulky frame.

First to arrive was Alex La Touche, who had taken all the photographs for the *Jamb Today* catalogue. He came armed with a pocket camera. He liked to record this sort of event – where the great and the good of the architectural world came together – for his own purposes rather than for publication. His archive of the last twenty years provided a fascinating insight into the mores of this bizarre tribe and the characters that it comprised.

Sid Dixon came on his own. His long suffering wife Veronica had gone off with one of her toyboys after the launch of The Infini T Tower. She had been furious when an interview written by Rachael Dove had described in rather too much detail some of Sid's extra marital activities.

"I don't mind us fucking around in private, but to splash it across the newspapers is bloody embarrassing!" she had screamed "The kids have seen it, my mum's seen it and all your randy designer friends have seen it and they can't keep their hands off me!"

Sid was soon in conversation with Astrid Sollit and thanked her for the Committee for Better Architecture's support of Amanda Stone's designs for The Infini T Tower.

"Elegant and understated, high quality design you said. It looks great on the advertising hoardings." Sid enthused.

"I'm glad – I think we've helped Frampton get some really good architecture," Astrid was always keen to find good examples of the Committee's work to prove to Government Ministers, who were always trying to cut budgets, that it was an essential part of the planning process

Malvina Black the Argentinian landscape architect was outrageous in an outfit of fluorescent pink plastic and huge Cutler and Gross glasses. In contrast Amanda Stone had cured Petronella of her Pre Raphaelite tendencies and dressed her in a similar severe style to her own.

Sam Spurling from Ecoplastics looked relaxed from a couple of weeks in his new house in Provence. He had done well out of the EuroGames financially and had just signed a juicy contact with Riccardo to supply sustainable plastic parts for all Marsoni furniture. He took a glass of wine and walked down the steps to the garden where he saw Tariq Shah.

"What's happened to Carlos? I haven't seen him for ages" Sam asked. "I used to see him all the time when we were sorting out the seating for The Pearl."

"We had to let him go when the workload dropped. But he hasn't been well. I expect he's gone back to Brazil." Tariq did not mention that the firm had had to pay out a substantial sum after Carlos threatened to sue Frederick Shaw and Partners for wrongful dismissal. The deal included a confidentiality clause to stop Carlos leaking stories to the press.

"That must have been a big blow – he's an amazing designer."

"It was, but every cloud has a silver lining. It meant that we restructured the firm. We've given more responsibility to our younger designers. I've become Chief Executive – the first time my mum has stopped moaning that I didn't become a doctor – and it gives Freddie a more strategic role. Talk of the devil. . . here he is now."

Freddie emerged from the French windows of the house, walked out onto the raised patio and looked down onto the garden, now filled right up to its herbaceous borders by the cream of London's design world. His white collarless shirt, and newly shortened hair accentuated his tanned and slim features. He had recently taken up serious road cycling and planned to do the Cycle to Cannes ride the next year. As a result his face had the taut and muscular look of someone with a zero fat figure. Condor had recently built him the most beautiful Classico bike and he was regularly riding a couple of hundred miles a week.

He walked down the wisteria-decked steps as the group below, always attentive to who the new arrivals were, watched. He waved to faces he recognised. Harry stood at the bottom where he had been greeting guests and, as Freddie reached the ground, he opened his arms and gave his erstwhile partner a robust man hug, patting him firmly on the back. The chatter stopped as though someone had pressed the mute button and guest gawped at the embracing couple. There could be no doubt in anyone's mind that the rift was healed.

"Oh Daddy, I'm so pleased!" Amelia grabbed her father round the neck and kissed him hard on the cheek.

The party guests turned back to their conversations and the volume rose as Harry and Amelia held each other very tight and sobbed into each others' shoulders.

***

Mayor Jarvis scanned the Birthday Honours List in *The Gazette*. Under the heading 'Knights Bachelor' it read "Albert Eustace Merton, for services to planning and regeneration Frampton-on-Tees". He looked down the page: both Henry and Freddie had been made CBEs for their service to architecture. He picked up the phone.

"Congratulations, Sir Albert!" Jarvis said when he called the Planning Committee chairman "Didn't I tell you I'd get you a gong if you did what I said? Making sure the Games's buildings went through that smoothly was the best thing you could have done for Frampton. And do give my regards to Lady Merton!"

As he flicked through the rest of the paper he saw Rachael Dove's portrait heading the centre spread comment column. Her spicey coverage of the architecture of the Frampton Games had caught the eye of the paper's Editor and she had been promoted to the role of general columnist with a brief to comment on any subject that took her fancy.

Chapter 18

The opening of the Games was on one of those carefree summer's days when everyone seems to be happy. The sky was clear and blue, the light breeze that blew down from the Frampton Hills kept the air fresh and clean, while the bright sun warmed the skin and the hearts of the crowds that converged onto Jarvis Park. The Council had unanimously agreed to the name change when it had been clear that the Mayor had delivered the Games on time and in a way that seemed to have garnered the general support of the population of Frampton.

On the same day the Council had also passed the budget for the commission of a figure of Jarvis, by the sculptor Celia Maxwell, to be placed in the last remaining niche in the decorated façade of the Civic Centre.

They came in coaches and cars, which were parked on vast acres of brownfield land a good twenty minutes' walk from the stadium. Despite the complaints of the motoring lobby, Ed Clutton convinced them this was good planning – it meant the race to the roads would be spread out, thus alleviating the worst of the inevitable traffic jams. They came by train – extra services were laid on, especially those that linked up with the Eurostar connections to the continent, these were the EuroGames after all. They filled the hotels for fifty miles around and hundreds of Frampton homes laid on bed and breakfasts. Those staying in the town were encouraged to walk. As the pedestrians passed the Conway Estate they were tempted to teas and snacks laid on by the locals in the Community Hall. Jonny Spon had had the idea.

"Why shouldn't you make a bit of money out of the Games too? You can let a few rooms, you can hire out your parking spaces and you can sell them food," he had told them. The caterers who had won the concession for providing food on the Park complained to the Mayor, but the Frampton Council rejected the complaint after Councillor Bradley gave an impassioned speech along the lines of "what are we doing supporting these fat cat southerners instead of the working men and women of our own city!"

***

Mayor Jarvis also walked to the Stadium, eschewing the Mayoral Daimler in order to prove that he was a man of the people. He strode down Conway Road together with Ed Clutton, his red gown flowing behind him and lace jabot fluttering in the breeze, waving his tricorn hat to the bemused Framptonians who had been unlucky enough not to win a seat in The Pearl. He stopped by at the Conway Community Centre and sipped a cup of tea for the cameras and congratulated the ladies of the Conway Estate on their enterprise before making his way to the Stadium and into the VIP suite.

The spacious hospitality suite was crowded even as he arrived. Here were the major sponsors, European dignitaries, and politicians as well as the senior members of the team that had put the whole event together. The EU Sports Minister was due to arrive in 15 minutes and the greetings line had to be assembled.

A black suited events girl grabbed Josh Stern and placed him in the line according to her numbered plan. As he waited for others to be rounded up to join him he looked around the room which felt more like the lobby of a five star hotel than a sports facility.

The Jamb Today range of Marsoni furniture added to the feeling of luxury with its suede upholstery and stainless steel structure. Harry and Freddie were talking animatedly together and Harriet and Jenny seemed to be getting on well enough. The events girl grabbed the foursome and placed them next to Josh. Ed Clutton and Joe Porley joined them.

"Where's Jonny Spon?" asked Josh. "Shouldn't he be in the architects' line up too?"

"He wanted to be in The Pearl with the people from the Conway Estate." Ed answered. "You've got to hand it to him, his way of getting people involved has really worked. They're a tough lot on the Estate and I never expected them to get behind the Games in the way they have. I take my hat off to him."

Freddie looked as white as a sheet.

"I. . .I. . . I've got to go" he suddenly felt very sick and ran from the room.

Richard Jarvis looked curiously at Freddie as he dashed past. He walked over to the rest of the construction group and shook each one warmly by the hand. He was genuinely grateful because the name of Jarvis would go down in the history of Frampton as the Mayor who did more than anyone since the Victorians to put the city on the map, to regenerate its desolate brownfield sites and to focus the international spotlight on its culture and its economy.

"Thank you so much for your brilliant buildings – you have done Frampton proud!"

Next, the EU Sports Minister was led into the room and welcomed warmly by Mayor Jarvis. The two had become good friends during the build up to the Games.

After introducing the Minister to the line up, the Mayor called for silence.

"Before we move into the main ceremony I want to say 'thank you' to all you people here who have supported this great adventure and particularly to our team of architects. These buildings are Frampton's Sydney Opera House, its Bilbao Guggenheim, its Gherkin and its Burj Khalifa. The beautiful pavilions, The Pearl and the Hester Stadium will be our icons, not just for today but for the future of Frampton."

The room burst into applause.

"I don't want to put a dampener on things," Jarvis leaned over to Harry, "but where on earth is Hester? I thought this was going to be his big evening."

"Haven't a clue – and quite frankly I don't bloody well care" Harry answered curtly.

"It gives me great pleasure to present the Minister" Jarvis continued "with this souvenir print – a beautiful drawing of Jarvis Park – signed by Petronella Conway, one of our leading local artists."

***

Freddie ran out of the Hester Stadium towards the Swimming Complex. He could see the crowds from the Conway Estate making their way into the building. The thought of the bolts that Carlos had removed made his stomach churn again.

"Supposing that bastard took out more bolts than he said?" Freddie thought. "Did we put them back in the right place? Did we fix them properly?"

He sprinted into the swimmers' entrance and through the undercroft of the building to the pool area. He looked up at the banked seating as it gradually filled with spectators.

***

As Mayor Jarvis led the VIP party out into the blinding lights amidst the cheering crowds who filled the Hester Stadium, he thought back to a conversation he had had with John Veduty a few weeks before.

"The name of Gilgamesh of Uruk has survived for nearly 5,000 years because of his prowess at building," lectured the erudite conservationist, "so too were the reputations of Pericles of Athens – who, as I am sure you know, commissioned the Acropolis – the Medicis of Florence and even Prime Minister Joe Cahill of New South Wales, who started off the Sydney Opera House, but died before it was finished (although he's better known for a bit of motorway) reinforced by their roles as patrons of architecture. The names of their architects – Phidias, Brunelleschi, Utzon live on through history."

"The work of architects turns political power and economic success into recognisable, physical form. Their buildings create the identity of places long after their makers have shuffled off this mortal coil; buildings bestow immortality. Their use may change but their form remains."

***

The crowds cheered wildly and waved their EU flags as the party walked to the podium erected in the centre of the stadium. Jarvis approached the microphone and raised his hand. The noise subsided.

"Ladies and Gentlemen, *Mesdames et Messieurs, Frauen und Herren, Signore e Signori, Señoras y Señores*; welcome to the opening of the European Frampton Games!"

In rushed the flagwavers – Jason Vent's colourful designs spun and fluttered around the stadium synchronised with huge banners suspended from the curving roof and matching the beat of the massed brass bands, as athletes from Latvia, Lithuania and Luxembourg marched in unity with those from France, Germany and Italy. The Cavaliers and Roundheads re enacted the Battle of Frampton, an army of dancers armed with steel grinders shot cascades of sparks into the night sky and.teams of 'steelworkers' hammered at huge sheets of steel creating a piercing and insistent rhythm that rose to an almost painful climax before stopping dead. In the programme Jason had titled the piece "British Manufacturing Killed by Margaret Thatcher."

In the eerie silence that followed several spotlights focused on the slim figure of Romilly Smith, a Frampton singer who had reached the finals of the reality TV show *Pop Icon* and gave a lusty rendition of "Salute to the Athletes."

"And now ladies and gentlemen" boomed the fruity voice of Frampton Radio's top DJ Kent Scott "would you please stand as the EuroGames Baton which has travelled to all twenty seven member countries of the European Union enters the stadium!"

The spotlights moved across the floor of the Stadium and picked out a narrow ramp that created a slender bridge from the VIP area to the centre of the Stadium.

Kent Scott had been sworn to secrecy, he was one of a handful of people who knew the identity of the athlete who would carry the baton on its last 100 metre journey. But as the lights picked out the white track-suited figure poised at the top of the top of the ramp the seasoned broadcaster could hardly get the words out.

"A huge welcome please. . . " Scott caught his breath and tears welled in his eyes "a huge welcome for one of Frampton's real heroes. . . " his voice shook and his catching throat electrified the atmosphere around the stadium. The figure moved slowly forward ". . . ladies and gentlemen I give you Frampton-on-Tees's very own Martin Hesssssterrrrrrr!!!"

Hester's wheelchair moved onto the slope. It sped down the ramp at what seemed to the crowd to be an alarming speed – the wild cheering was interspersed with gasps of horror. What they couldn't see were the tracks that kept the chair securely on course. Jason had calculated the steepness of the ramp so that Hester could travel the 100 metre distance in precisely 9.89 seconds – the speed with which Hester had won his Gold Medal nearly fifty years before. What they could see, magnified a thousand times on the giant screen, was Hester's face, the adrenalin-fuelled excitement, the thrill of moving at speed in contrast to his cumbersome chin-controlled wheelchair. He counted down the seconds just as he used to, his head thrust forward as though about to breast the tape, the roar of the crowd urging him on.

Scott switched off the microphone. He looked out at the spectators around the commentary box – there wasn't a dry eye to be seen. He couldn't speak. But it didn't matter. No words were needed. Amongst all the hullabaloo of the Games, the millions of pounds spent, the competition, the jingoism and the spectacular architecture, it struck Scott that the courage of one man in his struggle against appalling adversity had the power to inspire and move beyond even the world's top able-bodied athletes who would be competing in this Stadium over the following fourteen days.

The baton was held in a robotic arm fixed to Hester's wheelchair. As the athlete came to a halt in the centre of the stadium that bore his name, the arm unfolded and docked the silver cylinder into a digital cradle.

Instantly the screens around the stadium came alive with messages in all the languages of the EU. Texted messages from countries the baton had passed through had been stored in a chip embedded in its handle and were now released to the world.

"Frampton-on-Tees's future in the digital age," ran the programme.

The noise in the stadium subsided as the Sports Minister was guided towards the microphone by an events girl according to the strict schedule of the Opening Ceremony. Live TV coverage across Europe had been timed to make sure that the programme climaxed with the Minister's opening speech together with the massive firework display spectacularly recreating the historic furnaces of Frampton, cradle of the industrial revolution, and its phoenix future which would rise out of the EuroGames.

"No! no! no!" cried the events girl "Mr Hester you're supposed to stay on the dais!" Martin, his eyes still bright from the excitement of his spectacular descent was speeding toward the row of VIPS. He jammed on his brakes in front of Harry.

"Harry, I'm sorry. I didn't mean to hurt you. But I know I did, and I've paid the price. Now, come with me!" and Hester turned his wheelchair back towards the dais. Harry hesitated. The stadium was silent as the lighting controller realised his script was about to be rewritten. The spotlights were picking out the two men.

"For fuck's sake, Harry! Follow me. Do it now!"

Harry followed as the chair whirred up the ramp to the microphone. The Sports Minister looked on, unable to disguise his astonishment.
"Ladies and gentleman, as you know this Stadium is named after me," Hester began "and for which I am immensely proud. . .but I want to introduce you to the man whose name will always be

linked to this wonderful masterpiece. His name is Harry Jamb, designer of the Hester Stadium. I'm very grateful to him for creating this great new showpiece for Frampton. Please give a big Hester Stadium applause for Harry who has proved himself to be one of the *best. . . architects. . . in. . . the. . . world*!"

The crowd clapped and cheered. Harry waved and bowed towards the steeply raked seats. He was gratified how intimate the huge space felt. As Martin Hester spun his wheelchair round to return to the platform he looked at Harry and shouted above the noise.

"You should get a few jobs out of that!"

Harry nodded dumbly. It was all a bit too much. First Freddie and now Hester. While he was happy to restore relations with his old partner – it felt like it did when they first worked together – he still felt it hard to forgive Hester.

***

Eleanor watched the Opening Ceremony on television from her Tuscan retreat. She was shocked when Martin appeared in his wheelchair. Tears rolled down her cheeks as she recalled the lithe athletic figure for whom she had destroyed her life and as she watched Harry take the limelight. But she was in another existence now; better to forget the past. It was all too painful. She felt at home in Italy and among the local community. She was building up a new existence for herself.

"Hey, this must be bringing back some painful memories, eh?"

Thor Christensen stood behind Eleanor and gently stroked her cheeks and her hair as he watched Harry Jamb and Martin Hester together on the TV screen.

Christensen had retired as Head of the London Academy of Architecture two years previously, but had continued to help the school to raise funds for student scholarships. He thus had regular contact with Riccardo Scappi as the Academy's major benefactor.

The previous summer he had been staying at the Villa Scappi when Eleanor came to visit her father.

The old lecher had not forgotten Eleanor's rebuttal of him when she was a student and he had been determined to make a better fist of it this time.

But he need not have worried. Eleanor was not opposed to her former teachers' attentions. He was a good looking man with rugged Scandinavian features and a shock of white hair; for his age he was incredibly fit. She felt reassured by his presence and realised she was attracted to older men anyway – Thor was the same age as Martin Hester.

"It hurts but it's history. This is my world now, I feel comfortable here. It's close to the Villa and Amelia and Tom can come and stay with their baby whenever they like. The weather's warm and the people warmer." Martin Hester started to speak ". . . as you know this Stadium. . ." And she flicked off the screen.

***

Freddie breathed as sigh of relief. The audience had leapt from their seats in the Pearl when they saw Martin Hester appear on the big screen. They had stamped on the floor and finished with a Mexican wave. And the structure hadn't budged.

***

The Duke and Duchess of Frampton watched Jason Vent's firework display from the balcony of the Hall. As the golden showers erupted from the roof of the Stadium the Duke was forced to admit that pyrotechnics did a pretty good job of recreating the sight of the great Bessemer converters that had spewed out molten steel in the heyday of the Industrial Revolution. Indeed, the view looked remarkably like the painting by Joseph Wright of Derby *The Furnaces of Frampton* which hung in the Hall's drawing room.

With one final and massive eruption the fireworks stopped and bright lights flooded the Stadium and The Pearl, changing through the colours of the spectrum they highlight the profiles of the two new icons of Frampton. Pink, blue, yellow, red, green; the colours seemed to be taunting the old aristocrat.

"I've had enough! This whole thing is a bloody disaster," the Duke grunted as he turned to walk back into the house.

He stepped inside the French windows. The rococo room, all maroon and gold, was a great comfort to him. Around the walls portraits of previous Dukes looked down on him. These were the ancestors who had built up Frampton Hall, who had dug the coal and developed the steelworks. They were modernisers who had created the wealth and the means to bring about the greatest change in the human condition in the history of the world.

"Well. What would you have done?" Duke called out to a Gainsborough portrait of an eighteenth century predecessor which was partially obscured by a steel acrow prop. Large cracks had started to appear in the room, tearing the damask wallpaper, which the engineers blamed on the old Frampton coal mines deep below the Hall.

"Don't worry, Peter," calmed the Duchess, "the new City Library will show what good architecture is all about."

Try as he might to hold them back, the forces of change were too great. Yes, he was building the new library, it would have columns and arches but it would be just a shell – it wouldn't be the sort of library he dreamed of, magnificent great rooms like Hawksmoor's Library at All Souls, Barry's Reform Club or Trinity College Dublin's long barrel vaulted space – lined floor to ceiling with leather bound volumes. It would be full of students with laptops, community meeting spaces, a coffee shop and a media centre. The grand staircase he had wanted had been abandoned because of difficulties with disabled access, and he was having to dig deep into the Frampton coffers to pay for the carving of the Corinthian capitals on the main façade. He had grown tired of the fight. His ancestors had embraced change. They had no desire to retain the impoverished landscape of pre-industrial Britain and they and generations of Conways as well as the people of Frampton-on-Tees had been richer for it.

He was tired. He had won plenty of battles, he had fought against change and had delayed and stopped lots of buildings and developments he didn't like. But he had lost the war. Perhaps he just wasn't cut out for the twenty first century. Retreat to the comforting redoubt of the Frampton estate was an enticing option.

"One building won't make a difference, my dear," the Duke said resignedly "We have lost. We're just out of tune with the times. The world today is driven by growth and change rather than certainty. Buildings used to represent permanence and moral values, not transience and finance. They claim they are bringing order to our lives, but actually the architects of today are instruments of chaos."

Epilogue

"We'll have to get more staff!" Jenny urged Harry as the two stood in the empty shell of the docklands warehouse that was about to become the new offices for Harry Jamb Associates. "Either that or we're going to have to start turning down some seriously interesting jobs."

Six months after the end of what had turned out to be a highly successful EuroGames, the madness had hardly died down. The firm seemed to be invited to enter competitions for almost every major project around the world – as did Frederick Shaw and Partners. The website was receiving hundreds of hits a day and the firm was inundated with job applications from hopeful young architects. Harry had been forced to refuse invitations to lecture at schools of architecture, which he regretted. He liked keeping in touch with students, but there just weren't enough hours in the day.

"As it is we've been asked to submit proposals for the Hunan Opera House, a housing scheme in Moscow, a hotel in Valencia and the new Portsmouth Art Gallery," Jenny continued "and they are all offering fees: not a lot of money, but these are all the sort of projects we've always wanted to do and its worth the gamble. Our cash flow is looking healthy so we can afford to do it."

Jenny has become increasingly confident in her role as Office Manager. She had controlled Harry's less commercial activities and bought order to the firm's finances.

"I agree with Jenny," said Alex Rich at the partners' meeting the next day. He had been promoted as part of a programme of bringing on the younger members of the practice. "We're really stretched at the moment, everyone's working big chunks of the weekends and lots of late nights."

"I'm really nervous about the firm getting any bigger," Harry joined in "what are we now? About 60?"

"72" Jenny replied.

"I'm losing touch with projects. We've always prided ourselves on our attention to detail and the care we put into each project. We're in danger of losing that."

"You've got to learn to delegate Harry. I know I keep saying it, but you're burning the candle at both ends as well. . ." Jenny paused, "again" she added darkly.

After the EuroGames all the clients wanted Harry and Harry alone. When Alex turned up to meetings in his stead, they felt cheated.

"We can't just grow for the sake of it. We want the right sort of jobs and the right clients – for the first time in my life I can choose who we work with, and on what! If we grow too big we'll find ourselves on a treadmill, having to take any job we can to feed hundreds of mouths. I don't want to get like Freddie!"

***

Frederick Shaw and Partners – after the games it was officially rebranded as FSP – was a lot bigger than Harry Jamb Associates – and had been even before the Games. Now as the practice's fame spread worldwide, the work was pouring in and Freddie had no qualms about hiring more staff to deal with the influx. Freddie had told Harry when they met for their monthly catch-up lunch at Le Caprice how he spent very little time designing any more and was increasingly involved in management and finance.

Tariq was in his element: "Our profits are up, our turnover is up and we're in the top ten largest practices according to the latest *Building News* survey."

Freddie was happy. He travelled the world meeting and gladhanding clients. He lectured regularly at architecture schools and found that his post EuroGames and 'Divergent Paths' celebrity status was a great advantage in attracting young and nubile women to his bed.

***

"You know, Richard" Sid had told the Mayor soon after the EuroGames were over, "there are two key ingredients to successful property development – local knowledge and money. I've got the money and you've got the knowledge. All this work you've been putting into Frampton has increased values enormously. Why don't you benefit from your labours and join me in developing the area around the Games complex? You know everyone there is to know, you know what's needed in Frampton – and obviously getting planning permission with you on board should be a doddle!"

Jarvis accepted Sid's offer with enthusiasm.

***

"How much!?" Ed Clutton could not contain his astonishment as the CEO of Howard and Perkins, the sports and leisure masterplanners, spelt out the salary they were offering him to head up their Olympic delivery team advising cities on how to bid for and manage Olympic events. Ed had thought he earned a reasonable package at Frampton, But this was ridiculous.

"I'm very happy, *very* happy to accept!" and shook his new employer's hand. Since Mayor Jarvis had retired from his civic duties, life at Frampton had seemed a bit slow. This would be a great new challenge and a very well paid one at that!

***

Belo Horizonte was hardly the sort of place that Carlos de Souza ever imagined he would be practising architecture, but after his experiences in Frampton he had little appetite for the cut and thrust of conventional architecture. Instead, he threw himself into the *Vila Viva* ('living village') programme in the city's self-built slums, the *favelas* perched precariously on hilly sites around the city, cheek by jowl with some of Brazil's smartest neighbourhoods. Carlos worked on flood reduction programmes, paving projects and designed new public spaces.

"I can't believe the change that has taken place in my architecture since the days of The Pearl," he wrote to some of his old colleagues at Frederick Shaw and Partners, "but this is such rewarding work. I set out as an architect to give people better places to live and work in, and here, I really feel I'm finally making a difference."

It took several months for the news to reach England that soon after writing that letter, de Souza had been measuring out a plot for a new children's playground when he was caught up in crossfire between Brazilian police and local drug dealers. He was hit in head and chest, and was dead on arrival when they finally got him to the hospital.

***

"It gives me great pleasure," intoned Prince William as he stood in front of Frampton City Hall, "to unveil this splendid new statue," a chilly breeze ruffled the light fabric draped over the figure standing in the final niche of the ornately decorated building "of Sir Richard Jarvis. As Alderman and Mayor of this town he has done so much for its development and regeneration. He joins other great figures from Frampton-on-Tees' history who have made their mark on its urban development."

The crowd clapped as the young Prince tugged at the cords that released the statue's shroud.

The sculptor had created a good likeness of Jarvis and clothed him in his mayoral garb. His hands were outstretched and in one of them he held a model of the Swimming Complex – The Pearl, which as Ed Clutton had forecast had quickly become the icon of Frampton, its spherical profile recognised around the globe.

"Looks just like you!" exclaimed Martin Hester as he wheeled himself towards the ex-Mayor "Well deserved, if I may say so. The EuroGames has truly transformed this city, and people have a real hope for the future. They even like you on the Conway Estate and that's a real turnaround. You've got that young chap Spon to thank for that. I know you didn't like him, but he's worked miracles for the area."

"He seemed such an arrogant little sod at first – like a lot of those architects. They all took a bit of getting used to, but I have to admit they've done us proud."

***

"Let me draw you like that," Petronella said to Amanda, as the architect lay naked on the Zaha Hadid-designed sofa that was the centrepiece of their Clerkenwell loft.

Amanda Stone was 42 and in good shape – she ate like a bird and had a personal trainer three times a week who helped her keep her muscles tones and her skin wrinkle-free. She stretched out across the sinuous curves of the rich red seat.

Petronella quickly sketched her partner with the sort of attention to detail and three dimensional form that she lavished upon the architecture that was now her more usual subject matter. She was getting together work for an exhibition at the Savile Street Gallery; her agent had suggested a collection of drawings of new architecture following the success of her images of The Infini T Tower.

As she put the finishing touches to her portrait of Amanda, the elegant curve of her breast, the neat rectangular landing strip of her pubic hair and the red lips that chimed with the background, Petronella realised here was something more powerful and more *her* than the inanimate architectural subjects that filled her portfolio. She had done life drawing at art school and had enjoyed it, but now, her relationship with Amanda seemed to have brought out a rich strength and fluidity to her line. Her passionate engagement with her subject matter leapt off the paper.

"This is really working well!" she said excitedly to Amanda. "So well in fact that you're going to be the subject of my exhibition!"

She attacked a new piece of cartridge with a charcoal stick. She felt liberated, free of constraints and expectations, she was drawing flesh and blood, something that was live and vital and a total contrast to the old stones that had fascinated so much in the past.

***

"Boudin's Threadneedle Street office design a disaster" ran the headline in *Building News*. The critics were not being kind to Emily's first building following her split with Amanda.

Because Emily had worked closely and successfully with a number of Amanda's clients, they had been happy to give their jobs to her, thinking they would get the same sort of service and same sort of end product. But Emily was keen to create her own identity. Not only was she hurt by Amanda's rejection and keen to distance herself from everything Amanda stood for, but Emily also wanted to investigate architectural ideas of her own.

"The architects who set up in practice on their own" wrote Rachael Dove in *The Gazette* "set the tone for the work done under their name but which may well be carried out by others in their team. The founding partners create the DNA which infiltrates through everything a practice does. Designers who, while working for one firm produce very good work, sometimes lose their way when they leave and set up their own. This seems to have been the case as far as Emily Boudin is concerned. Without Amanda Stone to rein in her exuberance, the buildings she has designed in her new practice are coarse and poorly detailed, lacking the restraint and finesse of the projects of her former partner."

***

After the EuroGames, Josh and Jason had discussed the idea of moving in together but Jason's work on the logo and Opening Ceremony had caught the attention of Uberbrand, the New York ad agency who asked Jason to be their Creative Director.

"It's too good an opportunity to miss, Josh, I'm sorry," he explained when they met for breakfast at The Wolseley one morning.

"I wouldn't dream of trying to stop you, Jace. And anyway I'd like to get AAP to expand their workload in the States so I can easily come over as often as you like."

"Hey! Look at this!" Josh was leafing through a copy of *The Gazette*. He read: "Lord Frith, the former Chancellor of Frampton on Tees University has said he will champion gay rights when he takes his seat in the House of Lords. Lord Frith told *The Gazette* 'My generation was on the cusp between the decriminalisation of homosexuality and a younger generation where it almost ceased to be an issue. My elevation to the peerage has given me the confidence to speak out and a platform from which to do so.' Good for Nigel!"

***

Tom and Amelia took over the running of Marsoni Furniture when Riccardo Scappi retired. Tom was CEO and Amelia Creative Director, responsible for commissioning new designers.

Amelia was keen to get younger designers involved in new ranges for the company. She liked the stuff her father had done – Jamb Today was the best selling range in the catalogue – but felt it was too conventional. They needed some funkier designs that appealed to the emerging generation of architects who would be the future customers of Marsoni, designs that would make the headlines at the Milan Furniture Fair.

Jonny Spon was the natural choice. He had become the hottest designer in town. His edginess, popular appeal and powerful imagery had caught the attention of the press. There was hardly an issue of *Wallpaper* or *Monocle* that didn't include some new project by Jonny. He wasn't the easiest person to work with, but as the designs for his new office range started to emerge, Amelia knew she was on to a winner.

She flew out to Tuscany to show Spon's sketches to her grandfather. He was ecstatic; although the designs were not what he would have commissioned himself, it was clear that Amelia had inherited his instinct for making and selling innovative and beautifully crafted furniture.

Eleanor and Sven came over for a relaxed lunch at the villa.

Riccardo raised his glass "Here's to you Amelia. I had always dreamed a Scappi would carry on my business. You have made me a very happy grandfather!"

***

The man who probably received the most job offers following the EuroGames was Joe Porley. Every report of the Frampton event in every magazine and newspaper around the world included the words "on budget and on schedule". These were the magic words that excited the majority of clients. The architecture may be important, but whether the clients were directors of private companies reporting to shareholders, or elected officials having to defend their spending programmes to voters, cost and time remained top of their agendas.

After sifting through the pile of proposals Joe elected to deliver a new city in the Middle East. The budgets were phenomenal, the aspirations of the client were astonishing, and the salary mind boggling. After four years in the desert, he reckoned he would be able to comfortably retire to his dream ranch in Arizona where he could breed horses and ride among the cottonwood trees and mesquite-covered hills.

***

Harry and Freddie kept in touch and remained on good terms. They met for lunch each month, and would frequently pass each other in the reception areas of prospective clients as they went in or out of a presentation for a new job. They were as competitive as ever professionally, but they determined that neither their work – nor their wives – would ever again destroy their friendship.